Lucky Enough
by K.A Wesorick

Table of Contents

Dedication

For my grandparents

About the Author

Katie Wesorick grew up in western Michigan and currently lives in Chicago. This is her first book, which she was inspired to write after her grandpa passed away, as a way to honor and remember him. Her writing is focused on young adult characters who are searching to find their self-worth and confidence while coming of age.

Acknowledgment

Thank you to my parents, who repeatedly encouraged me to write this book. All your support brought this story to life.

Prologue

For once, I nailed it, the perfect first-day outfit. I turn from side to side admiring my unicorn print dress. My long strawberry blonde hair flows along with the sway of the dress. All it needs is the final touch, adding my black booties to give my outfit a little edge. During the summer I'm away at the cottage on Lake Michigan, and I always feel out of touch on the first day of school. Today is my first day of high school, which is making me extra nervous. One last look in the mirror before heading off to high school, here goes nothing.

"Becks, you ready? Don't want to miss the bus on your first day!" Mom yells up to me. As I run downstairs and out the door I try to give myself a mini pep talk, convincing myself this will be the best year ever.

"Bye, mom!" I say as she stops me in my tracks.

"Hey, wait a minute! I need at least one photo!" She says, smiling, as I sigh. There is no use in fighting it, so I smile for the camera before she gives me a hug, and I run out the door. The bus is pulling up just as I reach the end of the driveway. My hands start sweating as I firmly grip my backpack, nerves kicking in.

"Becks!" Trina yells with a smile and wave, and instantly, my death grip on my backpack relaxes. Trina! We have been best friends for as long as I can remember, and seeing her make my nerves disappear.

"Hey!" I say as I sit down and suddenly second-guess my perfect outfit. Oh no, not again. Trina is wearing an army green vintage t-shirt and ripped jeans that just scream 'cool girl', and I'm over here in a unicorn dress that screams 'middle school.' What was I thinking!? No, no, no!

"I did the outfit thing wrong again, didn't I?" I ask Trina, as I can feel the heat rise in my cheeks. It's bad enough to feel this way, but even worse, I always give myself away with my red face. My confidence is fading quickly as I see the agreement in Trina's face.

"It's fine. It would have been perfect for last year!" She says with a hesitant smile.

"Last year was middle school; I look like a kid, don't I?" Oh no, this happened in middle school, too. All the girls changed their style while I was away at the cottage. My look was stuck in elementary school while everyone else had moved on to the next big thing. It sounds simple, but the teasing is all too real.

"I mean, it's okay. Maybe they will let it slide this time. I should have called you to see what you were wearing, but my mind has been full of dance studio drama. Why didn't you call me to see what I was wearing?" Trina asked.

"I don't know. I should have. I honestly thought I nailed it with this outfit," I admit, feeling sheepish. Even worse, I'm just that out of touch. I really thought she would be impressed with my outfit.

"Well, the shoes are cool." Thank goodness I went with an edgier shoe! Why are outfits such a big thing?!

"I thought I had the perfect outfit and was excited-nervous to see Nate. Now I'm just really nervous!" This makes Trina laugh. She knows how after Nate and I had a "moment" on the last day of 8th grade, I've been obsessing over him all summer. He's always been nice to everyone, but something happened when we talked after the 8th-grade talent show. It felt different, and I'm hoping maybe a spark could still be there this year. If I didn't imagine the spark to begin with, that is.

"You look great, Becks, but you know how people can be. I've heard the upperclassmen like to pick on the freshman. If they do, just know that it's their first-day tradition; don't take it personally." Trina says, with an encouraging tap on the shoulder.

"Enough about my disastrous outfit. What's going on with your dance studio drama? Did they announce who will be submitted to the competition this year?" I ask Trina, knowing she was supposed to hear any day now if she will be one of two girls from the studio selected to try for the youth International Ballet Competition. She is the most talented dancer at the studio and should be getting good news any day. Looking at her face, I know it's not good news.

"Yeah, I wasn't selected." Trina's eyes are glossy as if she is trying not to cry, as her gaze turns downward. Her body slowly turns into a slouch, unlike her typical straight ballerina posture. All she can do is shake her head no as I give her a hug.

The lady who runs the studio, Miss Jackie, has been mean to Trina since the moment she met her. The ballet instructors recruited Trina to join the studio because her talent is unmatched, but the owner made Trina try out four times! Four! Usually, only one time is required. I have no doubt it is the owner who is blocking Trina from being a competitor now.

Trina releases my hug and starts to vent.

"I keep getting positive feedback from my instructors, but they never choose me. I've asked if there is a technique I need to work on or if they think I'm lacking in artistry, but the answer is always the same." She imitates her teacher, saying, "'You're great, Trina, the best dancer we have. I'm sorry, but Miss Jackie thinks that the others fulfill more of the criteria.'" Her eyes start to water, and I can tell she's holding back tears. "I'm just never enough. I do everything they ask, and it's still not good enough."

"That doesn't make any sense. You are by far the best dancer at your studio. Everyone knows that. It's that owner. I know it is; she has always been the problem. Did they explain what this criteria is that they are talking about?" I ask, my tone upset because this is wrong. Nobody treats my best friend this way!

"I had a heart-to-heart with my instructor and my mom. I am going to do some solo training and am giving the studio one more year. If I'm not chosen for the next competition, then I will switch studios over the summer. My instructor is baffled as to why I wasn't selected. She even told me that all the instructors recommended me as their first choice, but ultimately, the decision is the owner's. Miss Jackie never liked me. Remember how she had me do all those extra tryouts to get into the competitive classes? She didn't do that to anyone else. " Trina says with a huge sigh, "I just want to be so good that she can't hold me back, even if she wants to."

"I'm so sorry, Trina. I know how much you deserve to be the one competing. I wish you didn't have to go through all this. It's so unfair." I always think of Trina as unstoppable with her confidence, her outgoing nature and her talent. It makes it even more upsetting to see her down. She's always been my rock. Listening to her talk about this with such strength makes her even more amazing in my eyes.

"Well, it feels good to have a plan, and I will try my best the rest of this year. If it happens this way again, then I'm leaving, and so is my instructor. We made a pact." She shoots me a mischievous grin, knowing the studio would be losing one of their best teachers.

"Sounds like a plan!" I say, glad to see Trina has someone at the studio fully in her corner. As the bus turns the corner and arrives at the entrance at school, I add, "Let's make this the best year ever!" My outfit mishap now seems so ridiculous after hearing everything that Trina is going through.

"Best year ever, now that sounds fun!" Trina says with a laugh, her spirits lifting just as we get up to leave the bus.

The entrance seems so grand, with steps leading to the main door that are steeped in tradition. The upperclassmen and cool kids rule the steps. The doors are propped open and its full of activity as the buses are lined up one after another, letting the students off. I take a deep breath, trying to build up confidence before walking into my new home for the next four years.

"Welcome, Freshman!" An intimidatingly large senior boy greets us by standing right in our way, blocking us once again as we try to move around him.

"Yeah, thanks. But you're kinda in our way." Trina says back, matching his aggressiveness.

"Okay, okay. Have a nice first day, ladies." He puts his arms up in surrender with a fake smile and moves to the side. Everything in his tone of voice makes me uncomfortable, and I am already second-guessing my declaration of the best year ever. If Trina wasn't with me, that would have been much worse. I know it.

The hallway was filled with similar activity, putting the freshman in their place. The upperclassmen 'owned' this school and wanted to make sure we knew it. Trina, being confident Trina, just gave it right back and continued walking. I followed her with my head down, trying hide myself.

As we reach my locker, Trina looks at me concerned. "You gonna be alright?"

"Yeah," I say, though it doesn't sound very believable.

"My locker is just down there if you need me. I'll see you at lunch." Watching Trina walk away, I feel a huge knot in my gut.

I start to put away the books I won't need and grab my math book for 1st period. As I turn to go to class I notice Ryan stuck between two guys, probably seniors, and his back against the lockers. Ryan is in my grade and a smaller kid who likes to keep to himself. He has always been nice to me, and tried to help when people have teased me in the past. I was always grateful to him for sticking up for me. I can't believe it myself when I find that I'm walking over toward him.

"Hey Ryan, are you going to walk me to my class?" I ask trying to save him, but not daring to look the seniors in the eye the way Trina does. I know I'm being too sheepish and force myself to face them. I stand as tall as I can while looking them in the eye. "Let him go," I demand, although it comes out weak, more of a suggestion than a command.

They have smirks on their face and start laughing. "Who is this? Your little girlfriend trying to save you?" They ask Ryan before turning back to me.

"No, sweetie, Ryan isn't going to walk you to your class. Nice outfit, by the way. What is that? My little pony? My sister loved those when she was, like, 6." They say, laughing. "Nice try, little girl, but we have business with him. If you want, we can include you in it..." The threatening tone used makes me back away.

"No, no, that's okay," I say as I start to back away and lip the word sorry to Ryan before turning to leave. As I walk away, I hear them shove him against the locker, and just then, I walk into a teacher.

"Are you okay? The seniors?" He asks once he sees how shaken I am and clearly aware of how the upperclassmen treat the newbies.

"Umm, yeah, I guess." I hear another bang, making me cringe, and I look in the direction of Ryan. The teacher follows my gaze, nods his head and taps my shoulder as if to say, I got this.

"Hey, hey, Blake, Craig. Enough! You two get to class. Now!" He yells, calling out their names. The minute I hear their names, I know exactly who they are. Blake, a junior and the varsity quarterback. Along with Craig, a senior on the football team. They are known for being best friends. Infamous in the town, even though I only know them by name and story, that is who I end up encountering on my first day.

"Nice work, Teacher's Pet. We won't forget this." Blake says and purposely bumps into me while walking to his class. It's at this moment I decide from now on I'm going to stay under the radar.

"Hey, you okay?" Nate comes over. Nate, of all people, and my heart starts beating so hard I think he must be able to hear it. I don't know where he was, but he must have seen what happened. As I look up at him, I can't believe it's the same Nate as my 8th-grade crush. He must have grown a foot, and he looks strong. He certainly isn't the skinny, smaller kid he was at the end of last year. It's still Nate, though, with that same curly dark hair and kind eyes. The boy I was crushing on all summer is now HOT! Forget wondering if there is a spark. It's more like an explosion! Well…at least on my end.

"Yeah, I'm okay. Thanks." I say, looking down and full of shyness all of a sudden, not knowing what to say. The bell rings, and I add, "I should get to class."

"Okay. Yeah, me too." He says and shoots me a smile that makes me melt. As he turns down the hall I see Stacy, the most popular girl in our class, walk over to him and link her arm through his. He grins ear to ear, and I know I've lost my sweet Nate to the popular crowd.

Chapter One
Invisible

Staring at the clock, it reads 11:59, only one minute left before school is out for summer. The final minute of freshman year is taking forever. I keep thinking about how much that first day impacted my whole year. That was the day I decided to spend all year trying to stay under the radar. Today is a half-day, and nobody feels like doing anything, including Mr. Jackson. He let the class pick from a list of school-approved movies and brought in popcorn for a snack. Nobody is paying attention; half the kids are sleeping, and the rest are packed up, ready to leave the second the bell rings. Mr. Jackson is leaning back in his chair with his feet kicked up on his desk, maybe a little too comfortable since he fell asleep about 20 minutes ago. The bell finally rings. Startled, he jumps a foot off his chair. That makes me chuckle. I totally saw that coming. Managing to quickly recover, he gets to the door in time to wish us well. "Bye, have a great summer," he repeats as each of us file out of his class. Freshman year is finally over.

Once out the door, the crowd engulfs me as I head down the hall. A couple of the girls from the freshman dance team spot me and yell across the crowd, "Bye, Becks! Have a great summer!"

"You too!" I yell back with a smile and wave as they turn the corner and disappear. This is impossible. I'll never find Trina in this crowd. We're supposed to meet at her locker after class, which is in the wrong direction. The sea of people forces me to follow the crowd, there's no use trying to fight it. Everyone is exiting the school out of the main entrance today, and that is where the crowd leads me. Once outside, I'm greeted by sunshine, a sign that summer has officially begun.

The warm sun is inviting, and I close my eyes to look up. I love the warmth of the sun on my face. Suddenly, my whole body lunges forward as someone bumps me, "Hey, watch it!" they yell at me. I look at them in disbelief as they walk away, saying loudly to their friend, "Stupid freshman." The steps of the school are covered with students, but I find an open spot where I can wait for Trina. All the cool kids hang out on the steps, and it's obvious I don't belong. Where is Trina? I hate standing here alone. Obsessively watching as everyone exits the school, hoping she will be in the crowd. She isn't. Instead, I see that short, dark, wavy hair that instantly makes my heart skip a beat, and I know it's Nate.

My heart flutters at the sight of him. He is tall for a freshman, although he didn't start out that way. He used to get teased about his size in middle school, being smaller than most guys. It never seemed to bother him. He took it all in stride, and always just smiled through all the small kid jokes. Part of his nonchalance probably came from the fact that even though he was smaller than most of the guys, he was still more athletic than just about all of them. I used to feel bad for him, being teased about his height. Now that he's grown into this tall, athletic man, every girl is crushing on him, including me.

As he starts walking down the stairs, he looks in my direction. Swallowing nervously, I stare as he continues to walk towards me. All year, I've been daydreaming about this moment. The moment Nate and I finally have a conversation, my heart is racing. This is my chance.

He's close enough that I could reach out and touch him. Smiling at me as he walks toward me, I keep looking at his bright blue eyes as he reaches me. Finally, finding the courage I take a step towards him, saying one simple word.

"Hi." It's all I can manage.

Every ounce of courage is needed, but it's the last day. I haven't talked to him all year, except for one sentence on the first day. I need to do *something.* Just as the word falls out of my mouth I realize he is looking *past* me.

He completely ignores me as he nods his head at someone behind me. He didn't even *see* me. I'm dying of embarrassment. Of course, he wasn't walking towards me. What was I thinking? At least he has no idea what happened; to him, I don't even exist. Mortified, I look around, hoping nobody witnessed this. Nate's out of my league now. He's no longer that scrawny kid who complimented me after the 8th-grade talent show. Now, he is everyone's crush. All year, its been a constant on-and-off thing with him and Stacy, the most popular girl in our grade.

Across the stairway, the senior guys are snickering, and I know they saw it. Oh no! Any second now, and the teasing is going to start.

"Nice try!" Blake yells over while he and his friends start laughing. "Hey guys, looks like Teacher's Pet has a thing for Nate! Good luck with that!" This makes the guys laugh even harder. All year, I've been known as Teacher's Pet since that first day trying to help Ryan. I just want to disappear. I'm so embarrassed.

"*Hiii, Nate. Nate, you want to go out?*" One of them says loudly, in a girly tone, acting like a love-struck girl. The guys behind him are mocking me making smooching noises.

"*Ooo, Nate, why won't you come talk to me?*" His friend adds in the same tone as they start laughing.

"Did you see that? He totally blew her off!" They say, laughing and pointing me out to another friend.

Nate turns towards them, "What are you guys talking about?" He is oblivious, thankfully. I need to disappear before he figures it out.

"Your girl! You totally ignored her!" They say, pointing at me, followed by them asking me "Didn't he, Teacher's Pet?" Again, they are laughing and pointing at me. I need to get out of here now! Screw this, I'm waiting for Trina on the bus.

Nate looks at me; his expression is confused, and for a split second, we lock eyes. My whole body responds; my heart races, my palms sweat, and that familiar burning sensation starts on my cheeks. I know I'm turning bright red. The moment lasts maybe one second before I look away and run off the staircase towards the bus, mortified.

As I run away, I hear Nate "Becky, you okay?" Followed by, "You guys are the worst! Leave her alone."

It's nice to hear him sticking up for me, but I continue to run towards the safety of the bus.

The warm, stale air of the bus hits me as I reach the top of the steps. It smells of Lysol and sweat; so gross. The bus is empty. Everyone else is gathered around the school entrance, saying goodbye to their friends. I let out a sigh of relief now that I'm away from the crowd. The warm air of the bus is already suffocating me, but I'm still more comfortable here than outside. Air circulation is all I need. The windows are stuck, and it takes all my strength to pull the window open. Finally, the breeze hits my face as the window releases. Sitting at the back of the bus, I watch through the small window as people say their goodbyes.

Teachers and students are all smiles, celebrating and cheerfully making plans for summer. There are yells of "See you tonight," followed by hugs. Friends wave goodbye while heading to their cars. A group of sophomores walk below the bus window and are excitedly making plans for all the parties that follow the last day of school. But not me. All year, I was invisible, and that's how this year will end. Alone. It wasn't supposed to be this way. I started the year with such high hopes.

As I look out the window of the bus once more, I feel a tug at my heart, wishing I was out there. It's one of those rare moments when everyone is in high spirits. All drama is pushed to the side on the last school day. I should be happy looking at all the smiling faces, but it just makes me feel so withdrawn.

Trina has finally exited the school and is making her way towards the bus. We ride the same bus since we grew up down the street from each other. There is no way I would have survived this year without her. Typical Trina, she stops every few feet to chat with whoever she passes, and I realize that's why it's taking her forever to get to me. It doesn't matter who is along her path. She literally talks to everyone. She doesn't realize how beautiful she is. Her strong ballerina body, blemish-free dark skin, and contrasting white smile are truly stunning. There isn't too much diversity at our school, and I know that gets to her. Everyone likes her, but I know she wishes more people truly understood her.

A group of juniors are standing together in the corner of the main landing, probably making plans for some big party tonight. On the main steps of the entrance, the girls from the competitive dance team are talking with the senior guys. The juniors yell something over to them, shifting Trina's attention toward them. She walks over to them and starts talking to them for a couple of minutes. Honestly, how does she do that? I would never just talk to upperclassmen like that! I'm full of pride watching my friend, in awe of her confidence.

My stomach turns, and my heart starts racing as she approaches Nate. Oh no, what if they talk about me? Not today, after what just happened. As I start to worry, my thoughts get interrupted as beautiful Stacy sneaks up behind him, effortlessly wrapping her arms around him and says something to Nate with a cheerful smile. He turns and smiles back at her with that smile of his that makes me melt. Stacy and Nate were on Sweetheart court together this year, and ever since, they've been the talk of the school. I never had a chance with Nate once Stacy was into him.

She is beautiful and popular and just has this way about her. I remember walking by her locker, and she literally had people surrounding her, listening intently to her tell some interesting story. It's incredible how she captivates people. It feels like I'm punishing myself watching the two of them together, yet I can't look away.

Nate looks over at me, or at least in my direction. Instinctively, I look down, still mortified from earlier. Did he just look at me?

Daring to look out the window once more, the moment has passed, his face now turned away from me as he flirts with Stacy.

"Hey, what are you looking at?" Trina asks as she sits next to me on the bus. Following my gaze, she finds Nate talking to Stacy and gives me an encouraging nudge. "Hey, don't worry about them. A lot can change over the summer. He didn't have the chance to get to know you this year, but once he does…watch out, Stacy!" At least Trina has some confidence in me.

"Yeah, I know. That's never going to happen, though. The school year is over, and I didn't talk to him all year." I say with a sigh. "Thank goodness I'm getting out of here for a week. What did Nate say?" I ask, feeling suddenly anxious, wondering if they talked about me.

"He just asked if I was going to Blake's party tonight. You know, you are welcome to go. Nate will be there. I mean, there really is no reason that he wouldn't be totally into you once he gets to know you better." She says with a smile, trying to cheer me up. Blake, ugh, definitely not going. Blake is a typical jock; Popular, handsome, and totally obnoxious. Not to mention, he only ever refers to me as Teacher's Pet. No thanks.

"Thanks, Trina. I have to pack, though. We leave for our family 'school's out' trip tomorrow." As I say it, a pang of jealousy hits me, knowing everyone else will be at a party tonight. Although, I do love that we always head to Florida for a week to celebrate the end of the school year.

The bus starts to pull away, leaving the school behind. I look out the window once more, just in time to see Nate give Stacy a kiss on her forehead while he takes her hand in his. My heart sinks, wishing it was me instead.

"Becks, don't sweat it. I'm sure by the time school starts next year, this 'Nate and Stacy thing ' will be history." Trina's trying to comfort me, but right now, I just want to get out of this town.

"I just wish I didn't like him so much. It's ridiculous. I barely even talk to him." I say with a loud sigh of frustration. All year I wasted any chance I had to get to know Nate better, because I was too afraid.

"Well, maybe you'll find some cute guys in Florida!" Trina adds cheerfully, and that makes me smile. It's time to change the subject, and we both start talking about all the surfer boys I could potentially meet.

"I mean, there are worse things than having to settle for a hot surfer," I say, teasing. We keep coming up with silly opening lines to use to start a conversation with these imaginary surfers. All the surfer lingo we can remember is "hang ten" and "gnarly dude." We are laughing now. My mood vastly improved.

"Enough about me. When will you find out if the studio chose you for the summer competition?" I ask, knowing it will be any day now that Trina and her dance instructor either prepare for the next competition or prepare to leave the studio.

"Today." She says, and her normal confidence dwindles.

"Are you nervous?" I know I should say something more encouraging, but I don't know what else to say.

"Yeah, a little. I just want to feel like I actually have the same chance as everyone else at the studio. I never feel that way with Miss Jackie." Trina says.

"You deserve it, T. You really do." I say, knowing she works so hard and is so talented.

"Thanks, Becks."

Arriving at my stop, I give Trina a hug goodbye. "I'm going to miss you so much! Let me know as soon as you hear, okay?" I won't see her much during the summer. I'll be at the cottage, and she'll be busy with her summer dance season.

"I will, promise. And I'll see you whenever you're in town." Turning to wave goodbye once more as I exit the bus.

Just as I was finishing packing up for Florida, I got a text from Trina. All it says is, 'Can I come over? The studio just called.' I reply yes, and immediately head downstairs and out the door. She only lives a few houses down and will be here any minute.

As I watch Trina walk towards my house, I try to decipher from her body language what the news will be. My hands are sweaty from all the nervous energy beating through my body. Please, please, please is the only thought in my mind. Trina knows if she will finally get to compete in the youth international ballet competition. She is the best dancer in the studio but has been overlooked to compete for years now. I know it will break her heart if they don't choose her again! She's worked so hard and even added extra solo coaching with her teacher this year. She deserves this!

"Well??" I yell as I run over to Trina, who is walking up the driveway. As I get closer, my excited run slows to a stop. Trina's eyes are red and glossy, as if she has been crying. My heart sinks as I think, 'Oh no, not again!' I am angry and heartbroken for her and have no idea how to make her feel any better.

She looks me in the eye. Her body slouched, so unlike her typical perfect ballerina posture. All she can do is shake her head 'No' before crying into my shoulder as I give her a hug. Looks like she will be changing studios this summer after all.

Chapter Two
The Necklace

The hot Florida sun penetrates my bedroom window. Even with the air conditioning on, I can feel the heat as I get ready for the beach. My hands are full with my beach bag, towel and hat. As I open my bedroom door, I can hear my Grandpa talking to my mom. "It just seems like she's been a bit down lately, that's all." I quietly wait at the door, listening, knowing they are talking about me. Nothing more is said, so I yell to Mom, "I'm hitting the beach!"

"Okay, Gramps and I will head down for a walk in a little bit." She calls back. The beach is right outside the condo, and there is a spot near the shore where I set up my chair. Finally seated, I kick off my flip-flops and dig my toes into the sand. Listening to the crashing waves, I try not to worry about what I overheard. I know grandpa always picks up on my moods and is worried about me. Instead of thinking about that, my mind wonders to Nate. Once again, for the millionth time, I imagine myself flirting with him as we talk and laugh for hours. I slyly touch his arm, and we look into each other's eyes. I've completely lost myself in this daydream. Once again, I've won the heart of Nate.

"Hey, Becks, your Gramps and I are going to walk to the pier. Want to join us?" My mom says, bringing me back to earth, as they set down their beach chairs.

"No thanks, I'm just going to chill here," I say while still on a high from my daydream.

"Okay, well, if you need to go to the condo for anything, Grandma is there to let you in." Grandma always hides from the sun. She can't handle the heat for long. I'm starting to understand her point. I don't think I can sit here much longer, either.

As my mom and Gramps start walking down the beach, my mind takes over once more, but this time, I decide to take Trina's advice. This time, my daydream is about meeting a hot surfer who is tall and tan, with his bright blue eyes and bleached hair hanging loose around his face. He teaches me to surf, using all the slang Trina and I thought up while on the bus; it is a daydream, after all. Suddenly, the heat snaps me back to earth. The intense southern sun tends to sneak up on me, and I don't want my fair skin to get burnt. It's time to head inside.

Off in the distance, I notice my mom and grandpa walking the beach; they won't be too much longer. Grandpa's walk always gives him away. There's something distinct about the way he swings his arms as he meanders down the beach, periodically stopping to pick up shells along the way. Daytona Beach has unique hard-packed sand that makes shells stand out very distinctly, and I can't wait to see what he finds this time. He has the best luck finding the most magnificent shells along the ocean shore. Actually, he's amazing, lucky with everything, and likes to claim it's because he's Irish.

Gramps looks particularly delighted with himself as they approach and calls out, "Becks, I found something for you!" He must have found a really cool seashell, maybe a whole sand dollar! Those are my favorite, but its rare to find one still intact. As he gets closer, there is something in his hand that is shimmering in the sunlight. What is catching the light like that? As he opens his hand, the shining object falls a few inches, revealing what he found. It's a pendant that's catching the light.

Grandpa walks over to me, he holds out the pendant, "Would you look at this? It's in the shape of a four-leaf clover!" He laughs, his contagious, whooping laugh, before explaining, "I asked around where I found it, and nobody claimed it. Can you believe it? I can't imagine how it ended up on the beach." He is shaking his head in astonishment at his luck. This kind of 'lucky' thing happens to him all the time. Honestly, I'm amused that he's even surprised by it anymore.

"I just know this necklace is meant for you. Let me put it on and see how it looks." He looks at me with a proud smile as he clasps it on the back of my neck. He adds, "Irish luck will be with you anytime you wear it, it's your lucky necklace! I just know it's a sign of a great year for you, kiddo." Chills run up my spine as if he unknowingly cast a spell.

"I'll wear it every day! Thanks, Gramps." I say while hugging him. I've always been in awe of my grandpa, and maybe somehow, having this with me will help me be more like him. He can make anyone laugh and will talk with any stranger, easily turning them into a friend. I wish I was more like him. I sigh at the thought as I instinctively grab the necklace. If only he would've passed down those genes to me.

Everyone is tired from traveling and spending the day in the sun, so we decided to stay in tonight. We're watching a Lifetime movie when I get a major craving for ice cream. "Do we have any ice cream?"

"No, we only got the essentials today. We can pick some up tomorrow, though." Mom says, which is a total disappointment.

"That does sound good, though," Grandma adds while looking at Grandpa with encouraging eyes.

"Well, I guess I can make a quick run to the store. Want to come with me?" Gramps asks, looking in my direction.

"Of course, I want to pick the flavors!" I'm already standing; this ice cream craving is serious. Grandpa and I head to the grocery store to pick up a couple of half gallons. I have thoughts of mint chocolate chip and Rocky Road. As he walks in the door, the first thing he notices is the scratch-off lottery tickets, and he immediately veers towards the machine. He looks over at me with a smile and says, "Well, Becks, pick a winner. You have your lucky necklace on, right?"

"I do." Feeling silly, I reach up for the necklace as I look at the different scratch-offs. I chose a purple one because I like the color.

Grandpa buys the scratch-off before we continue to the ice cream aisle.

We arrive home with our ice cream and the scratch-off lottery ticket. As I start putting the ice cream in the freezer, he sits down to start scratching off the ticket. Slowly, with each scratch it is revealing different numbers and dollar amounts.

"Becks, I think we have a winner!" He yells and whoops. Running over, I lean over his shoulder as he scratches the final spot on the card. It looks like we really won, and we double-check it against the rules. Immediately laughing in amazement, he says, "Well, would you look at that!? We just won $200! Maybe it was your lucky necklace after all!" It's fantastic he includes me in on his luck, but I'm not exactly convinced it has anything to do with the necklace. He is the lucky one, not me. After overhearing him talking to mom earlier today, I think he'd do anything to cheer me up.

"Well, I guess we should celebrate with some ice cream!" Grandma says as she starts to scoop ice cream for everyone. She gives everyone a bowl, and as I head to sit down, she asks me, "So, do you think that necklace really is lucky?"

"Maybe. What do you think?" I ask, curious about what Grandma will say.

"I think if you believe it's lucky, then it is." She says with a smile, but I'm not sure what to make of it.

The next couple of days were beautiful, and we were all getting nice tans, except Grandma, still hiding from the sun. She watches us from the shaded balcony of the condo and waves down to us every day. Today, though, wasn't so nice out. It's the first day that's overcast and windy. It isn't nice enough to lay out in the sun, walking the beach is the next best thing. "Mom, I'm going to walk to the pier," I call out to her.

"Okay, we'll have lunch ready for you when you get back." She yells back to me. The pier is only about a mile away, so I shouldn't be gone too long.

"Look for shells, Becks. I bet those waves brought in some good ones! I found a couple this morning!" Grandpa yells as I walk out the door.

"Okay, I'll keep my eye out for some good ones." I yell back before adding, "I have my lucky necklace on, so maybe I'll find something good!" Grandpa's whooping laugh fills the condo; I knew he would get a kick out of that.

The wind on the beach is intense; despite my best efforts, I'm making slow progress walking against the wind. Waves are breaking far out in the ocean, and a red flag is flying at the lifeguard station to warn against swimming. It's pretty 'gnarly' out here. The thought makes me laugh, and I wish Trina was here to appreciate my surfer slang. We always make each other laugh; she'd get my joke. A few people are walking the beach, and some surfers are taking advantage of the huge waves closer to the pier, but overall, the beach is empty. My ears whistling from the wind, along with the surf crashing, is creating an almost hypnotic sound. The plan was to listen to music during the walk, but I am too entranced with the sound of the waves. There is something spiky sticking out of the sand, and I'm reminded of Grandpa telling me to look for cool shells. I'm closer to the pier now, and sometimes shells get stuck over here. I bend over to see if it's anything worthwhile, digging around it to pick it up, and am looking at a broken shell when I hear someone say, "Hey."

Looking up, I'm hit with total shock. It reminds me of the time Nate talked to me at the end of 8th grade. "Hey, uhh…um, what's up?" I'm stammering in disbelief. I'm looking into the eyes of my surfer. It's my tall, tan, blue-eyed surfer from my daydream. I turn around to make sure he is actually talking to me, suddenly re-living that mortifying moment with Nate. Nobody is behind me, he really is talking to me. He's leaning against his surfboard with his wetsuit half on, casually letting the top hang behind him. He is gorgeous, like, Nate who? I could definitely get over Nate quickly with this guy around.

"I was just wondering if you happen to know what time it is?" He asks.

"Oh, um, yeah." I fumble as I grab the phone out of my pocket and say, "It's quarter after 1:00."

"Thanks. I probably have time for a couple more." He says, shooting me a smile.

"Sweet, hang ten!" I say enthusiastically and immediately regret it. Why am I so awkward? Trina and I were incorporating 'hang ten' into our imaginary surfer conversations, so I'm sure that's why I blurted it out.

He laughs at me, smiles, and shoots me the "hang loose" hand signal. Then he adds, "Thanks again!" before he runs off.

I don't move, I can't. Instead, I watch him further down the beach as he puts his wetsuit back on before running into the water to catch a wave. Staring in astonishment, I can't stop myself. It's like he came out of nowhere. Literally, it's the surfer I've been daydreaming about all week. It seems absurd, but it really feels like I created this moment. All my daydreaming made this happen, could that have been a premonition, or the necklace? Adrenaline has taken over my body, and the rush of that encounter makes me feel unstoppable. Bring it on, world!

The next day, the shoreline of the beach is peaceful, with waves softly crashing in the background. The ocean has calmed, but my hope was still raging from yesterday. Playfully moving the necklace back and forth on its chain, wondering if it has some luck to it after all.

Chapter Three
Sophomore

The start of sophomore year is looming. My summer was spent at the cottage, away from the daily gossip that surrounded my neighborhood. Most people assume I have boring summers because I'm not around town hanging with friends. The truth is, I love my summers at the cottage. My introverted side thrives there. I'm not popular enough to get any summer party invites, and I never really keep up with the gossip. Besides, I'd rather live through my daydreams where my life is perfect and much more exciting than my real life. I haven't seen anybody all summer except Trina. She almost died when I told her about my encounter with the hot surfer while on vacation. She made me retell that story over and over. In her defense, it does make us laugh every time. I'll never live down my now infamous "hang ten."

Reality is hitting, and anxiety is starting to wash over me. Tomorrow is the first day of school. This year has to be better, and it all starts with my outfit. Freshman year flashbacks flood my mind, no unicorns this year. It's essential to pick the right outfit, something that says, 'I'm cool and confident!' It's a fine line between looking casually cool and looking like I tried too hard. It'll be judged by all the other girls, and I need to pull out all the stops on the first day. I hate it. So much pressure. If I get it wrong, I'll be an immediate target for ridicule again.

Magazines are piled up on my desk alongside pages full of ideas, my search for inspiration for my first-day outfit is so far unsuccessful. On top of my bed, there is a heap of clothes, which continues to grow larger as I reject another outfit attempt. It was a hopeless idea to try to revive this sundress from last year. None of my clothes exude confidence. The next option is a button-down shirt dress with booties. It's simple but effective. I try it on and do a few spins in the full-length mirror. Finally, I feel comfortable and trendy, but not so trendy that it's risky. As usual, I'm going with the safe bet.

I hated middle school when it first started too, and it did get better. It wasn't until 8th grade that I started to look and feel more confident. Goodbye braces, hello contacts. Nate even noticed me after the talent show at the end of 8th grade. It took until the end of middle school to find my confidence, only to lose it again on the first day of high school. I have to make this year count; no more hiding in the shadows. The only plan I have is to dress cool and try to open up more. Easier said than done.

After Freshman year, I'm not even sure what's worse: feeling invisible or being picked on. I'll never forget how withdrawn it felt sitting alone on the bus, watching as everyone else celebrated the start of summer. I don't ever want to feel that way again. I made a promise to myself that I'd be more outgoing this year. Although, I'm having second thoughts, instinctively I reach for the necklace. It does seem to calm my nerves when I start to overthink things.

Stevie starts barking; someone must be here. He always alerts us when someone has arrived. There is no need for a doorbell at our house. Our little rescue dog has a bark that doesn't match his size. He's only 10 pounds, and most of his size comes from his fluffy white fur, but his bark fills the entire house. Peeking out my window I see Grandpa and Grandma's car pull into the driveway. It's nice that they are around so much, especially since they always ease my mind. I'm not sure if they are stopping by to check on me, but I already feel lighter knowing they're here.

"Hey, Becks, are you excited for your first day of sophomore year?" Grandpa asks once he notices me walking down the stairway.

"Uh, yeah, I guess." My tone matches the unenthusiastic shrug off my shoulders.

"You don't sound so sure." He says with a knowing look.

"I always worry before the first day; I haven't seen anybody all summer."

"I like the outfit. Is that what you're wearing tomorrow?" Grandma asks, knowing how important an outfit can be. She has an amazing style, so hearing she likes it makes me feel better.

"Yeah, this is my first-day outfit, I just decided. I'm so glad you like it!"

"You look great! Are you excited to see Trina and the girls from the dance team?" Grandma asks with an encouraging smile.

"Yeah, it will be nice to see them," I say with a sigh. I know she's trying to find something for me to look forward to, but I'm still nervous. "The upperclassmen are so intimidating though, I can't think about it."

"Well, kiddo, I'm not worried. You have great friends, and I know they will be excited to see you. Don't let those older kids bother you. Besides, the Freshman will be intimidated by you this year!" Grandpa says with a laugh as he puts his arm around me, playfully giving me half a hug. He would never have to worry about something like this; everyone loves him.

"Easy for you to say," I say, which makes him laugh as he shakes his head at that.

"You'll have a great first day back, no doubt in my mind," Grandma says. It's her turn to give me a hug. She looks at the time and says, "We need to head home, Joe. I need to start the oven, or we'll be eating too late." Is she serious? It's only 3:30. They eat dinner so early!

"That was a quick visit, you're leaving already?" I ask since they just got here.

"We just had to return your mother's Tupperware and wanted to check on you before your first day." Grandma says, adding, "It'll be great, Becks."

Grandpa comes over to hug me goodbye and says, "Now, don't forget that this is your year, kiddo! Don't let anything change your mind about that. Remember, you have the luck of the Irish on your side!" He says with a wink, and I can't help but think about the necklace.

"Thanks, Grandpa. Thanks, Grandma. Love you!" I yell as they are getting into their car.

"Love you too, Becks. You'll be great! Go get 'em." Grandpa yells back.

"Love you too, Sweetie. Have a great first day!" Grandma says as she waves goodbye.

It was so nice to see them and get a little reassurance. This year will be better. I have the perfect back-to-school outfit, complete with my lucky charm.

Chapter Four
Week One

Two major things are at the top of my wish list: Nate McNeil and the competitive dance team. It's so easy for me to picture it…I'm sitting in class, and who other than Nate McNeil sits right next to me. He walks in wearing his classic t-shirt and jeans with his curly brown hair falling unruly on his forehead. He keeps smiling at me, leaning over and flirting with me during class. After class, he asks me out and holds my hand as we walk down the hallway. We walk right into the dance competition, and there I am with the dance team being awarded the regional trophy. A pep rally follows, where the team performs for the school, and we show off our trophy to everyone. The crowd is full of applause and admiration. I see Nate walking over to me, and he kisses me in front of the whole school. "I'm so lucky you're my girl," he says and leans…

"Becky, earth to Becky…" Trina interrupts my daydream and snaps me out of it.

"Oh, uh, sorry. I was.."

"Daydreaming about Nate again?" She asks, laughing and shaking her head as I shoot her a guilty look. "I knew it! You're always dreaming about him. What class do you have next? The bell is about to ring."

"I have history with Mr. Whitman."

"I had class with him first period, and he seems alright. I guess I'll see you at lunch then?"

"Yeah, sounds good." I agree as I pack up my books to head to my next class.

My first day was going pretty well so far. At least the harassment was not focused on the sophomore class, it was saved solely for the Freshman. A few times, I was able to step in and save them or offer them some kind words. Luckily, I've been spared from that stress. Speaking of luck, Trina made plans for Ally to drive us to school from now on since she lives down the street. Trina met Ally through her new dance studio, and they became fast friends over the summer. No more buses! Should I add this to the list of lucky things that have happened since my necklace? Ally is super popular, a year older, and now she's my ride to school every day! This year I have one class with Trina, so things are already looking up.

I reach my history class and I find a seat halfway to the back in the row closest to the door, the perfect spot to leave class quickly. I get out my notebook and search my bag for a pen. Found it! Looking up, my heart jumps into my throat.

It's Nate.

This is not a daydream; this is real. As he walks into class, he looks around for a seat and spots me. For some reason, he starts heading towards me. Nate: the most popular kid in school. The same guy I spent my summer, and, as a matter of fact, my last class, daydreaming about. He's much closer to me now, we lock eyes, and he smiles. Why would Nate sit by me? Seats are open all over, including next to Alesha and Stacy in the popular crowd section. Nate and Stacy continued to be a thing over the summer, but apparently now she is dating Blake. Instinctively, I look over at her, but her eyes are glued to Nate. As he puts his bag down next to me, she catches my eye and shoots me a fake smile. I hate when girls do that. The last thing I need is an enemy like Stacy, so I smile back and wave. She doesn't wave back, instead turning away in a huff, obviously not happy.

He sits down next to me and gives me a friendly smile. I smile back but don't dare say a word. Memories of the last time I tried to talk to him flood me, and I'm dying inside. Nate isn't just some guy in school. He is *the* guy in school. Well, *the* guy in the sophomore class, anyway. He's funny, smart, athletic, and everyone likes him. Over the summer, he made the varsity soccer team and now hangs out with a bunch of upperclassmen. Of all people, I honestly can't fathom why he chose to sit by me.

My thoughts are interrupted by Nate leaning over, asking, "Hey, are you alright?" Oh no, I must be making one of my faces. Anytime I'm really lost in thought, my face generally gives me away. Mom always tells me that everyone knows exactly what I'm thinking.

"Oh yeah, yeah, I'm good. Umm, how was your summer?" So far, I'm definitely not smooth like in my daydream, but at least I said something. Act normal, Becky. It's just some guy. As I try to regain my composure, I take a deep breath, but I am all too aware that it's not just some guy. It's Nate! Nate is sitting next to me! It's my chance to finally redeem myself. Another daydream is coming true! I can't believe this.

"My summer was good. I spent a lot of time playing soccer. How about you?" He asks.

"Me? What about me?" I'm so distracted by my thoughts that I don't understand what he is asking. He has a little smirk on his face, looking at me like he thinks I'm cute. Or… on second thought, it's more likely he's thinking I'm awkward. I mean, I'm not exactly acting normal at the moment. Relax, Becky, calm down.

"How was your summer?" he asks again. Seriously, after all my conversations with him in all my dreams, this really should be going better.

"Oh, it was good. I spent a lot of time at the beach, um, at our cottage. But no soccer for me. I'm not very coordinated, ha. I read a lot of books, too." He nods as he listens, but this is not the charming conversation I had envisioned. Just stop talking and smile; maybe he will say something. He doesn't.

Mr. Whitman starts class, "Welcome to class. I'm Mr. Whitman, this week we are going to discuss…" Whew. He started class just in time before I ended up doing something really embarrassing.

Suddenly, my instinct to grab my necklace is overwhelming, and as I hold the shamrock between my fingers, 'thank you' is what comes to mind. Grandpa could be right, this necklace really does bring me luck. I've dreamt this would happen for so long. 'If only I would sit by Nate, and we could talk and get to know each other. We could become close friends until he suddenly realized he loved me.' That was always the gist of my daydreams. It starts with us sitting by each other in class and ends with us in love. This, though, was real life, and he is literally sitting next to me in class. Unbelievable.

I can't stop sneaking glances at Nate. This is really happening. He catches me and gives me the most adorable smile. I look away quickly as my heart races. He's not full of himself like you might think. Actually, he's genuinely nice. Last year, I think he wasn't prepared for all the attention. After his growth spurt, he became incredibly handsome and the girls were flocking to him. For me, I always liked his fun, outgoing energy, along with his striking blue eyes that stand out against his contrasting dark brown hair and his smile. I swear, that smile can uplift anyone's mood. Those features haven't changed. He's still the boy I liked before he was on everyone's radar.

To avoid staring at him, I look directly at Mr. Whitman during class as if I'm enthralled by his lecture. Nate already caught me looking at him once, and I can sense him looking over at me periodically during class. My whole body responds to Nate's glances, everything from a racing heart to sweaty hands. This chance can't pass me by. I promised myself I would not be invisible this year. Should I ask him to borrow something? But what, a pen? I hope my face isn't noticeably red, giving me away as I pretend to be nonchalant.

"Hey. Nate." I loudly whisper as my heart starts beating out of its chest. He turns toward me with a questioning look.

"Uh, um, do you have an extra pen? My ink ran out." Lies. I'm a terrible liar. He knows I'm making it up. My palms are sweating. I'm so nervous.

He smiles and nods before digging through his bag. Finding a pen, he holds it up proudly and reaches it over to me. As I grab it our fingers touch, and it sends a rocket of energy through my body.

"Thanks. I'll give it back after..." I whisper before he cuts me off.

"No worries, you can keep it." He says with that smile of his. I'm so proud of myself.

Mr. Whitman isn't really all that interesting today, but he seems to appreciate my undivided attention. Most of the other students are ignoring him, so his eyes keep finding me as he lectures. Little does he know I'm only paying attention to distract myself from Nate.

The bell rings, and Nate is still gathering his books as I jump up to leave. I'm avoiding him because I'm not ready to talk to him again. Anytime I try to talk to him without a plan, I'm silent or just ramble on about nothing. Trina is going to die when I tell her what just happened. She's always encouraging me to talk to him. Walking down the hall, I'm urgently looking for her, but there are so many people in my way. Finally, I find her, and surprisingly, she's running towards me excitedly. It's as if she already knows I have great news to share.

"Did you hear?" She yells over to me. The halls are crowded. Everyone is moving in different directions, making it hard for her to actually reach me. Instead of yelling over the crowd, I shake my head; I don't know what she's talking about.

"Have I heard what? I have news, too!" I say as she finally manages to cross the hall over to me.

"They announced they are going to expand the high school competitive team this year! The team is adding two more spots! We really have a shot!" She exclaims. This is huge news for us. The competitive dance team adding two more spots will change the odds significantly in our favor. Reaching for my necklace, all I can hear is my Grandpa's words replaying in my mind. 'This necklace will bring you luck anytime you wear it. It's a sign of a great year for you, kiddo.'

The varsity girls' dance coach will soon start auditions for the competitive dance team. It's the second part of my daydream: making the team and winning the regional championship. The rules are that only sophomores and above can join, so this will be the first year we can try out. After the first round, there is always a huge cut, and if you even make it to the second round, it's a big deal. The second round is very selective and incredibly competitive. The addition of two spots on the team is definitely to our advantage but is still far from any kind of guarantee we'll make the team. Auditions for the first round of tryouts are next week.

Trina is still talking as we walk down the hall, but I'm not paying attention. My focus is on how amazing this is and the possibility that I could get everything I want this year.

"Let's practice at your house tonight!" Trina says excitedly, interrupting my thoughts.

"Definitely!" I agree with her and instinctively reach for my necklace. This necklace really could change everything. All I know is I believe it, and in my mind, I start repeating, 'Thank you, thank you, thank you!'

Trina came over after school to practice our routine for tryouts, and I finally got the chance to tell her about Nate. It was impossible during school. There was too much excitement about the competitive dance team. She's listened to me obsess about Nate for years. Once I finish telling her my story from history class, all she says is, "Well, at least now you'll have the chance to talk to the guy. You've only been crushing on him since when? Like, 8th grade? Keep me posted on him, but right now, we really need to practice." Her tone suggests that she doesn't think anything will really happen with Nate. It's also likely she's worried it will distract me from dance and doesn't want me to get too excited. Nothing is more important than dance in Trina's world. Honestly, she doesn't even need to worry about making the competitive team, she is so talented they are practically holding a spot for her. I really believe she would have been on the team last year if there wasn't a rule that excludes freshman.

"You know they're practically holding a spot for you, right? You're the best dancer in our school! I'm so glad you're helping me, though. I really need it." I haven't danced as long as everyone else trying out. Every time I practice with her, she really takes the time to make me a better dancer.

"My whole life, I've had to work twice as hard just to be taken seriously, especially in ballet. I never take making the team or winning a competition for granted." Trina's dream is to be like Misty Copeland, her idol. She is the first female African American Principal Dancer at American Ballet Theater, a very prestigious theater. Trina dreams of breaking down barriers and becoming a successful ballerina. I know she will do exactly that.

"I know you work hard! That's exactly why you will be on the team!"

"Thanks, Becks. It's just been my experience that it doesn't always work out that way." It's one of those moments where I'm glad Trina shares what she's thinking. She's been through so much with ballet. In the beginning, she had to fight to be allowed into the better dance studios but eventually came to win those battles. She's well known for her skills as a dancer now, and that's no small feat. I've always admired Trina. She's so accomplished and self-assured. Sometimes, I forget that she still has moments of self-doubt because, to me, she's always the most talented person in the room.

"I know, but you've been through so much and have proved yourself repeatedly! It'd be absolutely ridiculous if you didn't make the team. You're basically a professional! We are both making this team, no matter what!" I add, making Trina laugh at my newfound passion.

We plan to audition together, and the better we do together, the better our chances to both move on. Practice is essential, and nobody prepares like Trina. It's hard for me to keep up with her.

Since I started dancing, many people have complimented me on my performances, but I still doubt my ability. I'm grateful for their compliments, but deep down, I'm unsure of myself. It feels like I'm always a step behind since I started so late, but something feels different now. It could be the necklace, or maybe I'm just starting to believe in my dancing ability. It's a nice thought; maybe I really can get everything I've been dreaming about. Luck is on my side, and this is going to be my year! That's something Grandpa would say, which makes me smile to myself.

Trina turns and yells, "Ready?"

It snaps me out of my thoughts; she turns on the music and quickly runs into position. She yells, "5, 6, 7, 8..." and we start our hip-hop routine. I lose myself in the dance; it's like I become one with the music, and my body is taken over by the beats. Time disappears when I dance; it seems to stand still and speed up all at once. It feels like she just called the opening count, but we're already done.

"Great job, Becks. I really think this is going to be our year!" Trina says, echoing my thoughts exactly. You have no idea, I think to myself as I absentmindedly reach for the necklace. "Let's practice every night this week." She adds as she packs up her bag and gets ready to walk home.

"Perfect!" I say as I walk Trina to the door, "See you in the morning!"

One dilemma about having a class with Nate is picking out my outfits for school. It used to be just a first day of school thing, but now I can't get lazy as the year goes on. After trying on multiple outfits, I finally picked a blue and cream sundress that fits me perfectly. It is a skater dress, and I love it because it makes me feel like a dancer. The style is similar to what a figure skater would wear, but the skirt length is longer. I add a cardigan over it since it's always a little chilly in the classrooms. I love simple dresses, so I want to take advantage while the weather is still warm enough. As I look in the mirror, it hits me how much my body has changed over the summer. I've thinned out and am a little taller. My face looks less girlish and more mature. My usual ponytail has been replaced with wearing my hair down, which also makes me look more sophisticated. I'll be seeing Nate for sure in class today. The thought makes me excited and nervous all at once. At least I love my outfit. That makes me feel better already. For the final touch, I put on the necklace and turn to run out the door.

"You forgot your lunch!" Mom yells, and I turn around to grab it.

"Thanks, Mom!" I say as I give her a quick hug goodbye.

"Have a great day, sweetie."

"I will, thanks!" and I'm out the door to catch my ride. It feels so empowering to get a ride with someone as cool as Ally. It's a major improvement over arriving at school on a bus. I'm so lucky to have Trina as a friend. Despite my inevitable awkwardness, she pushes me to open up. My shyness tends to make things a little uncomfortable at times, but Trina saves me if needed. Ally happens to be gorgeous, on the dance team, and a year older. That combination is ridiculously intimidating to me, and I'm just hoping this ride goes smoothly.

"How was your summer, Ally?" I ask from the backseat, trying to be more outgoing. She drives a beat-up old Toyota Camry, and that instantly makes her more down-to-earth to me.

"It was good; I spent a lot of time in the dance studio. I ended up hanging out with Mark and Nate a lot over the summer. You know Nate? He's in your grade." She asks, which makes me laugh to myself. She doesn't wait for me to answer and just continues on. "It's funny to me now, but at first, I kinda thought he was trying to date me or something. He was around so much this summer. After a while, I realized he was just really good friends with Mark. The more I hung out with Nate, I started to understand why Mark was hanging out with him so much. Nate's really nice and fun. He's good-looking, too, for a younger guy. It's too bad I'm not into younger guys. Maybe I could have had a summer fling with Nate." She says with a laugh.

"Oh, um, well, he's not that much younger if you really are interested." I stammer, but I don't know why I'm saying this. The last thing I want is for Ally to date Nate! Instead, I should be reinforcing how young he is, not the other way around. My heart is beating so fast just from hearing his name. Instinctively my hand reaches for the necklace for help with this situation.

"Oh, please…" Trina says, glancing back at me with a knowing look, adding, "Becks is just playing it cool. She has a major thing for Nate. She's been into him since, like, 8th grade."

"I mean, it's not that big of a…" I start to deny it but get cut off by Ally.

"Oh my God, really, Becks!? You should totally go for him! I'm really into Mark, and they play soccer together now since Nate made varsity. We should all hang out together. It could be a double date!" She says and glances back at me before correcting what she meant. "I mean, they won't know it's a date. That would be our secret. Honestly, if I keep waiting for Mark to make a move, it will never happen. I thought for sure he was interested in me over the summer, but…nothing." Clearly exasperated with Mark's lack of action, she seems to think this secret date is some grand idea. There is no reason Nate would agree to hang out with me. And what if he actually is interested in Ally? Why would I want to go and spend time watching him flirt with her? This seems like a lousy idea.

"I don't know. He barely knows who I am." It comes out in a whiny tone. On the one hand, I want this more than anything, but on the other hand, this could all go horribly wrong.

"He sat next to you in class. He clearly knows who you are, Becks. Stop being so insecure, and go for it. I'm sick of hearing about how much you like him, yet you never even try to spend time with him. Personally, I think it's a great idea!" Trina says with an encouraging nod. My heart is pounding so hard I wonder if they can hear it. This is it. It's time to have a little faith; with that, I grab the necklace. Once again, remembering my promise to myself: I will not be invisible this year. It's time to take that risk.

"I'm in!" I agree and immediately start to regret it. My nerves are getting to me. This could be an epic disaster.

As I walk over to history class, I notice Ally just down the hall, she's all smiles and waving at me excitedly as she heads toward me. What is this all about? Oh boy, her excitement could be about our secret date. My heart leaps into my throat. She reaches me, grabs my arm excitedly, and squeals excitedly, "I've got news!"

"Oh yeah, what's the word?" I ask, and I wonder if that's even something people say. Definitely inherited the same 'condition' my dad has, where he says something wrong every time he wants to seem cool.

"Well, girl, the word is that Mark is totally down and is going to talk to Nate at practice tonight!" Mocking tone noted on the use of 'the word.' It's definitely not something people say. She continues excitedly, "He said Saturday would work best because they have a Friday night game. Can you believe it? He seemed totally excited and was definitely interested in hooking you up with Nate!" She is talking fast, jumping up and down while holding onto my arms.

Slowly, as I process what she said, it hits me. 'Interested in hooking you up with Nate' replays in my mind, making me stop dead in my tracks.

"Wait…WHAT?" I exclaim and stop jumping with her. Now, I'm staring at her. Please tell me I'm mistaken. "You told Mark about my crush on Nate? I thought you were going to play it cool! I thought this was a secret double date!" I'm dying. I must have misunderstood her. Once I see the look on her face, I know immediately, I'm not mistaken. It tells me everything I need to know. I hide my face with my hands, wanting to run away. I'm in total shock. What am I going to do now? No, no, no; this can't be happening now! Literally, my next class is with Nate. Invisibility seems like a brilliant idea at the moment, I'd do anything to disappear. I knew this was a bad idea.

Ally is trying to pull my hands off my face gently. She looks sheepish as she says, "I couldn't come up with another reason to ask

Mark and Nate to hang out. Sorry, hun, but your crush was the perfect excuse. I'm so sorry to throw you under the bus like that, but it worked out. Right?" She gives me a hopeful smile.

"How in the world do you think this has worked out?! I'm going to die of mortification; I can't even think straight right now. And I have a class with Nate next period!" My face was turning bright red. It's impossible. I can't face him in a couple of minutes. I hide my face in my hands once again. The only hope I have is that he won't make it to class today, or maybe someone else will sit in his spot. Ugh, good thing I wore my hair down. I can use it to hide my face from him. This is beyond horrible.

"Mark said he would talk to Nate at practice, so Nate hasn't heard anything about it yet," Ally reassures me while walking me to my next class. That does make me feel a little better; he won't know anything…yet. "Go in, act normal, it'll be fine," she says with a smile and encouraging pat on the shoulder.

"Ugh" is all I could manage to say to her as I open the door.

Nate's not in class yet, and a huge sigh of relief escapes me. Thank goodness I got here first. Now, he can choose to sit next to me or not. The clock is winding down. Class is about to start. Everyone else is already in their seats, and now there are only two open seats left. At this point, unless he wants to sit in the back with the stoners, he has no choice but to sit by me. The bell rings, and Mr. Whitman starts to hand out worksheets. Nate's skipping class today! Crisis averted. My heart rate slows as I take a deep breath and feel myself calm down. I get my worksheet and review what the topic will be today. Mr. Whitman starts explaining our assignment. I look up to see what he's writing on the board, and the door opens. Oh no.

It's Nate.

He's walking toward me, and I want to look away but can't. His gorgeous eyes have me entranced. Something in the way he's looking at me gives me the sense he knows. Oh my God, he knows. Mark talked to him, I know it. My heart is racing, my palms sweating, and there is a lump in my throat. Heat starts rising on my face alerting me it's turning a brighter shade of red. I need to get out of here. Now.

He sits down next to me, leans over, and whispers, "Sorry I'm late. I was talking to Mark."

Mark. My stomach drops. My heart can't handle this; honestly, it feels like I can't even breathe. Is this a panic attack? The only idea I have is to smile calmly, but I can't look him in the eye. He opens his notebook and reaches into his bag, giving me the courage to glance over at him. He turns toward me, and he gives me a knowing smirk. I'm so busted.

"Glad to see you could make class today, Nate." Mr. Whitman says. Uhhh, I let out a huge sigh of relief, saved once again by Mr. Whitman. My hand instinctively reaches for the necklace, needing all the luck in the world to survive this situation.

"I'm sorry I got hung up talking to my ride for soccer practice. I lost track of time. It won't happen again." Nate explains his tardiness to Mr. Whitman.

Mr. Whitman looks disappointed. "It better not," he says sternly, turns his back and begins to write on the board. Nate glances over at me, catching me staring at him. Embarrassed, I quickly look away and feel my face flush once more. A couple more times, I catch him glancing at me, and each time, I pretend I am looking past him at Mr. Whitman. This is going to be the longest class ever; I really need to get out of here. Honestly, if I were a good liar, I would totally make an excuse to leave. That's hopeless; I'm the world's worst liar.

The bell finally rings. I'm packed up and ready to get out of here as fast as possible. I jump up to leave, but Nate says, "Oh, Becky, wait!" His voice makes me stop cold. He caught me just in time; I was standing just ahead of him. Before I turn around to face him, I reach for the necklace, needing help through this. Necklace in hand,

I close my eyes, take a deep breath, and think, 'Please help' before slowly turning around.

"Yeah, what is it?" I'm trying my best to act nonchalant.

"I wanted to talk to you. Can I walk with you?"

"Uhh-huh, uh, sure." I barely manage to get a word out, so much for keeping my cool. Please don't bring up the date, please don't bring up the date. I'm scared to death. This isn't how this is supposed to happen. I'm not ready for this!

"I was talking to Mark, he mentioned you and Ally want to hang out Saturday, and I was…" He's about to let me down gently. I know it. I feel sick; this can't be happening! Why did I agree to any of this? There has to be a way to stop him.

"You don't have to go if you don't want to. I mean, Ally has a thing for Mark. It was all her idea; don't feel obligated or anything. I'm sure they can go out, just the two of them. It's no big deal." Extra emphasis is put on Ally's role in all this. The speed at which I'm talking gives me away. I'm obviously full of nerves. I had to cut him off before he could finish. I didn't want to hear him try and let me down gently.

Nate interrupts my thoughts as he touches my arm. He looks me directly in the eyes and says, "Hey, I don't feel obligated. I want to go." He shoots me that smile of his, and I melt.

He is looking at me with his kind, piercing blue eyes. Mesmerized, all I can say is, "Really?" Is he just being nice, or does he actually want to go? I want to clarify, but the only word that follows is "But…"

"No buts, we're going. I just wanted to ask if it's okay if we drive separately."

"Oh, um, I can't drive yet. Maybe my mom could bring me?"

"Oh, that's not what I meant. I'll pick you up, and Mark will pick up Ally."

"Really? Okay, I didn't realize you could drive."

"Well, I can't. I'll have to get my brother to bring us. It's just that it gives Mark a chance to be alone with Ally. He's really into her, too."

It all makes sense now. Of course, this was about Mark and Ally. The dreamer in me thought for a minute that Nate wanted to have alone time with me. My heart sinks. As usual, my thoughts must be written all over my face because he leans over with a flirty smile and adds, "It's too bad I can't drive." A jolt of electricity shoots through my body from the way he's looking at me.

We reach the door to his classroom, and he nods toward it, saying, "This is me. We can finalize everything on Friday." Before heading in the door, he turns back, touching my arm adding, "Have a good class," then walks into his classroom. Every time he touches me, my whole body feels electric and, somehow, magically calm at the same time. There wasn't a chance to respond before he was inside the door. It's probably a good thing, considering I never know what will come out of my mouth in moments like this. As I walk the rest of the way to my class, I can't keep the smile off my face.

After school, I head over to meet up with Ally and Trina for my ride home. They're leaning on her car, casually talking. I can't wait to talk to them about everything that happened. Taking the risk seems well worth it now. I'm so glad I agreed to this! At first, it was pure mortification, and I was upset with Ally, but now I love her and feel so alive. I'm almost in the car when I notice Ally looking at me with eyes like daggers. Goodbye, good mood.

"Uh, hi. What's up?" I ask tentatively, wondering why I am getting the stink eye. It has something to do with me overreacting to Nate, I'm sure of it. It was wrong to emphasize that this was Ally's idea so she could spend time with Mark. Oh man, here we go.

"What's up?" She repeats, sounding annoyed, as if I should know what's wrong. "What do you think is up, Becks? Oh, let's see…maybe it's the fact that Nate came over to me at my locker and mentioned he never knew I had a thing for Mark! He said you told him!" Fear confirmed, she found out that I was blurting everything to Nate.

"I'm so sorry, Ally, but I totally freaked out when Nate started talking to me about Saturday. You know how awkward I can be, and it just came out. Besides, Nate told me that Mark has a thing for you! That's exciting news, right?" I ask, hoping it will take the sting away. My face was keeping a hopeful smile, waiting for her to say something, anything.

There's no emotion on her face until, finally, she starts laughing. "I know! I was just giving you a hard time, and you totally believed it!" My whole body relaxes. I'm so relieved! Totally fell for it. She explains, "Nate told me Mark has a thing for me too! I mean, you did kinda throw me under the bus, so I had to mess with you."

"I got the idea from you, ya know. Mark totally talked to Nate before my class. I was beside myself, I can only imagine how red my face was when Nate walked into that classroom." We're all laughing now. Thank goodness she was just teasing, it would've been horrible if she was upset with me. "I really didn't mean to throw you under the bus, though, Ally. I'm really sorry." I add to make sure we are good.

"Oh, yeah, I know Becks. Your face was so classic. You really believed I was mad at you." She laughs again, turns away to get into her car, but then changes her mind. "I almost forgot, Nate did mention he thought the double date was a great idea…because he's been wanting to spend time with you too!" She's watching me intently with a huge grin, waiting to see my reaction. I'm in utter disbelief, and I'm sure my face shows it.

"Are you just messing with me again? You totally are, aren't you?" There's no way he actually said that! This must be another prank.

"Not messing with you; he's definitely interested in you, girl! Promise, I really wouldn't joke about that." She's serious, and somehow, I believe her. Suddenly, she squeals and adds, "Man, I can't wait for Saturday! We are going to have the best time!"

"I really can't believe he said that! Saturday can't get here soon enough!" I exclaim, and wonder, is this my real life? Catching rides with Ally and planning double dates with the coolest guys in school is too good. This would happen in a daydream of mine, sure, but this is real life! I'm going on a date with Nate! My Nate. Well, at least I think it's a date. Whatever. More importantly, what am I going to wear?

"Hey Ally, what are you going to wear on Saturday?" I ask, knowing it'll take me all week to figure this out.

Before Ally can answer, Trina interrupts all the excitement. "Okay, you two. It's only Tuesday. You have plenty of time to figure it out. What I want to know is if Ally will come to watch us practice our routine for tryouts and give us pointers." Trina asks, bringing us back to earth. "So….Ally? Will you help?" Trina is shooting her a pleading smile.

"You guys know we aren't really supposed to help others to keep it fair." Ally sounds unsure. It is true since she was already on the competitive dance team, but it's a grey area. Last year, she was one of the alternate captains, but she isn't a judge at the auditions. Technically, she has to try out herself, so it's not like it's completely against the rules.

"Oh, yeah, we understand, but this is only round one. We would never ask you to help for the next round." Trina continues to make her case.

"Uh, well, I guess. But just this round, okay, guys? We really want to keep it fair. I doubt you need any help. You two are the strongest dancers in your class." Ally says.

I can't believe Trina got her to agree. Ally's insight for the first round will really make our routine stand out. Again, there's that feeling, the need to touch the necklace and the knowing that comes with it. This is my year. Nate. The competitive team. It's all coming true!

It's Friday, and my anxiety is out of control. Tomorrow, I'm going out with Nate McNeil! Every day that gets closer to the double date, the anticipation gets more intense. The stress of picking an outfit for the date is really getting to me. Ally agreed to shop with me, so we are going after dance practice tonight. Nothing like waiting until the last minute to figure out my outfit.

Practice was great today. It got my mind off the date for a while. Our sophomore dance team is really good. We could give the varsity team a run for their money. Ally mentioned she thought I was one of the better sophomore dancers. That's a real compliment. Most of the girls on our team have been dancing since they were little, unlike me. The middle school dance team lets anyone join, and that's how I found dance. Instantly, I fell in love. I've worked hard to catch up with everyone else who has danced for longer, but my confidence is a work in progress. Everyone knows Trina is the best dancer in our grade. Dance is her life. She's been dancing basically since she could walk. Ally dances outside of school, too, and last year became the first sophomore who was an alternate captain. I have two of the best talents in school helping me perfect my routine for the audition. Indeed, it's unbelievable how different things are for me already this year. There's no way I would've dared to even talk to Ally last year! Yet somehow, now she's helping me with dance, and we're going shopping together for a double date. It's unreal!

"I'll see you Monday. Let's practice after school again!" Trina yells as she runs out the door. She has to leave right after practice tonight. Unfortunately, she can't join our shopping trip. We don't have regular dance practice on Monday, so we'll work on our tryout routine instead. The varsity dance team is practicing in the main gym, and I catch the last half of their routine. The song ends, and they take their final pose. Wow! Never mind, the sophomore team is good, but varsity is definitely a step or two ahead of us. I'm really going to have to step up my game if I'm going to make the competitive team this year.

"Hey Becks! Are you ready to do some shopping?" Ally runs over with a huge smile on her face. She is practically straight out of a magazine, with her classic blonde-hair and blue-eyes, yet she is still really down to earth. Mark is fortunate, I'm sure every guy must want to date her.

"I'm so ready," I say excitedly. At least I already have a simple sundress picked out. The only problem is that it's too plain. It needs something to make it stand out more.

"So how has the rest of the week been, you know, after Nate found out about your crush on him?" she asks while teasing me.

"He's been great, I think? He hasn't done anything too different. He always sits by me in class, and now he walks me to my locker in between a couple of classes. I mean, he doesn't go out of his way or anything. He only walks with me if we are heading in the same direction. I think that's still good, right?" I'm suddenly feeling unsure. It's not like we are holding hands, and he isn't going out of his way to walk with me. Although, he also found out about my crush and isn't avoiding me. That's a positive in my book.

It's astounding how much has changed this week since the news of my crush came out. Nate really has made an effort to talk to me, and it's making me so much more comfortable with him. Anytime we walk down the hall together, we get looks from people. He doesn't seem to notice at all, but I do. Everyone must be wondering why he is giving me so much attention. I'm going to have to get used to that. After all, I am getting everything I've ever wanted. Definitely no longer invisible.

"Of course that's good! He is finding time to be with you!" Ally says, easing my mind. My insecurity is that he's just being friendly, and I'm reading too much into it. It helps to get some encouragement from her.

"I noticed you've been sitting by Mark at lunch," I say, raising my eyebrows.

"Yeah, can you believe that? That usually doesn't happen right away, I mean, unless you were already friends and sitting together. Usually, guys don't want you sitting with them until it's more official, ya know?" I didn't know. But now I do.

"So, how did that happen?"

"Oh, it was real casual. We walked together into the cafeteria, and I headed to sit at my usual table. He touched my arm and nodded his head toward his table. Like asking, 'wanna sit with us?' I just smiled at him and followed him to his table. We didn't talk about it; it just felt right. Now it's turning into the new normal." Ally explained nonchalantly. "I mean, it surprised me that he did that before Saturday, but the guy knows what he wants! I really like that about him, no games. It's been so easy and comfortable with him. I haven't had any of those moments where I'm not sure where he stands. Ah, man, I really like him." She is totally gushing over Mark.

It's impossible not to compare her story to mine. Nate and I were definitely not in the same place as Ally and Mark. I hope that's not a bad sign. I mean, we found out about our crushes literally on the same day. Compared to them, we are on a turtle pace. Who cares if we aren't holding hands, sitting by each other at lunch…or even acknowledging each other during lunch, now that I think about it. I'm trying to convince myself that I have nothing to worry about. Not that long ago I was only dreaming Nate would talk to me, and now he is walking me to my classes. Calm down. Take it one step at a time!

"What are you thinking about? I asked if you liked this shirt like 4 times!" Ally says while laughing and shaking her head at me.

"Ugh, Nate. What else?"

"What about him?"

"You think that he and I are good, right? I mean, he doesn't even talk to me in the cafeteria or anything. And we definitely won't be sitting by each other at lunch anytime soon." I ask nervously, hoping I'm just getting in my own head about all this.

"You guys are good, trust me! Every relationship is different, so don't even try to compare them. Mark and I were hanging out a ton over the summer, and we already knew each other. We are just in a different place than you two. The best thing to do is to enjoy it when you spend time with him. Don't worry about it or force anything, Becks."

"I'm so glad I have you here! I don't know what to expect and have no idea what I would do without you." I really mean it. Ally has dated way more than Trina or me.

"What about this dress?" Ally asks as she holds up a short sundress that has a vintage vibe.

"Mark will love that dress!" I say with a nod of approval. Looking at it, just behind her, I see the perfect piece for my outfit on a mannequin. "Ooo, I love this jacket!" I point to the cropped leather jacket. It's exactly what I need to give my outfit just a touch of edge.

"Thanks, I love it too!" Ally says as she spins around with her dress. "That jacket is exactly what you need! We are going to look so good. Man, these guys are lucky!" Ally says, and we both laugh.

"I can't wait for tomorrow!" I couldn't contain my excitement.

Chapter Five
Saturday

Groggily, I'm awoken by the sunlight seeping through my bedroom window. I didn't close the blinds well enough, and it's shining through the cracks, ruining my ability to sleep in. It's still taking me a while to fully wake up until suddenly it hit me: It's Saturday! Immediately, it jolts me awake, and I sit up straight, full of anticipation. I'm going out with Nate tonight!

The day has finally arrived, it felt like the longest week of my life, but it's finally here. It's a wonder I slept at all last night. This week must have been more exhausting than I realized. Ugh, 7 pm is never going to get here. Time always moves in slow motion whenever I'm excited about something. Nate and his brother will be picking me up at 7:00, and then we are meeting Ally and Mark at the taco place before the movie. I need to distract myself. It's the only solution. I could always do some homework, but I doubt I'll be able to concentrate. Maybe Trina will come over and practice our tryout routine a couple more times. Dance always calms my nerves, and it makes time fly. It's just what I need.

Tryouts are next Wednesday, so we have this whole weekend and the beginning of next week to really master our routine for the first round. Ally loved the routine when she watched it the other day and thought it was even good enough to use for the second round of auditions. She gave us a couple of pointers, and it was advice we easily incorporated. It enhanced our routine without changing it too much. Her input made both of us feel so much more confident. Trina said she will come over but can only stay an hour. Well, at least that's one hour that will pass by quickly. When Trina arrives, we head to the finished basement so we have enough space to practice.

"Are you excited about tonight? I can't wait to hear all about it. After all this time listening to you crushing on him, it's finally happening!" Trina says, sounding genuinely excited for me. I don't know why that surprises me. I guess I thought she was getting annoyed always hearing about Nate. Although she was probably more annoyed with the fact that I would never even talk to him, it's different now that we are going out. She is super excited for me.

"I'm so glad you practically forced me to agree to this crazy idea in the first place. I would have never gone along with Ally's double date plan otherwise." It's true. I needed Trina's encouragement that day. "Now it's actually happening! I feel like 7 o'clock will never get here. Thankfully, Ally and Mark will be with us. That will help a ton with my nerves."

"You are so much more comfortable with him now. I can tell when I see you guys talking in the halls. You haven't had any stories about him lately that include 'I'm so embarrassed' or 'I'm so awkward.' You're finally starting to just be yourself. It's great to see, and everyone thinks you two are super cute together."

This shocks me. People think we look cute together? No way, I always thought they were thinking, 'What is he doing with her?' Never in a million years would I imagine they would think we looked cute together! A weight is lifted off my shoulders, and I realize just how much anxiety I have been carrying. I worry too much about what other people think.

"I can't believe that! I guess I was wrong. I noticed people were looking at us when we were walking in the halls. It made me self-conscious, to be honest. I always assumed they thought I wasn't good enough for him."

"Oh, well, I'm sure some girls are jealous too. Especially Stacy, she hasn't been very nice about it, but she hasn't been nice to anyone this year. She's probably just mad he broke it off with her. But, yeah, most people talk about how cute you guys are together. They think you are becoming more outgoing, too. I've heard that a few times."

"I've always been outgoing…or, umm." As I say it, I know that's not true. I don't even know why I said that. It's always been Trina who is outgoing, and I'm just always around when she starts talking to people. It's never me who starts those conversations. I'm too self-conscious. Trina, though, doesn't have a self-conscious bone in her body.

"You've always been nice but not outgoing. I'm outgoing. I'll talk to anyone!" Trina says with a laugh.

"No kidding. I think it's because you were born to be a star!" I say, really meaning it. She has that star quality about her. I've always imagined her becoming famous.

"That's right darling…" she says with some crazy made-up accent that makes us both laugh hysterically. We're chatting so much that we only run through the routine one time. That didn't matter, though; her company made the time pass quickly and helped me relax. It's just what I needed today.

Stevie starts barking and I know someone must be here. It's the only time he barks. He has the best life; most of his day is spent sleeping on someone's lap or chasing the biggest ball he can find. It's hilarious to watch this little white fluff ball chasing around a ball that is twice his size. We both head upstairs to see what all the fuss is about. As I get closer to the door, I hear Grandpa's voice talking to Mom.

"Hi, Gramps!" I say as I come up the stairs.

"Hey Becks! Hi Trina!" Grandpa says as he sees us enter the kitchen. "Your mom was just telling me about some big date you have tonight. Who is this Nate character?" Grandpa asks, sounding very suspicious, which is really just his way of teasing me

"Nate Character?" I ask with a laugh. "You'd like him, Grandpa, don't worry."

"Nate is the best. You don't need to worry," Trina adds, helping ease Grandpa's mind. "Have fun tonight, Becks. I can't wait to hear all about it!" She's heading out the door to make it home in time for her brother's game.

"Thanks! I will!" I yell after her as she closes the door behind her.

"I knew you would only pick a good guy. I see you're wearing the necklace I found. Has it brought you any luck?" Grandpa asks, giving me a wink and glancing at the pendant. He's not being serious, but little does he know just how much luck it has brought me.

"I always wear it. I love it. And, believe it or not, I think it is lucky! Or maybe your luck is finally rubbing off on me!"

"Oh, you really think so, huh? I'm sure your newfound luck has more to do with you than anything else. As long as good things are happening, I'm all for it!" He says with a chuckle. I feel like there was some extra wisdom in his words, but I often feel that way with Grandpa. "I've got to go pick up grandma from the salon now. Have fun tonight, Becks, and thanks for the cookies!" He says as he grabs a couple more of my mom's homemade cookies while walking out the door.

"What did he stop by for?" I asked Mom. He didn't stay very long.

"Oh, you know him. He was just killing time waiting for Grandma to finish up. And I think he really did just want a cookie. I told him earlier I was baking, and sure enough, he shows up." Mom said with a laugh. I don't blame him. She really does make the best cookies. Grandpa and Grandma stop by often; they only live a few miles away. I still have time to kill before I can get ready. Time is so slow sometimes! I guess I will attempt homework since I doubt I'll be able to focus on it any better tomorrow after my date. The time passed slowly as I worked on math until finally, I decided to get ready early; this waiting game was killing me. My heart starts fluttering. It's really happening.

I get out of the shower and look at the outfit I have planned. It seemed so edgy and cool in the store when I was with Ally, but now

I'm not so sure. The sundress is simple. It's knee-length with a simple floral pattern. The idea was to add a little edge by throwing on my new cropped motorcycle jacket and bold black leather booties. Turning side to side, I check out how it looks in the full-length mirror. I've always been naturally thin; sometimes, booties can look weird with my skinny legs, but these actually work well.

"Mom!! Can you come in here?" I yell, needing outfit advice ASAP.

"Hey, I'm right here! There's no need to yell. Oh, you look great, honey!" She says immediately when she sees me. She was just in her bedroom down the hall from mine, so she got to me faster than I had expected.

"Oh, sorry, I didn't realize you were just down the hall. Do you really like the outfit? It's warmer out than I was expecting, is it too plain without the jacket?" I ask as I take off the jacket to show her.

"You look great. Really. And it's supposed to cool off tonight, so I'm guessing you will need the jacket. Nate is one lucky guy if you ask me." She says with a wink.

"Thanks, mom," I needed that extra input, even though I knew my mom would say I looked great in anything I wore. Now, it's time to add the last, and most important touch; the necklace. It makes me feel instantly better once it's hanging around my neck.

"It's going to be so fun!" I exclaim, full of hopeful expectation.

Mom laughs at my enthusiasm. "My baby is all grown up!" She says with a mixture of sadness and joy. I'm a little relieved that Dad is working tonight. You never know what he'll say when first meeting a guy about to take out his daughter. I'm not sure if he would try to be cool or if he'd be protective. He's done both with my sister, and they are both a little embarrassing for different reasons. We all know he means the best, but dads meeting boyfriends is always a little awkward. I really want Nate to have a good first experience when picking me up, so at least I don't need to worry that Dad will break out into a lecture with a bunch of rules for tonight.

I'm blow-drying my thick strawberry-blonde hair, which falls a few inches below my shoulders. Rarely do I wear it down, usually throwing it in a ponytail because it's easier and more comfortable. This year, with Nate around, I've been wearing it down more. It is actually much prettier than the ponytail, but it can get so hot and windblown. It's hard to keep it down for very long. Tonight, I'm going all out and starting to curl it section by section until I have those cool beach waves I see in magazines. I never curl my hair, partially because I don't wake up early enough before school to have the time. Also, I don't know how to make it look good, I had to watch a YouTube video to learn how to curl my hair like this. Once I finish the curling, I look in the mirror, and I'm impressed. The waves just add something special. I hope Nate likes it. I put on my makeup, which is minimal. I've never been very good at makeup, so I'm keeping it safe. One last look in the full-length mirror, twirling around, reviewing my completed look, and I feel pretty good.

Stevie is going crazy downstairs. Someone must have pulled into the driveway. He must be here and I run over to my bedroom window to peek through the blinds. It's him getting out of his brother's jeep, and my heart leaps into my throat. Literally, one minute ago, I was perfectly fine. All it takes is a glimpse of Nate, and my heart is practically beating outside of my chest. A quick glance at the clock, 6:30 pm. He's early.

"Becky, Nate's here!" Mom yells up the stairs to me. One more quick look in the mirror, outfit is good, hair looks good. I'm as ready as I'll ever be. I reach for my necklace for a last touch of luck before heading downstairs.

As I start down the stairs, I see Nate waiting in the entryway for me. He's holding a bouquet of flowers. He brought me flowers! Who does that anymore? It's so sweet and better than anything I ever imagined. The sight of the flowers calms me, and I walk over to him with a giddy smile. "Are those for me?" I ask as I finally reach him.

He turns to me with a shy smile and says, "Yeah, I thought you'd like them," and shrugs.

"I LOVE them," I say and kiss him on the cheek. I've never kissed him on the cheek before. We haven't even held hands. There was just something about him looking shy and unsure that made me want to reassure him. It felt natural, and when I looked at his face, I knew it worked. He seems rather pleased with himself now.

"Mom, will you put these in a vase for me?" I ask as I hand her my bouquet.

"Of course, honey, how very thoughtful of you, Nate," Mom says, and I can tell she is impressed with him. Nate seems awfully proud of himself now that he knows the flowers are a hit. "You two have fun tonight and tell Ally I said hi. Remember, curfew is midnight, no later." She says, giving Nate a look like it's his responsibility.

"We won't be out that late, at least I don't think we will," I quickly say, not wanting Nate to think I had any expectations for the night.

"Thanks, Mrs. Lewis. She's in good hands," he says as we walk out the door. His brother's sitting in the driver's seat of his older Jeep Wrangler, listening to old-school rock. He was in my sister's grade, but I don't know him well. He was already in college when we started high school. He was popular in high school, I know, and lives at home while he goes to community college. He's still around town, but I never really talk to him.

"Hi Becky, I'm Chris." His brother says, turning around to introduce himself as I get in the jeep.

"Hi, thanks for driving us. Nice car," I say

"Thanks. So we're off to the plaza?" He asks, looking at Nate.

"Yup, the plaza it is," Nate says.

The plaza has a movie theater, restaurants, boutique shops, and a small playground for kids to play while adults are shopping. It's the place to be on the weekends since everything is all in one spot. Suddenly, it hits me that we're going to run into a bunch of people from school, and for some reason, that makes me nervous. I always imagined it being just the four of us. Chris pulls into the plaza and stops in front of the movie theater to let us out.

"Call me if you need a ride back. It was nice meeting you, Becky." Chris says. We thank him again, and he pulls away. It's just Nate and me. Alone. This is unexpected; I wasn't planning on any alone time with him, and I feel a bit self-conscious.

"Hey, remember when I asked if we could ride separately so Mark could spend some time with Ally?" Nate asks, interrupting my thoughts.

"Yeah, I remember. Why?" Curious why he would bring that up now.

"It got me thinking, and I figured we could get dropped off early to have some alone time. I hope that's okay. We have a half-hour before we need to meet them for dinner." He says with a smirk, and just like that, I feel comfortable with him. I don't know how he does it, but all my self-consciousness disappears.

"Oh, you want extra time with me, huh?" I say while leaning into him, flirting.

"Yeah, I guess so." He says with his adorable smirk. "It's nice out, want to walk over there?" He's pointing to a bench in the vicinity of the kid's park, but a little further out so we would be alone. It's the ideal spot for privacy. I wonder why I've never noticed it before.

"Perfect," I say as he takes my hand for the first time and leads me over to the bench. We sit close together. It was a little chilly, just like my mom said it would be, which gave me the best excuse to cuddle in closer to him. Suddenly, I feel as though I am exactly where I am meant to be. I'm amazed at how natural this feels.

"Can I ask you something?" He has a serious tone that I haven't heard before. It was different, serious, but not intimidating. I liked it. It's nice he seems curious about me.

"Yeah, of course," I say, wondering what he's going to ask me.

"I remember trying to talk to you a few times last year, but you always seem a little bit in your own world. I'd try to get your attention, but sometimes you were somewhere else entirely. I always wondered, what is she thinking about? So, what are you always thinking about?" He asks, to my surprise. He was trying to get my attention? All I wanted was for him to talk to me, and somehow, I never even noticed he was trying! Too much daydreaming on my part. I really need to live in the real world a little more. I wonder what else I missed out on. If he only knew, I was most likely daydreaming about him. That makes me laugh, and Nate breaks my thought by asking, "What's so funny?"

"Oh, sorry. I've just been told that my whole life. I can get lost in a daydream, imagining the most amazing things happening. But, I get so lost in my daydreams that I tend to forget about the real world for a while." I explain, leaving out how most of those daydreams included him.

"What kind of things do you imagine?" He asks, and I wonder how honest I should be when answering this question.

"Well, for instance, I imagine my tryout for the dance team going flawlessly and making the team, and then winning regional finals. And, if I'm totally honest, I've imagined this moment with you a few times too." I don't know where I got the courage to tell him that, but it is true, and at the moment, I want him to know it. I look up at him nervously, wondering if I said too much. As he looks back at me, his eyes brighten, and he leans closer to me. For a minute, I'm convinced he's going to kiss me, but he doesn't.

"Do the things you daydream about usually come true?" he asks instead, with a flirty smile.

"Well, that's an interesting question. I never really thought about that. I'm always too busy daydreaming about the future. But, if I think about it, yeah, I guess they kind of do. I am here with you right now, aren't I?" Flirting as I say it, I don't know what's gotten into me. I'm so comfortable and confident. Quickly changing the tone of the conversation, I add, "I made the dance team both years and won the talent show in 8th grade against all odds. I mean, somehow, I beat out Trina, who is the most talented person I know! I daydreamed about that for months before it happened, but I didn't really stress about it happening in real life. If that makes any sense."

"That's cool. You know, you don't give yourself enough credit. You're extremely talented. The way you are on stage when you dance, you're so confident. You're really amazing to watch. I'll never forget your dance that night at that talent show. It was the first time I really noticed you. You looked so free on stage. You were beautiful." He says and looks at me with his piercing eyes. Nate just called me beautiful. Is he going to kiss me? My heart is racing, but I back away a little, feeling self-conscious all of a sudden.

"I remember you came up to me after, I think it was the first time we ever talked. I was so awkward." I say, looking down, feeling embarrassed at how I had acted. It was the first time he ever made a point to talk to me, and I was a bundle of nerves. I reach up to touch the necklace for reassurance; for some reason, I feel vulnerable when talking about that night.

"You weren't awkward. You just seemed a little shy. It was cute. I've been curious about you ever since that night." He says with his smile and gives me a flirty nudge before adding, "I finally get my chance."

"You were curious about me? I always thought you probably had a horrible impression of me. I wish I could talk to people as easily as you; you have such amazing confidence." I pause, thinking for a second before adding, "Can I ask you something?"

"Of course. Anything."

"You always seem so confident, like nothing bothers you. Do you really feel that way?" I've honestly always wanted to know this. He seems like he has no worries in the world; he's popular, plays for varsity, and gets good grades. I know there is more to him, but he never shows any kind of insecurity.

Now it's his turn to laugh. "Well, of course, things bother me. I am human." He says in a teasing tone before continuing on. "I know what you mean, though. People have that perception of me. You know, everyone thinks that making the varsity team was a given for me and that those guys welcomed me with open arms. Well, they didn't, and it wasn't a given. I beat out one of their friends, who got cut from the team. I worked so hard practicing and playing in travel leagues throughout middle school and worked twice as hard last year to become good enough to make varsity. The thing is, once I made the team, I hated it." He sounds defeated, like he is reliving it all, including the emotions. It makes me like him even more. He's being so honest and open with me.

"Why did you hate it?" I can't imagine him hating soccer. Everyone knows he loves it. It's hard to imagine him struggling with it so much.

"The guys were brutal to me all summer until it finally boiled over. We all got into this huge fight, and it felt like the whole team was against me. Coach made us sit down and talk, which is when I found out I beat out their friend for a spot on the team. As punishment for the fight, the coach assigned all these extra team-building drills. He made a rule that if one person lagged behind we would all have to do it over again. It was horrible, but it really did force us to help each other out, and now we're cool. To be honest, this summer was nothing but a test of my confidence. I was bothered by it every day and was pretending everything was cool when I was around everyone else. It honestly felt like I was being punished for working hard and achieving my dream." He says, seeming exhausted just from reliving the memory.

"I had no idea. I'm sorry to bring up bad memories. Thanks for sharing that with me." I say, not really knowing what else to say. That was the most vulnerable I'd ever seen him.

"You know, just now telling you about it made me realize I'm glad we went through all of that. It made our team closer, it made me stronger, and the guys treat me as an equal on the team now. Mark was one of the first guys to really take me under his wing. He's a great guy, and we became close. He really helped me keep my head up all summer long. I guess, looking back, maybe it wasn't really all that bad. It just felt horrible at the time. I didn't share that experience with anyone but my mom and brother. I think that added to the pressure. I was pretending to everyone else, letting them think that things were great. When they would ask me about soccer, it was just easier to pretend than to explain it to people, you know?" He asked, and I did know. I totally understood.

"Well, I'm glad you felt like you could tell me."

"Me too," he says, leaning in. He is for sure kissing me this time, and I close my eyes.

"Hey guys!" Ally's voice interrupts us, and my eyes fly open. Startled, I sit up straight. Turning around, I see her and Mark walking towards us. Ugh, she has the worst timing! I look over at Nate, who just shrugs and smiles like he is thinking the same thing.

"Hey," Nate and I say at the same time

"We were going to walk into the restaurant but saw you guys sitting over here. Are you ready to grab some tacos?" Mark asks, rubbing his hands together with excitement. "I love this place. They have the best Mexican food. I wish I was old enough to get a Margarita. They always look so good."

"Me too," we all say at the same time and start laughing. We walk over to the restaurant, hearing all about Ally's day. Apparently, she went car shopping because her car is getting too old. I was excited she might get a new car, knowing my ride to school would get an upgrade. Her car is really old, and her parents want her in something more reliable. It sounds like she might have to wait until her birthday, which is in May. The guys like talking about cars, though, so this is a good opening conversation.

I'm amazed at how comfortable I am, and as I look at the people I am sitting with on a Saturday night, it hits me: I'm with the popular crowd. Not only that, but I feel completely at ease as Mark talks non-stop in between the bites of his tacos. He's really funny and has all of us laughing hysterically at dinner. It's amazing how much he loves tacos, I've never seen anyone eat so much. Nate wasn't as talkative as I had imagined, but that was mostly because Mark stole the show. It didn't matter to me. Nate and I had our chance to talk before dinner. That's my favorite part of the night so far, and I'm so glad he had us arrive early.

After dinner, we head to the theater to see the new Marvel movie. The best part of the show is Nate holding my hand. It's hard to pay attention, even though the movie was action-packed and really good. Nate holding my hand was quite a distraction. At the end of the movie, it was almost 11:00 and time to head back home. Mark drove us all back to my house first. Nate, being a gentleman, walks me to my door. "You know, I would kiss you goodbye, but I feel like we are being watched." He says as he turns around and looks at Mark's car.

"I know," I say and kiss him on the cheek. He gives me a hug goodbye.

"I'll text you tomorrow. I had a really great time tonight, Becky." He says as he looks at me with a smile that melts my heart.

"Me too" was all I could say, and at that, he turned and headed to the car. He opens the door and waves goodbye. I wave back and hear Mark saying, "You didn't kiss her? What is wrong with…" and the door shuts. I can't help but laugh, imagining the conversation going on in that car right now. I feel like I'm floating. I'm just so happy, so very happy, and without realizing it, I touch my necklace and think, 'Thank you.'

Grandma and Grandpa came over after church the next morning, and as I greeted them, Grandpa was eyeing me as if he were assessing me. "You look awfully cheerful today, Becks." His tone sounds more like a question than a statement.

"I am, thanks," I say, not offering any extra information just to tease him.

He comes over and sits by me. "Does this have anything to do with that Nate character?" he asks quietly as if it's a secret between us.

"Maybe. Why do you keep calling him a 'character?'"

"Because I don't know who he is until I meet him. Until then, he is just some character taking out my granddaughter." He says with a smile

"Well, I'm sure you'd like him, Grandpa. Maybe you'll meet him someday."

"He must be something special. He's the first guy you've let take you out. And I know there are plenty of young men who would like to take out my beautiful, sweet granddaughter. So, what is it about this guy?" Grandpa asks in a teasing manner, but I know he really wants to hear about it.

"Well, he's really friendly and gets along with everyone. I really like him. He shared some things about himself he doesn't share with everyone. He was really struggling over the summer with the soccer team and was so different than I thought he would be. He always seemed so carefree and like everything just works out for him perfectly!" I sound astonished that he isn't as perfect as I had imagined. Last night was the first time I'd seen Nate in a different light, and it only made me like him more.

Grandpa starts laughing really hard. His boisterous, whooping laugh is contagious, and I start to laugh, too. Once he can finally talk, he says, "Oh, Becks, you're so funny! Did you really think his life was carefree and perfect?" He chuckles again and shakes his head. "Nobody's life is perfect, Becks, you know that! Often times, it's easier to hide problems from others and act as if everything is okay. The truth is, you never really know what is going on in other people's lives unless they share it with you. It's good he felt like he could share his true self with you. Everyone needs someone they can talk with freely."

"He just always seemed so perfect to me, but I like getting to know the real him."

"Well, I can guarantee you that nobody is perfect. The thing is, when it comes to the ones you love, it's important they can confide in you. I've always thought sharing insecurities is what makes relationships special. It's in sharing those parts of yourself that you don't share with everyone else that make relationships so precious."

"I know. I think I was just scared to let myself believe he could like me. It just seemed easier to daydream about it. I know I won't get hurt from a daydream. I didn't want to end up heartbroken and disappointed." I say with a sheepish laugh, knowing it sounds silly.

"Well, kiddo, at some point in life, you will have a heartbreak. It's not just boyfriends that will break your heart, either. You will be heartbroken when little Stevie's time comes to pass. I bet you wouldn't choose to miss out on all the love, laughter, and joy he has brought to your life just to avoid heartbreak. I know you'd still choose to have him in your life. The thing is, I don't want you to be closed off to people because you're scared of heartbreak. You could miss some of the best things life has to offer. Becks, you should always go for it when it comes to love." Grandpa says with a wink, but I knew he was telling me something truly important.

"Thanks, Gramps. You're the best." I lean over and give him a hug.

"I'm just sharing some thoughts from an old geezer." he laughs. True to form, Grandpa doesn't keep things serious for too long. "So, did he kiss you?" He asks with a laugh, nudge, and teasing smile.

"Grandpa! No, he didn't kiss me. It was a first date!" I say, pretending to be offended, but I was just teasing him right back. On that note, I head over to see what mom and grandma are doing. I don't want to talk about kissing with Grandpa!

Mom and Grandma are looking at some new curtains online, and they keep asking for opinions, so I ended up over by the computer. Dad and grandpa are watching the Lions game. They are yelling at the television, convinced they would be better coaches than the professionals. Mom and Grandma don't even notice the ruckus in the living room. They're used to it. The two coaches sitting over on the couch with all their comments always make me laugh; it's funny how passionate they get. We spend hours looking at different curtains and finally order the only style we all agree on. As the game wraps up, Grandma tells Grandpa it's time to go.

As I say goodbye, Grandma says, "I'm glad you had so much fun last night, and thanks for the help shopping — bye, sweetie," as she hugs me goodbye. "Bye Stevie," she says and pats him on the head since he is circling her feet.

Grandpa comes over and gives me a hug, and says, "I'm so happy for you. Always go for it." I know exactly what he means. He's talking about Nate.

I hug him tight and say, "I will Gramps."

My parents and I stand on the porch and wave goodbye to them as they back out of the driveway. Stevie is whining at the door, acting as if we forgot him. We open the door, and he starts twirling for us like we were gone for an hour. I pick him up and give him a hug. This love, I would never stay away from a love like this. As I think it, Stevie gives me a big wet dog kiss. "Thanks, buddy," I say, even though I'm leaning my head back to avoid his sloppy kisses. I put him down, and he spots a ball in the corner and immediately starts chasing the ball in circles around the living room.

Time to focus. I really need to finish my homework. This weekend, I've hardly been able to get any homework done. Nate is dominating my thoughts, so it's been taking me twice as long to get anything done. I can't wait to see him again. We almost kissed, and it keeps replaying in my mind, that moment on the bench. I'm positive he was going to kiss me until Ally showed up. My phone is next to me as I try to read, so I decided to look once more. Ugh, still no text. It's amazing how much nervous energy I have every time I look at my phone. I'm dying to hear from him. There's nothing to worry about. I mean, I'm just now sitting down myself. All day, I've been busy with my family, and I wouldn't have texted him until now. 'Ding,' my phone goes off, and immediately, my heart starts racing as I quickly grab my phone. It's just Trina.

T: How was your date?

B: Amazing! I thought he was going to kiss me, but Ally interrupted us. He said he would text today, but so far, nothing.

T: Really? OMG, he was going to kiss you! Did you finally hold hands?

B: Yes, we did when we were walking and during the movie. I'm screwed. I really like him

B: Also, Mark can eat more tacos than should be humanly possible, just saying

T: LOL, like, how many tacos?

B: I don't even know, 10? And these weren't small little taco bell tacos either. LOL

T: That is a lot of tacos!! Well, don't worry too much about Nate not texting. I think the soccer team was doing something together today. Ally mentioned it

B: Oh, thanks, good to know, maybe I can finally focus on homework then

T: Yeah, good luck. Anyway, I'll catch up more mañana

B: K, see ya tom

Now that Trina mentions it, I do recall them saying something about soccer. That makes me feel better immediately. I might actually be able to get through my homework now. About a half-hour passes before I start to daydream about Nate again. It's so easy to imagine us together. We really connect with each other. Opening up to Nate was easier than I thought. He seemed to genuinely care. I don't know why, but that surprised me. I can't believe last year, while I was moping around inside my own head and feeling invisible, he was trying to get my attention. Last night was unlike anything I had pictured. The expectation I had was that he'd just be goofy and fun-loving the whole time. It was a nice surprise that he opened up to me as much as he did, but it did make me feel a little guilty for pre-judging him. I love getting to know him and hope this is only the beginning.

Once again, I try to concentrate on my homework and look at my list to see what I have left. I've finished math, science, and history. A couple more chapters to read for English class, and then I'll be done.

"Ding!" I immediately reached to grab my phone, hoping it was him.

It's Nate, and my heart starts pounding. I'm so relieved that he finally texted.

N: Hey, how was your day?

I start to respond but stop myself. Am I supposed to play it cool? If I respond immediately, he'll know I'm dying to talk to him. I waited exactly one minute. That's all I could manage before thinking, 'Who cares?' and text him back.

B: Good, my grandparents came over to watch the Lions lose,

N: Yeah, too bad they couldn't pull it off today. There is always next week!

B: Of course, too bad they don't listen to my Dad and Grandpa's coaching ideas

B: How was your day?

N: Good, I had a soccer thing that went long.

N: I still have to do homework since I just got home, but I wanted to text first

B: It'll be a late night for you if you're just getting started

N: Nah, no worries, I'm used to late nights. But I should get started. See you tomorrow.

N: Night Becky 😮

B: Night Nate 😊

It was a simple conversation, but I still couldn't stop smiling. He was right. It was late. Once I finish this chapter, I'm going to get ready for bed. He hasn't even started; he's going to be exhausted. Soccer really takes a lot of time; I guess I didn't realize just how much time it takes out of his schedule. At least I can go to sleep knowing he still found time to text me. It's the best feeling in the world, knowing he was thinking about me. Sweet dreams for me tonight.

Chapter Six
Round One

Immediately after school, I will head to the locker room to meet Trina. I look at the clock; any second now, the final bell will ring. My hands are sweating; nerves are setting in, and I subconsciously grab the necklace. The bells ring, and I run out the door to get my dance stuff out of my locker. Nate runs over to my locker to wish me good luck. "I was hoping I would catch you! Good luck. You'll be great." He says as he hugs me. "Text me how it went when you're done. I probably won't be able to text until after practice, but I want to know right away, okay? You got this!" It felt so good to know he was cheering me on, even from a distance. He has been holding my hand when walking me to class now. Every time he reaches for my hand, I get butterflies, and I love it.

"Hey, are you ready for this?!" Trina comes running over. "I can't believe it's here! I feel like we have been practicing in your basement for a year!" It hasn't been that long, but I know what she means; it felt like this day would never come. The first round of auditions are finally here.

"I know, and then for the next round, we only have a week to master our routine," I say with an exasperated sigh. We have another routine planned for round two. It won't be too bad to refine the second routine; we just haven't practiced it much because we were super focused on the first round. First things first, we need to move on to the next round.

At the tryouts, there are so many girls I couldn't even count everyone. All the junior and senior dance team girls are trying out, plus a bunch of girls who aren't on the regular dance team. I don't know enough about them to be completely sure what I'm up against.

On our sophomore team, the top five dancers are all trying out. There is a ton of competition. Everyone, even last year's captains, need to try out, but they have the advantage of being allowed to use their routines from last year. I don't know if that is fair or not, but the tryout is more of a technicality for them anyway. We watch as Ally enters the room with last year's captains. They look so confident. We can go in alone or in a group of up to three people at a time, depending on your routine. Trina and I are listed in the middle of the pack, and I don't know if that's good or bad. We practiced the beginning counts a few times while waiting for our turn, and before we knew it, our names were being called.

"Next up is…Trina and Becky." The coach yells, reading from her list. Nervous energy overcomes my body the second I hear my name being called. I feel like I'm going to be sick. Deep breath, deep breath. Somehow, I manage to put a smile on my face as I stand up. I'm trying to hide my anxiety and instead exude confidence. I remember the necklace. It's the only cure I have at the moment. As I hold on to my necklace, I know it'll work its magic once more, and I'm calmed almost immediately.

"We're here!" Trina and I yell as we run over to coach. Once we reach her, Trina hands her our music. We are dancing to a hip-hop routine since the majority of the competitive dance routines will incorporate those moves.

"Okay, great. Stand in the middle, on the mascot, and we will ask you a few questions before starting your music." the coach says. I feel so small standing in the middle of the court with only Trina by my side. There is a panel of three judges, but they're the only other people. It makes the gym feel awkwardly empty.

"Becky, how long have you been dancing?" The first question was directed toward me.

"This is my fourth year, I started dancing in middle school. I was on the freshman dance team and am currently on the sophomore dance team." I had to yell my answer because I was far from the judges; everything about this process seemed to stress me out.

"And you, Trina?"

"I've been dancing for 11 years since I was 4." She says, and suddenly, I wonder if my experience will be an issue. There's a big difference between 11 years and 4 years of dancing. I'm going to need the luck of the necklace more than ever.

"Okay, great. Thank you. We will start your music now; don't be alarmed if we stop it before your time is up. We just need to keep the auditions moving. Once we've seen enough to make a decision, we will stop the music."

We both nod and then turn around to get into our starting positions. Thank goodness we start with our backs turned. 'Thank you' fills my mind as I grab hold of the necklace once more before tucking it safely away. As always, it calms my nerves. The first few notes of the music blare through the gym, finding the beats in my mind as I think '5,6,7,8...', and begin moving with the music. Turn..2, 3...down, up...7,8...and the music stops. It's too early. We stop dancing and walk back to the center of the mascot. We didn't finish our routine; they stopped us halfway through.

"Thank you, ladies, very nice." The judges say without showing any emotion. The coach adds, "Our decision will be posted tomorrow by noon. If your name is on the list, you will be moving on to the next round. You may go now." I feel like I just left everything out there on the floor. It feels amazing. I know I danced my heart out.

We walk out the door, and Ally runs over. "How did it go? I know you did great."

"They stopped us halfway through," Trina says, sounding disappointed

"Of course they did; they saw enough. They know you're good enough for the next round and don't want to be here all night. They're only halfway through auditions; don't be down about it." Ally says

"Did they stop you early?" I ask, suddenly feeling more unsure of myself after seeing Trina's reaction.

"Yeah, they've always stopped me early in the first round. I'm assuming they don't need to see us complete a whole routine once they've seen enough to make their decision. It'd take too long if everyone did a full routine. They don't want to be here all night." Ally explained with conviction.

"I was thinking the auditions were moving pretty fast." I feel better; her explanation makes a lot of sense.

"Let's put it this way: they stop you quickly if you are that terrible or that good. If they are on the fence, they'll keep you dancing longer to help make the decision. I know for a fact you two are NOT terrible, so I'm going to say you guys were that good!" Ally said, smiling and emphasizing the words to lift our spirits.

Trina let out a huge sigh. She must have been really worried. I've never heard her sound so nervous before. "Thank God, I was really worried," Trina says with a huge grin.

I reach for my phone and shoot Nate a text. 'We're done! They cut our routine short, but Ally says that it is a good sign. We'll know around 12 tmrw! ☺'

He didn't respond right away, but I knew he was in practice. We piled into Ally's car and couldn't stop talking about how great it would be if we were on the team together. They'll select one or two extras who will be alternates, so if someone gets hurt, they can perform. It's a similar role as an understudy in theater, but I want more. I want to make the team and earn my place to perform. One thing at a time. I'm trying not to get too far ahead of myself and get the impulse to grab the necklace. Once I feel the four-leaf clover between my fingers, it completely eases my mind. I'm going to make the team. Nothing is going to stop me now; after all, luck is on my side.

"Ding!" My phone alerts me, and I quickly look to see Nate's response to my text.

N: 'Just got out of practice. I know you killed it today!

N: Gotta get to my homework now, see you tmrw. We'll celebrate at lunch 😮

B: 'Thanks! Let's hope I'll get good news tmrw! Good night, Nate 😮'

N: 'You will.

N: Good night, Becky 😌'

By the time he texts, it's always late and he says something similar, but it still makes me feel special. This year's varsity soccer team is exceptional and under pressure to perform since they are expected to make it to the state finals. After spending time with Nate and Mark, it's incredible how hard they work, and I really want them to win the state championship. Nobody deserves it more. Typically, I'm getting ready for bed, and Nate is just starting his homework. It's crazy to me that he never complains; I can't imagine how late he stays up to get everything done. I'm pretty sure I would be exhausted.

The next day arrives, and all I can think about is the dance team cuts. The anticipation is killing me, and I know I'm not alone. Everyone who tried out is on high alert. The main bulletin board is located in the hallway near the lobby, and it's creating a bottleneck. Between every class, groups of girls stop to check if the list is posted as they walk by it. It's hard not to second-guess everything. After the audition, I felt good, but who knows if it was enough to make the team. At my locker before history class, I'm grabbing my book, when I feel someone's arms wrap around me.

"Hey, I've missed you all morning. I couldn't wait for history class." Nate says as he sneaks behind me and spins me around to kiss my forehead. Butterflies replaced my nervous energy; my mood immediately lifted. He grabs my hand as we walk together to Mr. Whitman's classroom. It feels so good whenever I'm around him; his presence just makes things better. My nerves are getting to me today, and I look up to him for support. Knowing exactly what I need, he smiles, saying, "It'll be good news." As usual, he seems to read my mind.

In history class, we are discussing the Civil War, and it's hard for me to imagine our country fighting within itself. This sounds like pop quiz material, I'm writing frantically when a folded piece of paper lands on top of my desk. Startled, I draw a line through my notes as I jump. It's from Nate. He can be so distracting! But who am I kidding? I love the attention and can't stop smiling. Opening the note, in Nate's boyish handwriting, it says, 'Sit with me at lunch today.' Overjoyed, I re-read the note. I'm so happy. It's finally happening. This is a huge deal!

Looking over at Nate with a questioning look trying to determine if he's sure. My heart starts racing. He shoots me that flirty smile of his before turning his attention back toward Mr. Whitman. In disbelief, I can't stop re-reading Nate's simple message over and over. Scribbled on a small piece of scrap paper is a dream come true. According to Ally, sitting with Nate at lunch means we are taking the next step in our relationship. Last year, it seemed impossible to even talk to him; I've come so far from that invisible girl.

As class starts to wind down, a sudden feeling of uneasiness consumes me. Once more, as I read his note, my heart explodes with excitement. But I'm also feeling unsure. I know this means we are taking our relationship to another level, but today is also the dance cut. More than anything, I want to sit with Nate, but I'm anxious about the uncertainty of the cuts. If I get cut, I'll be in a bad mood. If my friends get cut, I'll want to show them support and sit with them today. Trina and I usually sit with the dance team girls, and today isn't the best day to ditch them for Nate. It feels like bad timing. At the same time, I don't want to miss my chance to sit with Nate. I've waited for this for so long! Ugh, I'm so conflicted.

Instinctively, touching the necklace, I think through my options. Reaching for that magical touch has become a habit of mine anytime I'm feeling unsure. As always, that simple touch brings me confidence and belief that, somehow, it'll all work out. The bell rings.

There is only one more class before lunch — one more class before I find out my fate.

Nate looks over at me as we start to leave and says, "Well…"

"Well, what?" I ask, distracted as I'm lost in thought about the team cuts.

"My note. You want to sit with me today?" He asks with a hopeful smile as he holds my hand on our way out of class. He seems truly excited. I hate that I'm not as sure about it as he is.

"I do. Of course, I do. But…" I look at him as I try to find the words to explain my hesitation. He stops walking and turns towards me.

"But? But what?" He asks, looking hurt. It's written all over his face that he wasn't anticipating this reaction from me. Slowly, he begins pulling away just the tiniest bit. Oh no, he's misinterpreting. I want to sit with him so badly and just need to explain. Why did he have to ask me today, of all days? The timing is off.

"It's just that the list will be posted around lunchtime. I think the girls are going to want to talk about it, either way if the news is good or bad. I know if I don't make the team, I won't be the best company. Can we play it by ear, depending on how it goes with the list?" I ask pleadingly, wrapping my arms around his to pull him closer to me. He laughs at my attempt to cheer him up, and he comes around.

"Yeah, I was just thinking you'd want to celebrate with me. I'm positive you'll make the cut. I understand, though. We can play it by ear." He says with his bright eyes and a big smile.

"I do want to celebrate with you, but I'll also want to celebrate with Trina," I add, knowing there is no way I can leave her at a monumental moment like this!

"Have her sit with us! You know, Austin has a thing for her. He'd love it if she sat with us!" He says this with a conviction that makes me feel like this issue is settled.

Lunchtime arrives, and a crowd is surrounding the bulletin board. It's posted; my fate is on that list. Right now, it's impossible to get close enough to see the names listed. Extreme nerves hit me and I'm hesitant to look at the list. Most of the girls in the crowd will be eliminated; there are so many girls that tried out. Even if I manage to make this cut, I will face fierce competition in the next round. As I wait my turn, I watch as multiple girls leave with looks of disappointment, getting hugs from friends who are consoling them. The next girl looking at the board is a junior who is on the varsity dance team; she turns around with tears welling up in her eyes. Clearly, she got cut. This is horrible, my stomach is in knots. Trina is close to the board now, right in front, and my heart can't handle the tenseness. She turns around, her face beaming. It's obvious she made the cut. It's written all over her face. Trying not to be boastful, she hides her smile until she reaches me. Once she's next to me her beaming grin returns.

All I can think is what if she made it and I'm cut? If so, she should really simmer down. I don't know why I'm suddenly full of doubt; maybe it's all the disappointed faces surrounding me. Once she is close enough to me, she says quietly but urgently, "We made it! Time to prepare for round two!" Shock sets in. No way, we made it. I'm moving on! Unable to move while slowly trying to process what she just said, she pulls me into a hug.

"We made it, Becks! We're moving on." She repeats. It's amazing how much exuberance is in her voice while still being a whisper. We don't want to overdo it with the celebration since so many people around us did get cut. We look at each other, smiling so big it hurts. I wish I could shout the good news across the cafeteria to Nate! Oh, that reminds me, I need to ask Trina if she'll sit with us.

"I want to celebrate! Maybe I'll get one of those huge cookies at lunch today." Trina was saying with a laugh. She always eats healthy and follows a strict ballerina diet of foods rich in nutrients, which means no excess sugar. We're the total opposite that way. I love my sweets. She really does leave sweets to special occasions only, which I can't even comprehend.

"Do you feel like celebrating at Nate's table with me? He wants us to sit with him." My voice sounds hesitant, but I still smile hopefully. I don't want her to feel like I am forcing this on her, and I know she might want to sit with the girls, too. At the same time, I'm dying to tell Nate the good news, and I really want to sit with him.

"Finally!" She says with a big smile. "Of course, I'll sit with you! The cool kid table it is..." She's teasing; she could care less about who is considered cool or not. One of my favorite things about her is that she likes everyone. Honestly, she could choose to hang with only the cool kids if she wanted. Instead, she hangs out with whomever she wants, which is how she's friends with someone like me. Otherwise, she and I wouldn't have stayed friends. I've never been considered a 'cool kid.' Looking over at her, it seems like she's lost in thought, and then she adds, "Actually, I think that would be perfect timing today, you know, since we want to celebrate. I don't want to be rude about it in front of the girls who were cut. And we can sit with Ally since she will be with Mark." Wow, that worked out well! This necklace is amazing! All my worry for nothing. It seems impossible to keep all our excitement bottled up. She's right; it could be worse to sit with them today. Even so, I'm a little uncomfortable about it. Before I sit with Nate, I stop by the table and talk to the girls.

"Hey ladies, how are you guys doing?" I ask, tentatively approaching them as this is starting to feel like a bad idea.

"How do you think we're doing?" The girls are looking at me in disbelief. Everyone is looking at me as if they are thinking, 'How dare I ask them how they're doing at a moment like this.' Oh no, this is the exact opposite of my intent.

"I'm so sorry. You're all so talented, and you know they rarely take any sophomores. There's always next year." I'm trying to be cheerful, but I'm realizing quickly it's probably best to leave before I make things worse.

"Well, congrats to you and Trina…two sophomores moving on to the next round." The annoyed tone and avoidance of any eye contact are telling me everything I need to know. I know they're just upset at the moment. At least I tried, but this certainly isn't making anything better for anyone.

"Thank you. I just wanted to stop by and say no matter what, we all know you guys are great dancers. Try not to get discouraged. We still have our dance team." At that, I turn to leave but hear them exasperated.

"Stop by? You're not sitting with us?" Oh boy, this really couldn't be going any worse. All I want is to escape to the safety of Nate's table.

"Nate wants me to sit with him. Um, to celebrate. I'm really sorry." Sheepishly trying to explain, but can tell I'm not helping things. Trina and Nate were right. Today is a good day to get out of here. Clearly, my presence is only making things worse.

"Fine, go sit with your perfect boyfriend." She says, clearly upset.

"He's not my boyfriend. We're just…hanging out, I guess. I'll see you guys at dance practice tonight. I'm really sorry. You are all so talented." I say, trying to make some kind of amends, but I know the gesture fell short. Relieved to be leaving, I head towards Nate, my 'perfect boyfriend.' We haven't been hanging out long and haven't even kissed yet. Still, I couldn't help but love it when she called him my boyfriend, even if her intent was snarky.

As I reach Nate's table, he stands up and wraps his arms around me, giving me a congratulatory hug. Ecstatic, he lifts me off my feet, kisses my cheek, and says, "I knew you would be moving on. I'm so proud of you!" He's genuinely proud. His face is beaming. Trina is already conveniently sitting next to Austin. Hmm, wonder how they made that happen. I'll have to fill her in on that situation later.

"How did it go over there?" Trina asks, nodding over to the girl's table.

"Horrible," I say, shrugging. Nothing is going to take this moment away from me. For the first time in a long time, I'm starting to believe in myself and have worked so hard for this.

"Yeah, it usually doesn't matter what you say when the wound is still fresh. They just need a little time." Trina says. She would know she dances competitively outside of school and has dealt with similar situations many times. It's never easy. In the long run, it usually works out, and she has learned to just give them time. I thought I understood what she was going through, but this was my first time experiencing it firsthand. It's harder than I thought.

"Yeah, I figured it might be rough on you to be over there today. I was there with the sophomore guys when I was moved up to varsity. They will be happy for you eventually, but they are dealing with feeling rejected right now." Nate adds.

"Is that why you asked me to sit with you today?" My heart stops. Is that why he invited me to sit with him? Maybe this wasn't because our relationship was going to the next level, after all. This is about helping me get through today with the cuts being announced and has nothing to do with us as a 'couple'.

"Partly, but it was mostly because I missed you all week with the extra soccer games taking up so much of my time." He says with a pout on his face, which is so adorable. His explanation reassures me, and I take a calming breath. It occurs to me that I'm gripping my necklace. It's such a habit now anytime I feel anxious. I didn't even realize I was holding on to it. Nate just said he missed me. It's like I'm in a dream. I like him so much. He's right; we usually see each other much more than we have this week. Today, he was running late getting to school, and I was late in between classes, so we kept missing each other. It's been like that all week.

"I missed you too," I said, linking my arm through his and leaning my head on his shoulder as we finished up our lunch. I love being near him and feeling his strength, especially now. Even though I'm happy to have made it to the next level of tryouts, I still feel bad about the girls. I hate that they were upset, but leaning on Nate helps ease my mind. He kisses my forehead, and I wonder, how did I get so lucky?

"Let's grab lunch together next Saturday, just the two of us. I want you all to myself for once." He says quietly in my ear since I'm leaning on his shoulder. Looking up at him, I'm met with those kind, bright blue eyes of his.

"That sounds wonderful," I say, feeling euphoric. For once, it's like I belong here, with Nate, with these new friends, and on the dance team. This is the life that was meant for me.

"Can we go to the diner since we can both walk there? It's easier than figuring out a ride." Nate interrupts my thoughts.

"Of course. It's perfect." I say, adding, "I can't wait." He smiles at that and squeezes my hand in agreement.

Chapter Seven
Group Date

Lately, my life can be described in one word: practice, practice, practice. Body aches are the new normal. I've learned that Trina accepts nothing short of perfection. It's been non-stop. Constantly, she is pushing me to improve and teaching me new moves. I'm so lucky to have her on my side. At this point, we can do the routine in our sleep. The girls on the dance team have become really supportive of Trina and me. A few times, they even stayed late after practice to watch us perform our routine for the next round of auditions. They pointed out that we had a tendency to drift from the center while performing and gave us really great ideas on how to stay in our correct spots. It was so heartwarming when the girls came around. Trina and Nate were right. They just needed some time.

Trina and I are ready, and the day is finally here. Arriving at school full of angst over the tryouts, I head to my locker before the first bell rings. As I open it, a note falls out of my locker. Nate must have left it for me; in his distinct scribble, it says, 'You got this! xo, Nate.' It's all I needed and makes me feel so special. Nate and I have still been texting and walking to classes, but we haven't had any alone time. We still haven't had our first kiss, and I don't know exactly where we stand. Spending time alone with him this weekend will be so nice. I can't wait for this Saturday. First, I need to get through the second audition, and then I can think about Nate.

Today is going so slow. It feels like the auditions are never going to get here. It's only lunchtime. Trina and I sit with the boys every day now. Austin and Trina seem to be getting along. They tease each other constantly. I wonder how long this flirting will go on before Austin finally asks Trina out. Catching Nate's eye, I nod my head in their direction, saying quietly, "Is he ever going to ask her out?"

Nate smiles and says to the table, "Anyone want to go to the movies tonight?" I know he is giving Austin the opportunity to hang out with Trina outside of school. He is a little shy compared to the rest of the guys. It's sweet. In Austin's defense, Trina and I have been spending every available moment perfecting our routine. Even if he dared ask her out, she would have made him wait until after today's audition anyway.

"Trina and I would love to go to the movies! It'll keep our mind off the dance team." I say loudly while giving Trina the eye, trying to get her to agree. Hopefully, I'm helping with the idea. Plus, it's true. We will have to wait all weekend before the team is announced. Distractions are the best way to deal with the anxiety of waiting to find out if you made the team.

"Yeah, that's exactly what I need, I'm in." Trina says, smiling at me with a knowing glance, and then she looks over at Austin, "What about you?" She asks him.

"Definitely in," Austin says with a smirk.

"Us too!" Ally yells, she and Mark are sitting at the opposite end of the table today.

And just like that, we have a group date for the movies. Looking over at Nate, I notice he seems proud of himself as he shoots me a smirk. It's Trina's turn to get forced into a group date, but it did work out for me and Nate after all. "Nice job," I whisper as I nudge him.

"I'm just trying to help Austin out. He's been working up the nerve to ask her out." He says. "This will be an easier start for him. Plus, I don't mind sharing you since I know I will get you all to myself Saturday." He pulled me in closer as he mentioned Saturday.

"I can't wait" I say and I mean it. We haven't talked about Saturday in a while. It was nice to hear him mention it with so much enthusiasm. It's never just the two of us. We're always in groups or at school. Our practice schedules make it nearly impossible, but we make time where we can, which often means group activities. Saturday will be really nice.

"Good luck at the audition. I probably won't see you before, but I'll try." Nate says as he kisses my forehead before walking in the opposite direction of me.

"Thanks. I'll text you after." I yell after him.

"You'll kill it!" He yells down the hall with a smile.

The last bell rings and school is out for the weekend. Trina and I head straight to tryouts. This audition has fewer people but is stacked with top dancers. They cut most dancers after the first round and now only need to cut five people. We're the only two sophomores, and as I look around the room of people auditioning, my palms start to sweat. They are all really talented. I wouldn't cut anyone from this group. Suddenly, I don't feel as ready as I did earlier in the day; glancing over at Trina, she gives me a forced smile.

"All these girls are really good," I whisper nervously.

"I was thinking the same thing. We're ready, though. We know the routine inside and out. The question will be, 'Is our routine good enough to beat five of these girls?'" She says, trying to sound confident, but I can tell she's nervous, too.

"I'm nervous," I say, and instinctively grab my necklace. Calm immediately washes over me, and I get that burst of confidence I've come to expect. Somehow, by some miracle, we will make this team. I'm sure of it.

"We got this. The routine is amazing, and we will kill it!" I say with a smile.

"I like the confidence. Let's do this." Trina says, and I can tell she feels better, too. This necklace is incredible. One touch and I went from being a nervous wreck to having total confidence in myself.

"Next is Trina and Becky. Come on in, girls!" Coach yells.

We get into our places, and the coach says, "Go ahead and start the music." No questions or introductions this time. It's all down to the dancing. The music starts, and I get a rush of energy. The routine is flowing effortlessly, and I can see Trina in the corner of my eye. We are in perfect sync. Our music comes to an end, and I look at my spot; we haven't drifted. Perfect. "Great job girls. As you know, the team roster will be posted on Monday."

"Thank you." Trina and I both say as we run out of the gym and into the hall.

"I think we nailed it! Trina that was the best we have ever performed that routine." I'm overflowing with excitement.

"I think so too! I can't believe we have to wait a whole weekend to find out!" She says, with a huge sigh. "Waiting is the worst!"

"Hey guys, looks like it went well?" Ally asks as she spots us celebrating.

"It was as good as we could have possibly performed it. Now, we have to wait and see if the routine was strong enough to land us a spot. I hate the waiting game." Trina says, emphasizing it again. It's a really good thing she has her date tonight. I think she really needs a distraction.

"At least you know you performed it well; besides, I have a good feeling we will all be on the team this year!" Ally says confidently, then adds, "But, seriously, I'm so glad we're going out tonight! That will be a nice distraction." It's like she read my mind.

"Speaking of, you know Austin totally has a thing for you, right?" I asked Trina. I'd been meaning to tell her, but we were hyper-focused on dance. I kept forgetting.

"Well…I thought maybe…" she says, smiling shyly.

"Oh, he's been dying to ask you out, but he can be so shy," Ally says.

"Are you interested?" I ask. "I know for a fact he is, and you guys always seem pretty flirty."

"I guess I am, but we're always being sarcastic and goofing off, so it's hard to know for sure if I should take him seriously. He is cute and fun, so I'm not against it!" She says with a wink and a laugh. Ally and I both know she's totally interested, we just look at each other with a knowing smile before we start laughing with her.

On the big screen, the hero and villain are fighting, but that's not what has my attention. Once again, I lean forward to see if Austin has his arm around Trina or at least is holding her hand. Ouch! Nate pinched me as he whispered, "Stop it." I can't help it; I'm dying to see if they are hitting it off.

Austin is really nice, and he's artsier than the other guys, it's perfect for Trina. He isn't on the soccer team with Mark and Nate, but he's been good friends with Mark for a long time. Similar to Trina and I, they grew up together, living down the street from each other. Most likely, Austin wouldn't naturally be with the popular crowd if it wasn't for Mark, who is super popular in school. Unless Austin knows you well, he pretty much keeps to himself. He's more introverted than outgoing but has a genuine kindness to him. I've always felt like I could tell him anything, even when we first met. It's almost as if he is the glue of the group. Anytime he is comfortable, you really see the funny Austin; it often comes out when he is teasing Trina. She is literally the only person I have ever seen him tease and be sarcastic with besides Mark. All that teasing is a sign that he feels comfortable with them; it shows off his quick wit. No one else sees that side of him; to others, he's just seen as a nice guy.

After the movie, we ran to the restroom because we all drank huge drinks. Of course, there is already a line for the ladies' room. We're not the only girls who went directly to the restroom after the movie. "So, did he make a move?" I ask Trina, dying to know.

"Not really. I thought he was going to, but he kept noticing you leaning forward and looking at us. Thanks a lot, by the way." Trina says, trying to sound annoyed, but smiles, so I know she isn't.

"Sorry, Nate kept telling me to stop, too. I just couldn't wait to see how it was going." I give a shy laugh and hope she's not mad. "Well, the night is still young. We can see if the guys want to do something after, or maybe you and Austin could hang out alone." I say with a smile, the night isn't over yet, and he can still make his move.

"We'll see…" Trina says with a sly smile, making me laugh. They just have to get together. It would be so much fun for us to end up as three couples. Oops, there I go again, making myself a couple with Nate. Who knows where we stand? We like each other, but are we a couple? I have no idea. Of course, I'm all in, but I need to play it cool. It really hasn't been that long. Maybe I will figure it out on Saturday, or for sure around homecoming.

"Let's go see what the plan is," Ally says, interrupting my perpetual thoughts. We head over to our guys, who are standing in the hall with a bunch of other guys, all waiting for their girls to exit the restroom.

"Hey," I say to Nate, and he puts his arm around me. I could really get used to this.

"We were thinking about going back to my place and having a bonfire. Maybe get some stuff for S'mores." Nate says to the group.

"That sounds good to me. Did Austin say anything about Trina?" I ask Nate quietly.

"Yeah, that you kept looking at them, so he didn't feel comfortable making any kind of move. I told you to stop it." He says, and he grabs my side, which kind of tickles. I can't help but squeal and giggle, making Nate laugh.

"Come on, you two, you're going to miss your ride," Mark yells over to us with a big smile. I know he likes us together; he once mentioned to Ally how happy Nate is with me.

Arriving at Nate's house and walking through his door is like a dream; I can't believe I'm in his house. It's crazy. I have dreamt about this forever. I've always known where he lived but have never been inside. His mom is in the kitchen, and his dad is in the living room watching the news.

"Hey, mom, dad. We were thinking of having a fire in the pit and making some S'mores." Nate says as he walks in the door.

"Oh, hey honey, I thought you were home early. Hi, I'm Kristine, Nate's mom...you must be Becky," She says, reaching out her hand to me, but when I reach out to shake it, she changes her mind. Instead, she hugs me. "It's so nice to finally meet you! Nate talks about you all the time!"

"It's so nice to meet you, too."

"Mom..." Nate says, giving her the 'please stop' eye, smiles, and just shakes his head. He seems embarrassed that his mom admitted he talks about me, but I think this is great! I'm going to find out everything he's ever said about me.

"Hi," she says, giving her attention to Trina instead.

"Hi, I'm Trina," she says, reaching out her hand to Nate's mom, but she also gets a hug instead. I like how warm she is. "Justin, come say hi to the kids." Reluctantly, his dad gets off the couch, leaving his TV show to come over. Once he makes his way over to us, he is very friendly, too. He shook my hand as well as Trina's since we were the only people he didn't already know. Patting the guys on the back as a greeting, he says, "You guys are going to make some S'mores, huh? There should be everything you need out there. Let me make sure you have a lighter." The guys follow him into the kitchen and out to the patio to make the fire. That leaves us girls alone. I'm nervous being with Nate's mom, even though she's been very friendly. Never in a million years did I expect to meet his parents tonight.

"How was the movie?" His mom asks.

"Good," we say in unison. Ally starts telling her about the movie in more detail, and I'm so thankful for that. Strangely, I'm feeling a little shy and unsure of myself all of a sudden. Instinctively, I grab the necklace.

"That's a pretty necklace." Nate's mom says, looking closer at it.

"Thanks, my grandpa randomly found it on the beach. Nobody claimed it, so he gave it to me for good luck. He's Irish, so he found it fitting that it was a four-leaf clover." I explained, but I felt a little silly telling her about the good luck part.

"I love it, we're Irish too." His mom says, and I feel better about talking about it being lucky. She didn't seem to think I meant anything by it. Trina starts talking about the luck of the necklace again, though, and for some reason, it makes me self-conscious.

"I didn't know that about your necklace. I noticed you wore it during tryouts, and you normally never wear jewelry. Let's hope it brought us both good luck then." Trina says with a laugh and smile. I know she is being genuine, but for some reason, it makes me uncomfortable to talk about it. I've really started to believe in the necklace. Every one of my biggest dreams has come true. For example, I'm at Nate's house talking with his mom right now! And, if I'm really honest, I know I will make the competitive team, and I believe it has to do with the luck of this necklace. Suddenly, I'm aware that I've been kind of zoned out, and the girls are looking at me like, 'Say something.'

"Oh, sorry, I haven't thought about tryouts all night. I suddenly remembered our fate would be determined in the next couple of days." I say sheepishly, hoping that is an acceptable explanation for my wandering mind. I don't want to seem disinterested. For as long as I can remember, I would get in trouble for zoning out or daydreaming at bad times. It can come across as rude, and I'm trying to be better about it.

"I know! It's so hard to wait and not worry!" Trina says, putting her arm around me. "At least we're in this together."

"Hey girls, come on out, the fire is going good now." Nate's dad says as he comes back inside and heads towards the living room. "It was nice meeting you. Enjoy the S'mores."

"Have fun, but tell the boys to keep the noise to a reasonable level. Does anyone want to take something to drink outside?" Nate's mom asks.

We head over to the fridge and grab some drinks. Our hands are full of water and soda cans. "Thank you, Mrs…"

"Kristine, please, Becky, just call me Kristine," she corrected me, saying with a smile, "Have fun."

"Thanks, Kristine, we will," I say with a smile and head outside to the rest of them.

Nate sees me and pats his leg like he wants me to sit on his lap, but I hesitate. Does he really? "Sit right here," he says, patting his leg again. "At least for a little while, I want to put my arms around you." I sit on his lap, and he gives me a bear hug. I am the luckiest girl in the world.

"Your parents seem nice," I say.

"Yeah, they're great. My dad travels a lot, though, so he isn't around much. My mom is amazing. She is involved in everything, I swear. She always bakes the team cookies, so they all love her. Homemade cookies. That's all it takes to win over a group of guys." He says with a laugh but then adds with a serious tone, "Honestly, she was really there for me this summer when I was having a hard time with the guys on the team. And, she had to win over the guys and their parents in her own way, too."

"Well, I can't imagine anyone not liking her," I say, and I mean it. She is very warm and kind.

"It was never about her. It was always about the parents of the guys who felt like they were cut because of me. And there was more than one set of them, even though I only took one spot. We both got the blame. The other parents were siding with the guys who were cut, at least until we became a real team. Now they love us both."

"It sounds like it was really nasty for a while."

"Yeah, I think it was hard on her at first. She kept up a positive attitude for me, though, and Mark was always cool, thank god, or I may have even quit."

"That bad, huh? I honestly can't imagine you ever quitting."

"Me either, but I did think about it. I was pushed to my limit."

"I hope that doesn't happen if Trina or I make the competitive dance team; they rarely take sophomores. It would probably feel like we stole a spot from an upperclassman. Oh man, parents would be pissed."

"Yeah, I hope it doesn't go that way, but if it does, I have some miserable team workouts you guys can do! Suffering together is team building," he says with a laugh. "Ready to make some S'mores?" he asks, lightening the mood. The other couples were already eating theirs, but since I was on Nate's lap, we couldn't really roast marshmallows.

"Here you go," Nate says as he hands me my stick with a marshmallow on the end. My stick is immediately straight into the flame and catches the marshmallow on fire. Quickly, I blow it out before turning it to the unburnt side and doing it all over again.

"You're good at this. Just catch 'em on fire! That's the only way to roast marshmallows if you ask me." He says, impressed. Everyone has their own way of roasting a marshmallow. I like it that we agree. We're so in synch.

"Definitely, catching them on fire is the only way. We make lots of S'mores at our cottage during the summer, and that's how I've always done it." It floods me with positive memories of the cottage and all the bonfires we've had out there.

Glancing around the fire, I notice Trina sitting next to Austin with his arm around her. Well, well… it seems he isn't embarrassed anymore. Poking Nate to get his attention, I nod my head in their direction. He smiles and whispers in my ear, "About time," and we both laugh. Sitting next to Nate on this cool fall night, sharing a blanket to keep us warm, makes me so happy. It's still unreal to me that this is my life as I look around at my new group of friends.

"What are you thinking about? Are you daydreaming about your next big thing?" Nate teases while snapping me out of my thoughts.

"Actually, I was just thinking that so many of my daydreams are actually happening. It makes me so happy." Looking up at him, I know it's one of those moments. If we were alone, he would kiss me, but we're not. He leans over to kiss my forehead instead.

"You being happy makes me happy," Nate says.

"It's about that time, Becks, we have to get home for curfew," Trina says

"Ugh, okay, the night went so fast." Thank god Trina's parents have her on a strict curfew, too. It makes it so much easier. I'm so glad I'm not the only reason the fun has to end.

Nate walks me to the door and hugs me tight. "I'll see you tomorrow. We can finally have some alone time. I'll text you when I leave tomorrow and meet you at the diner." He kisses my forehead, and I feel like I'm floating on a cloud of happiness.

I walk over to Mark's car and wave goodbye to Nate, thinking, 'I can't wait until tomorrow.' Getting rides is a major perk of hanging out with people a year older. November is around the corner, which is Nate's 16th birthday, and I can't wait for him to drive. Trina has to wait until June, after the school year, so that's not helpful. And I'm a summer birthday, so I will be hitching rides all year. Austin is driving Trina home, so they will have some alone time. I can't wait to hear about her night. I haven't had a chance to talk about her about Austin since we've been at Nate's.

"What do you guys think of Austin and Trina?" I ask Mark and Ally.

"It's on!" says Mark.

Ally laughs and adds, "They are so cute together! I can't wait to hear all about it. Maybe we could meet at the diner for lunch with her tomorrow?"

"Oh, I can't, or, well…I'm already going to meet Nate at the diner for lunch."

"Oh, okay." She says, turning around to look at me with raised eyebrows.

"Um, well, I guess you could join?" My tone is hesitant because I really want to be alone with Nate. I only invited her because I didn't want to disappoint her. Please don't join us! I hope I didn't just ruin our only alone time.

"It's okay, maybe we could meet up later. Then you can tell me how it goes with Nate at lunch, too." She says with a laugh.

"Do you girls talk after every single time we hang out?" Mark asks, sounding a little worried.

"Nah, I don't kiss and tell," Ally says and leans over to kiss him on the cheek. Then she looks back at me and winks as Mark pulls into my driveway. Laughing at their exchange, I thank Mark for the ride as I exit the car.

Chapter Eight
The Tree

Time to pick out my outfit for lunch with Nate. Super casual, for sure, but it still needs to be cute. So far, I have picked out a pair of ripped jeans, and I'll definitely be wearing the leather jacket. It'll be perfect with my new favorite T-shirt, which is a crop top. I look in the full-length mirror. It's perfect. I'm so excited to spend the afternoon alone with Nate. Plus, he'll be the best distraction, so I won't be thinking about the dance team. Hopefully, we'll get some time away from the diner since, in this small town, we'll still know everyone there. My phone dings, and it's a text from Nate. He is out his door. It's time for me to leave. Running downstairs to head out the door, I pass Mom, who is in the kitchen.

"Hey honey, where are you off to?" She asks just as I'm about to walk out the door.

"I'm going to lunch with Nate at the diner, remember?"

"Are you walking or want a ride?" She asks

"I'll walk. I want to get some fresh air." The diner was halfway between my house and Nate's house. It's probably a 20-minute walk for both of us.

"Well, be back by dinner time, okay? I'm making grilled chicken and mashed potatoes because your sister is coming home for the night." She knows that's one of my favorite dinners; definitely not going to miss it!

"Oh, yum! I didn't realize Jen was coming home! I'll definitely be home for it."

"Well, yeah, she is going to Leslie's birthday party, so it's easier if she stays here."

Leslie has been a good friend of my sisters since high school. She's going to the community college her first couple years and then might transfer to Michigan State, where my sister goes. It's only about an hour's drive, so they still see each other often. Leslie dated Nate's brother in high school for a while, but he never came around our house. I forgot about that until now.

"I'll make sure I'm home for dinner. What time?"

"Around 6:00-6:30, your grandparents are coming too. They want to see Jen."

"Sounds good. I'll make sure I'm back in time. See you later." I say, and I grab my phone to text Nate that I'm out my door. I'm only a few minutes behind him. It should be perfect timing.

Walking over to the diner, I decided to listen to some new music my sister recommended to me. She always finds new bands and tells me to check them out. It feels so good being in the crisp fall air. The sun is shining, and there are moments I can feel the warmth on my face; it's a nice contrast to the chill in the air. I love Fall. I love the changing colors of leaves, the cool air, and wearing jeans.

Most importantly, it's the best weather for cuddling. Last night, when I was cuddled up with Nate, I felt so comfortable and genuinely happy. Anytime I'm with him, all my doubts melt away. For once, my mind wasn't stuck worrying about one thing or another. The only other time I feel truly confident the way I did last night is after I touch my necklace. Nate is walking into the diner just up ahead, and he beats me inside by only a few minutes.

"Hey," I say as I walk in the door. "You were just a few minutes ahead of me."

"Yeah, it must be exactly halfway between our houses," he says with a smile and shifts his backpack off, dropping it on the floor. It's full of stuff. Maybe he has a surprise in store for me?

"So...I was thinking we should order food to go." He says with a sly smile.

"Okay, and where will we be eating then?" curious as to what he has planned. I look at his backpack and then over to him with questioning eyes as if to ask what's inside.

"Oh, I just brought a blanket and some drinks. I was thinking we could eat in the park by the river. This place gets so busy, and we're going to know just about everyone here. The more I thought about it, the more I wanted to go somewhere that would be a little more private."

"A picnic?" I ask with raised eyebrows. He always surprises me, and I would never have guessed that he would think of planning a picnic.

"Yeah, good idea, right?" He says, sounding very proud of himself. It's adorable.

"Best idea ever." Leaning into him in agreement, he throws his arm around me. My excitement just shot through the roof, a picnic with Nate. It's exactly what we need: real alone time. We walk up to the counter and order burgers and fries from Rob, the owner of the diner.

"Hey kids, what'll it be?" Rob asks in his happy voice.

"Two burgers with fries. To go." Nate says, looking at me to make sure I don't want anything else. I nod in agreement.

"To go? You kids going out to enjoy this beautiful day?" Rob asks, striking up a conversation with Nate while we wait for our food. Rob knows everyone in town, and he is part of why this place is so popular. It also doesn't hurt that Rob's Diner has the best burgers in the world. The location is in the prime spot in the center of the town. Main Street is made up of a diner, a pizza place, and an ice cream shop as far as food goes. The rest of the street has a bank, a convenience store, a few boutiques, and a library. It's cute and with a very quaint, small-town feel. The area around us is growing like crazy, and our little town is now surrounded by all kinds of chain restaurants, fast food, and shopping centers popping up all around our town. We can't walk to any of it, though, and I think that's perfect. It's far enough away that we still haven't lost the chill vibe of our little town.

"Here you go! You kids have fun!" Rob says as he hands our food over to Nate. I missed most of their conversation since it was too loud in the diner to hear.

"Thanks, Rob!" Nate and I say at the same time as we turn to head out the door.

We walk down the street a couple of blocks and into the park. The trail leads us along the river until finally, the street is out of sight. Instead, we're engulfed in the woods. We head off the trail and towards the river to find the perfect spot. There is a landing with a clearing of flat grass that's a few feet higher than the water level, overlooking the river. It's inviting, as if it existed just for us. Looking out at the view while Nate lays down the blanket, it's amazing how beautiful it is here. Water is flowing vigorously downstream, cascading effortlessly over the randomly placed boulders within the river. When I look a little further upriver, I notice there are boulders build-up that make the river look more like a waterfall. I've never paid attention to that in all the years I've walked through this park. Never once have I noticed this perfect spot; it's magical. The water shimmers as it catches a glimpse of sunlight, and I'm struck by the beauty. It's special here, an enchanted place.

There is a huge tree just behind us; it must be over a hundred years old. Its large branches stretch over the clearing, creating a canopy that shades us from the sunlight. Shade makes it just a touch cooler, but not bad. In awe of the tree trunk, I examine it, wondering how old the tree really is and see initials carved on it. Couples' initials with hearts around them; we weren't the first ones to discover this spot.

"Nate," I say, pointing out the initials to Nate.

"Yeah, it's the best spot. I think many couples have enjoyed a lunch or two here."

"Have you been here before?" Suddenly, the specialness of this place evaporates.

"Yeah, it's a great spot. I come here alone when I need to clear my head, and Stacy was here with me once over the summer." Stacy. The sound of her name gives me a pang of jealousy. I wish it didn't have that effect, but it does. She's beautiful and popular, much more the type of girl everyone would expect him to date. Of course, he was here with her. They dated over the summer. On the first day of school, I remember wondering why he wouldn't sit by her in history class, but they were already broken up. He chose to sit by me instead. Hopefully, it's a sign he's over her. Insecurity starts taking over my happiness, knowing I can't compete with her. As always, I reach for the necklace, and my worries fade away. Luck is on my side.

"Oh," I say, realizing I sound disappointed. My magical idea of this place was just smashed to smithereens. I just wanted this to be our special place.

"We were hanging out this summer, well, a little bit. I was always in a bad mood, though, because of soccer. She didn't know the real me and always wanted me to be the life of the party. She only liked my fun-loving side. I never felt like I could tell her what was going on with the team. I hated that. I felt like I was always acting when I was around her. It ended pretty quickly, but, yeah, she was here with me once." He explains, and, for some reason, it felt like a confession.

"It's okay. I just thought we had discovered this place together." I said, shrugging.

Nate laughs, "Oh, this spot is pretty famous in town. It doesn't get any better than this. It's amazing, somehow just about every time I come here, it's empty. Maybe people don't enjoy it like they used to, or maybe it's only famous in my family. The two sets of initials on that tree are from my grandparents and parents." He smiles at me, walks over to the tree, and points out his grandparent's initials and then his parents. They are the only sets of initials carved into the tree.

"You'll have to keep that tradition alive." As I say it, I'm visualizing R.L + N.M carved in the tree for Rebecca Lewis and Nathan McNeil.

"Yeah, I always thought I'd carve my initials here. Someday." He says with a smile, then adds, "This place has always been special to me, and I wanted to share it with you."

He is looking me in the eyes almost as if he wants to tell me something, and I wonder what he is thinking. He looks back at the initials and runs his hands over the carved letters. Then he looks at me with his kind, beautiful blue eyes as he pulls me close. I know he is going to kiss me, and this time, there were no interruptions. I feel his lips on mine, and it's as though I am floating. It's like a fairytale, our first kiss under this amazing tree in this magical, meaningful spot along the river. He pulls away and smiles. "I have been wanting to do that for a while now."

"Me too." That's all I can manage to say before he kisses me once more. I am breathless as he pulls away. I look up at him, searching his eyes, wondering if he knows how much I like him. At the moment, I don't say anything. Seemingly out of nowhere, he breaks the moment with the most boyish thing ever.

"Let's eat! I'm starving!" It's such a change in mood that I can't help but laugh. Knowing him, that's exactly what he was going for: time to relax and have a little fun.

Digging through his backpack, he pulls out drinks and another smaller blanket to warm us up. Eating our delicious burgers while we sit on the blanket covering the grass makes me realize that burgers are kind of weird picnic food. Oh well, the burgers are really good.

"These burgers are seriously the best," I say as I get ready to take another bite.

Nate just nods approvingly, as his mouth is full. He finishes his bite and says, "It's better than PB&J, that's for sure. That was my other option for food today. I really wanted the burger." He chuckles before taking another bite.

After we finish eating, my head is on his lap as I lay down while he sits under the tree. We are cuddled under the same small blanket. As I look towards the sky, the colorful leaves sway above me, and I am mesmerized. Soon, those branches will be bare as winter is around the corner. In the background, there is this soft sound of the river flowing peacefully over the rocks as I listen to Nate tell me childhood stories. It's fun and enlightening to learn more about his family. He shares the history of this special place and how his mom's parents met in high school. During their senior prom night, they carved their initials on the tree; it's where his Grandpa proposed to his grandma. His brother almost carved his initials with Leslie, my sister's friend. They were much more serious than I ever realized. He thought she was the one, but they broke up during their senior year. After I told Nate my sister was close friends with Leslie, the stories turned into me sharing some of my favorite family stories and memories. Leslie was involved in many of them since she and my sister were so close. He listened intently, asking questions as I told stories. He would sneak kisses here and there if he found something I shared to be particularly endearing. I loved how much he wanted to learn about my life.

It was starting to get late, and I had to get home in time for dinner with my family. It was so nice to spend the day under that tree alone with Nate. It felt like we learned so much about each other in one day. "I don't ever want to leave," I say as I'm cuddled in his arms.

"I know. I feel the same." He says as he kisses my forehead. "You know, I told you Stacy was here, but I didn't tell her the history of this place. I've never felt like I could open up to her. I feel like I can tell you anything, and I've told you things nobody else knows. It's so easy to talk to you."

"I feel the same. I could listen to you and share stories with you all day." I sit up and turn around so I can look at him. He kisses me again and says, "I really like you, Becky."

"I really like you too," I say, mesmerized by what just happened. But, then, notice the time. "Oh crap, Nate! I have to get home! My sister is coming home, and my grandparents are coming over for dinner."

"Okay, let's pack up and get you home." He says, laughing at my sudden urgency.

"My sister is home for Leslie's birthday. I never realized she was that serious with your brother." We continue to talk as we quickly pack up our picnic.

"Yeah, I think he's going to her party tonight. The problem was always that he was more serious than she was. At least, that's what it sounds like to me. He's still holding onto hope they will get back together, I think, but he won't admit it." He says with a shrug.

"Hm, want me to ask my sister about it?"

"Nah, let them figure it out." He says. Then, for some reason, he comes over and gives me a bear hug, picking me off the ground. I start laughing as my feet dangle, and he swings me around in a circle. It's pure happiness. This is better than I could have ever imagined.

We walk back to Main Street together before going our separate ways. He kisses me on the forehead and says, "Have a nice dinner with your family." For the rest of my walk home, I feel like I am walking on cloud nine.

Back at home, despite what Nate said, I have to ask Jen about Leslie and Chris. As she gets ready for the party, I try to get information about them out of her. "I never realized that Leslie and Chris were such a serious thing in high school," I say, trying to act nonchalant, even though I was dying of curiosity.

"Oh yeah, he was really into her. She really liked him too, but she didn't share too much about it with me. She said they broke up over something really weird. I know it was something that made her feel like they were getting too serious. A tradition in his family or something? I don't know what it was exactly. She kept it to herself."

Carving the initials in the tree, that has to be it. That's exactly what my sister is talking about. For some reason, though, I don't tell my sister about it. It seems private and silly if you don't understand the importance of that tradition in their family. It's so meaningful to them, and once you're in that special place, it almost seems sacred. I wonder if that's why Leslie never told my sister about it, too. "Nate said he thinks Chris is going tonight."

"I'm sure he is if he was invited. From what I can tell, he never stopped loving her. I don't really know what happened with them. So, what's going on with you and Nate?" She asks with a sly smile.

"I don't know for sure, but he kissed me today. We had this romantic picnic by the river. Ughh, I really like him." I could gush about him all night, even if talking about this makes me blush.

"Oh yeah? Well, I bet you're happy! I always knew you had a crush on him, and he kissed you! When did this happen? He always seemed like such a jock to me, but I don't know him well. He is very cute." She says in a teasing voice.

"He's so much more than a jock. You'll really like him once you spend time with him. I don't know when that will happen, but I hope you get to know him soon. We started hanging out at the beginning of the school year. First, we went on a double date with Mark and Ally from the junior class. Ever since, all of us have been hanging out a lot. Nate's so hot, isn't he?" I'm crushing so hard, and can't believe Nate kissed me today!

"Well, sounds to me like you have your first boyfriend! What a great start to a new school year! By the way, when do you hear back about the competitive team?" She asks, and nerves hit me. Nate was such a great distraction. I really wasn't thinking about it all day.

"On Monday. I hate waiting." Now I'm full of angst.

"You know, just making it to the second round is a huge deal. You know that, right? You should be really proud of that. Plus, I am positive you did great, and they would be crazy not to want you on their team."

"I know. I really want to make it on the team. I always dreamt I would be on the competitive team."

"All that matters is that you did your best. I'm sure you will make the team, Becks." She says unconvincingly, and I understand. It was a big deal just to make it past the first round of cuts. The chances of me making the team are slim. But then again, I grab my necklace and think, 'Or maybe I'll make the team after all.'

Chapter Nine
The Cut

My nerves are so intense I feel sick to my stomach. Trina is up ahead; it's almost lunchtime, and we are about to look at the board. There are a handful of girls surrounding one area of the bulletin board outside the cafeteria, and I know they have posted the final list of members for this year's competitive dance team. It's different from last time, not the same massive crowd of girls. They already dwindled it down to the best dancers, and for them to take two sophomores seems almost impossible.

Trina and I look at each other, both knowing our future is on that board. We start walking over slowly with mixed emotions about seeing the list. Someone behind us says, "Congratulations," and we turn around. It's Ally. She's all smiles.

"What?" Trina and I both say, not daring to react to her words.

"Congratulations. To you BOTH!" Ally squeals. My jaw drops. Literally, I'm shocked.

"No way!" Trina says, clasping her hands and jumping up and down.

"Let's go look. I want to see my name on the list!" I say, thinking to myself that Trina on the team is a no-brainer. I just can't believe I also made the cut. I need proof. My name is really on the list? I've imagined this moment so many times. I just need to see it to believe it.

"Me too. Let's go check it out!" Trina says, pulling me to the board much faster this time. We are no longer tentative, and we can't wait to see.

Reaching the board, we see names in alphabetical order, and sure enough, both of our names are listed. I grasp my necklace knowing that I truly believe now. It's magic.

"Let's go find the boys and tell them the good news," Ally says, and we head into the cafeteria. The guys are all sitting together, joking around when we make our way over.

"So… has it been posted?" Mark asks Ally hesitantly since if one of us was cut, it would be awkward.

"Yup." Says Ally.

"And…" Mark says, trying to gauge the reaction from her.

"We made the team!" We all say in unison.

The guys jump up and hug us all. "Congratulations" was repeated by everyone around us. I'm on such a high. I have everything I've ever wanted.

Nate comes over, picks me up off the ground, and spins me around with one of his bear hugs. He gives me a kiss on the cheek, saying, "I'm so proud of you."

"Thanks!" I say as he puts me down. Once I sit, I'm immediately getting pulled into conversations about practice and routines with Ally and Trina. Now, I will have practice every day after school, sometimes doubles, where we will have a competitive dance team practice right after our sophomore dance team practice. It's going to be a ton of work, but it's worth every second. My schedule is going to be much more like Nate's now, starting homework no earlier than 9 pm.

After school, the competitive dance team meets with the coaches to introduce everyone and get the practice schedule and rules. Luckily, the girls don't seem to be angry about having two sophomores on the team. We start right away. Our big competition will be right before Christmas break. The first major competition is regionals, and if we win, then we will be off to Nationals. We'll perform at some events leading up to regionals to refine the routine.

This year, there are going to be two alternates; in case someone gets hurt or can't make the show, then the alternates will step in. That might be why nobody is upset yet. They probably assume we will be the alternates. Those are the two new extra spots. The alternates will be determined by how we perform up until the first competition. I want to be dancing with the team in a competition, not an alternate. I'm going to do everything I can to make that happen.

"I don't want to be an alternate," Trina says to me as we are leaving.

"Nobody does," Says Ally.

"No kidding, we all need to be performing at the competition," I say as I grab my necklace, knowing with luck on our side, we'll all be performing on the big stage when the time comes.

Chapter Ten
Homecoming

Nate still hasn't asked me to Homecoming, and I'm so confused. Everyone is buying tickets and making plans, but I have no idea where I stand. We haven't talked about being a couple and haven't used the words boyfriend and girlfriend yet. I'm so bad at this stuff. Ally is always telling me we are together and not to worry. He has to ask me to homecoming, though. I can't just assume we're going together. Nobody has ever asked me to be their date to a school dance. Last year, I went with a group of girls from the dance team to every dance. The dance committee has been selling tickets all week. Should I buy my own ticket? Just as I look over at the ticket booth, I notice Nate buying tickets. How many did he buy? It's hard to tell, but I think it's two tickets.

"Hey," Nate says, walking over to me as he puts the tickets in his book bag.

"Hey," I say, "Did you buy a homecoming ticket?" I ask, trying to see if he bought one or two.

"Yeah, I got the tickets," He says, smiling.

"Tickets?" I clarify, hoping he will eventually ask me to go with him.

"Yes, tickets. Why?" Nate seems so confused by this conversation.

"Well, who are you bringing?" I ask quietly, feeling self-conscious.

"Are you serious?" He looks astonished and amused, then starts laughing. "You honestly don't know who I'm bringing?" He's shaking his head as he wraps his arm around me.

I just shrug, "I don't know." As I say it, I know it sounds ridiculous, but I just didn't want to assume.

"Was I supposed to ask you? I thought you knew we were going together since I'm your boyfriend. It would be ridiculous for us not to go together." He says as if this is a known fact or like we've discussed this before.

"Oh, okay." I say with a smile, "Well, I guess I can go with my boyfriend. I like the sound of that." He's never said that before, that he is my boyfriend. I know I shouldn't need to hear it from him, but I do.

"You're hilarious, and here I thought I was your boyfriend this whole time." He laughs, still shaking his head in amusement.

It was the first time we said anything about being together. Clearly, I needed to hear it before I could fully believe it. Nate McNeil is my boyfriend. It's beyond any feeling I could imagine. I'm over the moon. As I reach for my necklace, thinking 'Thank you,' I begin to wonder: If Grandpa never gave this to me, would any of this be happening?

Time flies when you're having fun, as they say, and it's so true. It feels like just yesterday was the first day of school, but now here we are, perfecting the performance as a competitive team. We are getting it ready to perform for the pep rally on Friday before homecoming. It is the start of what will become our routine for the competition; it's the short version, and all of us will dance since the competition rules don't apply. The routine starts with us all standing and then immediately dropping to the floor for a 6-count before hopping back up and changing formation. It's a dramatic beginning and my favorite part. I can't wait for Nate to see it.

Trina, Ally, and I are heading into practice when I hear Nate call my name. I turn around, and he is jogging over to me. I tell the girls I'll meet them in the gym.

"Hey." He says

"Hi, what's up?"

"Oh, nothing. I'm heading over to soccer practice, but I saw you and wanted to kiss you."

"Oh really?" That makes me laugh. It's so unlike him. We never kiss at school.

"Yeah, we've been so busy it's hard to get together, and I miss you." He says. It's a kiss straight out of one of my daydreams, where even though we're surrounded by people, it feels like we are the only two people in the world. I have really missed him too. He's never kissed me at school in front of people. After this kiss, I'm in total ecstasy.

"Thanks, that made my day." I can barely talk.

He just winks and says, "Gotta go! I'm glad I got to see you for a minute." He gives me a peck on my forehead and runs off. I'm in shock as he runs out the door. Finally able to move after the shock wore off, I entered the gym in the best mood. How did I get so lucky?

Today's practice is intense, repeating the routine over and over. Coach made sure we were ready to perform at the pep rally tomorrow. The week has been packed with activities and spirit days. Tomorrow, the competitive team will wear their dance outfits to school since the theme is 'school pride', and we'll be performing. I can't believe we will finally be performing in front of an audience! My heart jumps in my throat, excitement and nerves jumbled together. The pep rally will start with our routine. Our job is to get the crowd going with our performance. The coach will announce the football team after our routine, followed by one of his motivational speeches, preparing everyone for the game. The pep rally will end the school day as we head into homecoming weekend. It's going to set the mood for the whole weekend.

It's almost time. The dance team is waiting in the cafeteria while students take their seats on the bleachers. Once it's full, our coach tells us to get in line. We wait outside the gym doors until we are announced. As always, I get nervous before performing. I reach up to touch my necklace, say thank you, and tuck it into my shirt. It immediately soothes my nerves. Principle Davis is announcing our team; that's our cue, and I follow the girls as I run into the gym. We jump and wave to get the crowd energized as we make our way to our starting formation. Over the loudspeakers, the music starts as I find the beat, thinking, "5,6,7,8," and then drop to the floor. It's a dramatic start to the routine, which sets the tone for our fast-paced, dynamic routine. The song ends, and the students are on their feet, cheering us on! I'm used to dancing for the junior varsity games on the sophomore dance team, which has pretty low attendance, so this is shocking to me. I've never experienced a crowd applauding like that after a performance. It's a standing ovation! I am hooked. Let's do that again! The energy of the crowd is palpable, and I never want it to end.

We take our seats in the front row that is reserved for us. Looking up in the stands, I catch Nate's eye, and he looks so proud of me. He's sitting too far away to talk. I can't wait to hear what he thought of the routine, but I'll have to wait. The varsity football coach is announcing the football players, and everybody is cheering as the players run out. Someone whispers in my ear, "You were amazing." I turn around, and it's Nate. He must have made his way to me through the crowded bleachers. The guy behind me looks a little annoyed with him, but Nate doesn't notice.

"Seriously, that routine was killer. And you nailed it." He wraps his arms around me from behind and kisses my cheek. "You're amazing." Everyone was standing, so he came down and stood behind me with his arms around me for the rest of the pep rally.

"I can't wait for tomorrow," I say.

"Me too." He agrees.

Tonight is a big game; we are playing our rivals, and it's homecoming. There is a ton of pressure on the football team to win. My sister is in town to help me with my makeup, but she is going out with Leslie to a party instead of going to the game. I was hoping she would get a chance to spend more time with Nate, but I'm sure she doesn't want to go to a high school football game.

At the game, Nate and I are sharing a blanket. Mark is sitting on the other side of Nate, and they keep talking about the plays. They think the coach is being too conservative with his play-calling. It reminds me of when Dad and Grandpa pretend to be coaches as they watch the Lions play. We're tied, and the game is getting stressful. I'm sitting by Trina. She doesn't usually care about football, but even she is into this game. We have a chance to take the lead at the end of the half, but Blake, our quarterback, overthrows the pass. It was the last chance before the clock ran out, so on that note, the players head into the locker room.

The band is doing a mash-up of oldies that the parent section seems to really enjoy. Nate leans over to me and says, "I'm freezing, come closer." I was talking to Trina, so I had absentmindedly moved further away from him. It is always nice to be close to Nate, and he was right. The extra body heat really helped.

Once halftime is over, the guys run out onto the field, prepared to receive the kickoff. The kick is caught by one of our best players, who runs it back almost for a touchdown. The crowd is going crazy. Everyone is on their feet now. Blake heads out onto the field. He has high expectations placed on him, and he hasn't had the best game. Everyone watches as the first play is run, and they gain no yardage.

"They need to pass the ball to win this game. I don't know why they keep running." Nate says to Mark.

"Yeah, it's like they don't trust Blake tonight." Mark agrees.

The next play is a pass, and it is caught. The receiver turns and runs into the end zone for a touchdown.

"Yeah!!!!" Mark yells and high-fives Nate.

"Finally! The last thing we need is an angry Blake," Nate says. I wonder why Nate says that, but figure it's probably just sports stuff.

For the rest of the half, there was no score, except a field goal by our rival. It wasn't enough to tie us, so now we are running the clock out, waiting to celebrate our homecoming win. The game was a blast. Everyone is in a good mood as they exit the stands. It's late, but we still decide to go to the pizza parlor since the guys were hungry. It's packed with students coming from the game, and it feels like a post-game party. We hang out until the restaurant closes and decide to go home since tomorrow is a big night for all of us. I can't wait for the homecoming dance.

Sleeping in this morning is impossible; I am full of butterflies, the good kind, the exciting kind. I'm going to homecoming with Nate! It's just unbelievable how dramatically my life has changed, how much this necklace has brought me, and how much confidence I have now. It truly feels like I'm finally right where I belong. I really believe that with my good luck charm, nothing can go wrong. Hurry up, 6:00 pm! Trying to be productive while I wait for the time to pass is impossible. I can't concentrate on homework at all. Instead, I end up watching TV to pass the time.

Finally, it's time to get ready. My sister is home from college to help me with my make-up. She's always been good at make-up, and it's a great excuse to make her come home. There's no doubt I'll look amazing with her help, but more importantly, I really want to share this moment with her. After the dance, coming home to anyone else isn't the same. Sharing my excitement with her is something that only happens between sisters.

"Ouch! That's my eye, you know." Wincing, I yell at Jen as she jabs my eye with the eyeliner. She's never really had a gentle touch when helping me get ready.

"Sorry," she says, but sounds disinterested, followed by "You know I'm not a professional."

To be fair; I knew exactly what I was getting into by asking her for help.

"So, are you excited for Nate to see you all dressed up?" She asks.

"I'm so excited!" I squeal, hardly able to contain myself anymore.

"All done!" Jen says, sounding proud of her work. "What do you think?"

Turning around to look in the mirror, when I see myself, I barely recognize my face. It's not what I expected. I look different, not like the young girl I'm used to seeing. Instead, I look sophisticated and quite pretty. It's always shocking to me when I see my face after a full set of make-up.

"I love it, Jen! You're amazing!! Thank you." I say as I give her a hug. I can't wait to see the completed look.

Now that I'm ready, it's time to put on my dress. It's strapless and short, just above the knee. It has layers of sheer champagne-colored chiffon and dainty embroidered stars made of a material that shimmers when the light catches them just right. I love this dress. It makes me feel beautiful. My open-toe, nude heels give me a little extra height, but not too much. Time to look at myself in the full-length mirror. It's the first time I've seen my completed look. I'm stunned. I look so different and elegant. The dress, with my hair and make up done, makes me look like a princess. It's like I'm a whole new person. Nate's going to die when he sees me!

"Jen, look at me! I look like a whole new person. I hope Nate loves it!?" I say to Jen. "I can't wait for you to see us together." Jen knows who Nate is from his brother and being around town. She never really talked to him. I know she will see everything that I feel for him when she sees us together. For some reason, her opinion and validation mean a lot to me.

"I can tell you seem really happy. And, different, more confident. It looks good on you." She says and gives me a hug. "You're beautiful, Becks. Nate's going to love it."

"Thanks, sis."

"I'll be with Chris tonight; I guess Leslie is giving it another try with him. They got back together at her birthday party. These McNeil boys better treat my girls well. Crazy, my sister and my best friend are dating brothers. Who would have guessed?." she says with a laugh. "It's kinda perfect, though. We can pick you guys up from the dance, and all go out to a party at Chris' friends' place for a couple of hours after."

"Really? Cool! I'd love for you to get to know Nate better." I say excitedly, but then remember my real life and say with disappointment, "But I have a curfew."

"Yes, really! And I talked to Mom and Dad about curfew. We need you home by 1:00."

Running over to hug my sister, I wrap my arms around her, exclaiming, "Thank you!"

"Don't thank me, just behave tonight, and we'll be fine." She says with a huge smile.

It's time to head downstairs to show my parents my outfit, and Dad is the first one to see me. "WOW, that can't be my daughter! You are too grown up. Your sister really made you look like a foxy lady!" Dad says as Mom shakes her head and gives me a look that says, 'Your dad will never get the lingo right.' I have to laugh. "Really, sweetheart, you look amazing! Nate will be knocked off his feet." Dad says.

"Thanks, Dad," I say as I give him a hug.

My mom just looks teary-eyed and says, "My beautiful girl, come here," reaching out to me for a hug. Jen looks very proud of herself as she listens to Mom and Dad gushing at how grown up and amazing I look. As mom and I hug, Stevie starts barking to alert us that Nate must be here.

My dad says, "I'll get it," and heads over. He opens the door to Nate and says, "You behave tonight. I mean it." He doesn't even say hi to Nate first. I must look pretty. Dad is going to talk about rules tonight, which makes me laugh.

"I will," Nate says, knowing Dad is serious. He walks in, carrying a box with my corsage in it. He bends down to give Stevie a little love. The dog always comes first. Dogs have a way of making sure of that.

He looks up at me and looks shocked, as if he had just seen a ghost. Hopefully a pretty ghost, I'm thinking, just as he says, "You are breathtaking, Becky. I don't even think I knew exactly what people meant by that until now." In front of my family, he's just staring at me in admiration. "Oh, um, here, I got you a corsage." He says, and I get the sense that he's very aware of my family watching him as he stares at me. He suddenly seems uncomfortable.

"Thanks, Babe," I say, trying to change the vibe. I never call him babe. Maybe I was inspired by my dad's way with words.

Nate smirks, "Babe?"

"I don't know. It just came out," I say, shrugging.

"I like it, babe." He says, teasing me. We both laugh, and I'm glad he finds it funny. That's all it took for him to feel more comfortable. Even though I may look different, and my family is staring at us, it feels like us again.

"I can see why your dad made a point to tell me to behave. You look so beautiful." He says quietly while putting his arm around me for a picture. He knows my dad is being protective. Nate loves that about him, even though we like to joke about it. I smile at him, loving that he fits in with my family.

"Thank you," Is what I say to him, but 'I love you' is what I'm thinking. I can't say that to him yet though.

At that moment, I caught my sister's eye and could tell she saw exactly what I thought she would see. Nate and I really are great together, and she can see how happy I am. She always knows. It's like she has a sixth sense about these things. You can't get away with hiding your true feelings from her. Before leaving, we take a bunch of pictures in front of the fireplace. Chris and Leslie are waiting in the driveway for us to join them. They're going to dinner and a movie while we go dancing. After their movie, they will pick us up from the dance and bring us to the party. I've never been to a real party, and never thought my sister would be the one taking me to my very first party.

"You guys have fun! You look great! Text me when you get there safe and are on your way home." Mom yells as we get in the car, and in my mind, I hear, 'Nothing good happens after midnight.' This is always the response I get from her when I try to extend my curfew. Somehow, my sister convinced my parents to give me an extra hour, maybe they agreed since we Jen will be with me.

The dance is held in the high school gym with decorated tables, punch stands, balloons, and streamers. We walk in, and the first thing we see is the official photographer. We get in line, which moves quickly. I can't wait to see our photo. It's cheesy, but I'll cherish this photo with Nate. Right when we walk onto the dance floor, we find Mark and Ally kissing and have to harass them.

"Hey, you two," I say.

"We hope we're not interrupting anything," Nate says with a laugh.

"Very funny guys," Mark says, pretending to be annoyed. He and Ally are one of those couples that always seem to be kissing, and we love teasing them for it.

"I love your dress, Becks!" Ally says.

"Yours too!" Ally is wearing a royal blue sequin asymmetrical dress that fits her so well that I wonder if she had it tailored. I feel like my dress has a younger, princess vibe. It's still a dramatic shift from how I normally look. Our dresses really suit both of us. I notice Trina and Austin walking over to us.

"Hey guys!" Trina yells over the music.

"Love your dress!" Ally and I say at the same time. Trina looks good in everything. Tonight, she is wearing a fitted red dress that makes her look like a model.

Austin pulls her close, obviously proud to be with her. They're so happy together; as a slow song comes on, we join them on the dance floor. It's so nice to have Nate's arms wrapped around me. I'm lost in the moment until a hip-hop song changes the mood. We start dancing in a big semi-circle. The guys are pretty good dancers, but I'm most surprised by Austin. He has really great moves. It's totally unexpected since he can be so quiet. He's an excellent match for Trina, though, who can dance to anything and look amazing. Looking around the crowd at everyone dancing and singing along, I notice Stacy walk in with Blake. He's the superstar of the weekend after carrying our football team to victory over our rival. He's getting a ton of attention tonight. You could describe them as Ken and Barbie, the kind of couple that's too perfect. Even though Stacy is beautiful, it still surprises me that he would date a sophomore.

"Ugh," Nate grunts, annoyed as he watches them. Blake is getting high fives and praise from everyone while Stacy stands proudly at his side.

"What?" I ask while acting like I don't see what he is looking at.

"Oh, nothing. Let's make tonight the best night ever." He says, kissing me on the dance floor. We must look like Mark and Ally. It's so out of character for us. I like it, though. Nate is my man, and now everyone knows it. Suddenly, doubt sets in. I hope he didn't do that to make Stacy jealous. He had such a weird reaction to seeing her with Blake. Why would he care? It doesn't make sense unless something is going on with Nate and Stacy. Insecurity is starting to take over. As usual, the feel of the four-leaf clover between my grip is reassuring as I hold onto it. It changes my whole mood. Everything is working out for me. Even if Stacy wanted Nate, she doesn't have magic on her side.

"Since when do we kiss in public like that?" I ask breathlessly.

"I couldn't help myself. You are so beautiful. Plus, I love the expression on your face right now."

"What expression is that, exactly?"

"It's hard to explain; it's a mixture of shock and happiness. It's cute." He says with that flirtatious smirk of his that I've grown to love.

"Oh, well, as long as you like it," I say with a laugh.

"I do." He says and kisses me again. I'm the luckiest girl in the world.

We danced the night away with our group. Austin and Trina were basically having a dance-off with each other, trying to one-up each other with their dance moves. They were all smiles, though, and laughing as each time, it got more and more ridiculous. It was hilarious to watch, and before we knew it, a group of people had formed around them. They are such a great match. I never knew Austin could dance like that. It suddenly switches to a slow song, ending the dance-off and changing the mood of the crowd. Once more, I was wrapping my arms around Nate. As we slowly danced, we turned a half turn, and in the distance, it was Blake and Stacy, looking like they are arguing. Blake seems angry, and he starts pulling Stacy out of the gym by her arm. Well, it sure looks like their night is over. A couple more songs played before Nate gets a text from his brother to come out to the car.

"We have to go!" Nate says, surprised at how quickly the time has flown by.

"Where are you guys going? There is still at least a half-hour left of the dance." Mark asks, almost insulted we would leave early.

"Well, Chris is here. He's taking us to a party. Becky can stay out until 1:00 tonight!" He says, beaming.

"Okay, cool. We'll follow Chris. Can you guys come?" Mark asks Austin and Trina.

"My parents still need me home at midnight," Trina says sheepishly.

"Well, Ally, you want to go to the party or stay here?" Mark asks.

"Um, let's stay, but text us the address if it's fun, and we can meet you later." She says.

"Will do, but we gotta go! See you guys later!" Nate says as he takes my hand and leads me off the dance floor. Before reaching the door, I turn and wave goodbye to the girls, who are waving back excitedly.

As we jumped into the car, Chris, Leslie and Jen all start asking us questions immediately. We tell them about the dance-off, how the dance was a blast, and informed them Mark might bring Ally to the party a little later. They seem cool with that. I wasn't sure how they would feel about it since it is a college party, but it must not be a big deal. I'm excited and a little nervous about going to my first party. At least my sister and Nate are by my side.

Chapter Eleven
Jungle Juice

As we arrive at the party, my sister starts telling me not to drink too much since I have no experience drinking. It's not like I've never tasted alcohol. I've had a little bit here and there, mostly a little taste of other people's drinks. As we look for a parking spot, she says once more, "Don't drink more than one glass of punch. It tastes good, but it is full of alcohol, and it will hit you hard. I mean it, promise me."

"Okay, okay, I promise. I don't want to get drunk!" I say, and I mean it. It'll ruin the first time I get to stay out late, and I'm hoping to prove to my parents I can stay out later.

"Well, if you don't want to be drunk, then stay away from the punch. It's called jungle juice. Have you ever heard of it?" She asks.

"No, I don't know what that is." I'm shaking my head because I've never heard of it.

"Well, just believe me and stay away from it." She reiterates. It must be a crazy drink. She really wants me to stay away from that Jungle Juice. Mental note: I need to google this punch later.

As we walk in together, people start yelling multiple greetings, some to Jen and Leslie, some to Chris and Nate, and none to me. Nobody knows me here, and I'm already feeling out of place. To make things worse, I notice Stacy walking over to me with an extra glass of punch. "Here, have some. It's delicious."

"Thanks," I say while taking the punch. What a start to the night! I'm already ignoring my sister's warning. Truthfully, I'm only drinking it to avoid looking weak in front of Stacy. This can be my one glass. Technically, Jen said I could have one glass and still be okay.

"So, you and Nate seem to be going strong. I never pictured you two together. You've never really been on Nate's level". Her tone is catty. She's not even trying to hide it. "What do I know? Opposites attract, I guess." It's a mystery to me why she even talked to me if that's what she has to say. Hasn't she ever heard the saying, 'If you have nothing nice to say, then say nothing at all?' Seriously, after all this time that I've admired her from a distance, now I learn she's not even nice.

"Uh, yeah, that's true. Opposites attract. So, how long have you been with Blake?" I'm dying to change the subject. Anything is better than listening to her talk about Nate, especially since she thinks we're "opposites" and I'm not "on his level." Whatever that means. It has to be a popularity thing, or maybe she thinks I'm not good-looking enough to be 'on his level.' One thing, for sure, is that she doesn't know me well enough to judge me on anything else.

"We've been together since this summer, soon after Nate and I took a break. It was such a fun summer with Nate, but he's not one to stick around too long." She says, and I know it's a purposeful dig. She's making a point to let me know she thinks we will be a short-term thing.

"Oh, well, you and Blake look great together. Thanks for the punch." I say, ending this conversation. Before I leave, I take another big sip of the punch and then turn around to find my sister. This punch is delicious. I would have never guessed it's full of alcohol.

"Ugh," I say to Jen as soon as I find her. "Stacy is getting to me. She keeps saying things about Nate just to get under my skin."

"Don't let her get to you. Why, what did she say about Nate?" Jen asks.

"I don't know. It's the way she says it. I can tell she is being a snob. She said she doesn't think I'm 'on his level,' whatever that means." I'm annoyed and drink more punch. It tastes so good.

Anytime I tried alcohol in the past, someone would give me a sip of whatever they were drinking, and it was always disgusting. Across the room, Nate is at the punch bowl, talking to Stacy. Great, she's probably telling him that I'm not good enough for him. She puts her hand on his shoulder, and he backs up a little. It's evident to me that he's uncomfortable. I wonder what really went on with them this summer.

"Hey," Leslie says.

"Hey, this punch is good," I say.

"Be careful with that. It will hit you hard. And don't let them bother you." She says, nodding her head toward Nate and Stacy.

"It's hard not to. She made it sound like Nate isn't interested in anyone for very long, and my time with him will be short-lived. I thought she was over Nate. I mean, she has a new boyfriend. You'd think she'd be happy enough with that, but it doesn't look that way to me."

"Nah, she was way more into Nate than he was into her over the summer. I do think she is trying to make him jealous of Blake. Nate's a good guy; you don't need to worry about him. He isn't the type of guy to just want a fling."

"He told me he wasn't that serious about her, but, he also took her to the tree by the river. I still don't know why he would do that if he wasn't serious about her."

"He did!? I can't imagine him taking her there! I don't know why he even tried to date her, and he was so miserable the whole time they were together, according to Chris." Leslie said, shocked, then asked, "When did he take you there? He must really like you. That place is practically sacred ground for the McNeil's."

"He took me there for our first real date. We had a little picnic. He said the only other person who had been there with him was Stacy."

"I still can't believe he would have taken her there. There is probably more to that story. Chris and I talked about carving our initials on that tree. Did Nate tell you about that tradition?" She asks, and I nod, so she continues, "I got scared and broke up with him instead. It just seemed too important, almost like an engagement or something. I didn't want to ruin the tradition if we didn't end up together. It felt like it would ruin that spot for the whole family and was just too much pressure. It seems silly now, but at the time, I just freaked out about it." She says, and then nods her head towards my left side. Following her gaze, I see Stacy standing near us. I look back at Leslie and shrug. Stacy was likely eavesdropping, but I don't know how long she's been there. She was by Nate only a few moments ago. I'm sure she didn't hear anything, and I just continued the conversation.

"I think I can understand that," I say.

"Yeah, now Chris said he decided only to carve initials when he is engaged."

"Do you guys talk about marriage?" I ask, shocked. She's not that much older than me.

She laughs, "Not really, not seriously or anything. We would wait a while. We're both too young."

Nate walks over with another glass of punch and hands it to me. My first glass is gone, and even though I'll be over my sister's limit, I take it anyway. Two glasses can't possibly be that bad. They are only small punch glasses. "What are you two ladies talking about?"

"Oh, just the McNeil boys." Leslie says with a laugh, and then starts walking over to Chris. She stops, turns around to add, "No more of that punch for you tonight, young lady," and walks away.

"How many glasses have you had?" Nate asks.

"This is my second. Stacy gave me my first glass." Adding her name to see his reaction. This glass is going down even easier than the first.

"Oh," he says without much emotion, so I figure everything's fine. We sit for awhile just enjoying being at a party together for once.

"Let's go over there and dance, shall we?" Nate asks since we've been sitting awhile, and I nod in agreement. As I stand up the affects of the punch hit me hard. "Whoa, I think Leslie is right; no more punch for you tonight. It's way stronger than you realize." He says as I stumble into him on our way over to the dance floor.

I recover from my stumble, and we make our way to the dance floor. We start dancing and are having a great time. I am not sure how much time has passed, but I start to feel a little unstable. I'm now standing with my arms wrapped around Nate, and I mumble, "I think I feel the punch."

He laughs and says, "Yeah, I think so." He just continues to hold me up as we sway to the music.

"I really like you." I say, "Like, a lot."

"Oh yeah? Well, I really like you too. Are you sure you didn't have more than two glasses?"

"Yeah, promise. Two." I say and hold up two fingers.

"Well, I think maybe some water is a good idea."

"Okay." Nate helps me walk over to the lounge area, and he has me sit down before finding Jen. In the corner, I can see him talking to my sister, who turns towards the kitchen while Nate comes back to sit by me.

"Nate," I say, as I lean my head on his chest. "I wonder if you like me for me or if you only like me because I'm lucky."

"Well, I don't know what that means, but I definitely like you for you. I do know that." He says, giving me a peck on the forehead. "I really like you, Becky."

I stare into his eyes and say, "I'm the luckiest girl in the world."

Jen comes over and says, "Here's your water. Drink up. I warned you about that punch. You never drink, so it will hit you a lot harder than the rest of us. We have enough time to get you in better shape before curfew, but no more drinks. If mom and dad see you like this, you'll never be able to come out again." She says to me with a stern look, then turns to Nate and asks, "Are you okay watching her?"

"Yeah, we're good." He says. I finish all my water and lean back on his chest. He has his arms wrapped around me, and I feel so happy. Stacy is looking at us from the corner of the room. It's like she's keeping tabs on Nate.

"What is her deal? Seriously." I say to myself, or I thought I did.

"Whose deal?" Nate asks.

"Stacy. She is being so weird tonight. She acts like she's my friend, bringing me punch, but then she starts making all these underhanded comments. I'm not a fan." I say, and then add, "Sorry, I know you liked her."

"It's okay. She is just going through some stuff with her and Blake." He says.

"Oh yeah, why is she telling you about that?"

"Well, we still talk sometimes. We broke up, but that doesn't mean we can't be friends."

"Seems weird…weird…weird. I mean, your ex-girlfriend is complaining to you about her current boyfriend? So weird." I say, but I'm getting super tired and want to close my eyes. That punch is strong.

"Are you asleep?" Nate says, half chuckling and half worried.

"Nope!" I say and sit up straight with my eyes wide open.

Nate laughs and says, "We should probably get you home."

"What time is it? I get to stay out late. I am not going home early!"

"Well, it's 12:30, so we should be heading out soon."

"Okie, dokie," I say, making him laugh.

"What are we going to do with you?" He asks with a smile.

Jen finds us and has another bottle of water for me to drink on the ride home. During the whole trip, she coaches me to just say hi to Mom and Dad and tell them I had a great time but am exhausted and going to bed. "Remember, don't talk too much; keep it simple." she keeps saying.

"Okie dokie." I say in agreement.

"And definitely don't say 'okie, dokie' to them!" She says, exasperated.

We get to our house, and Nate walks me to the door. He kisses me and says, "I had a great time tonight, even if you had too much punch." He winks and asks, "You going to be okay in there? I can't get in trouble with your dad, you know."

"I'll be fine. Plus, Jen can talk for me." He nods at Jen, who nods back, and he says, "Thanks, Jen, you're a lifesaver."

"Don't thank me, it's partially my fault. I should have totally banned the punch." She says with a smile. "We'll be fine."

"Good night, ladies."

"Night, Nate, I loveee…" and stop myself, terrified the word 'you' will fall out of my mouth. I'm literally frozen for a couple of seconds, not daring to move or do anything. Oh my God, I'm so close to saying I love you. Nate saves me by breaking the silence.

"You too," he says with a knowing smile, giving me one last kiss on the forehead. "Good night, Becky." He heads into the car while Jen and I walk inside.

Mom and Dad are waiting up, or attempting to wait up, but we can tell they fell asleep watching TV. "Hey, girls, how was your night?"

"It was awesome. We had so much fun. Thanks so much for letting me stay out late, but I'm really tired now. Can I tell you more tomorrow?" I ask.

"Sure, sweetie, we're glad you had fun."

"Okay, night, guys," I say and head upstairs to my room. Crisis averted, I think. It sounded good to me, but who am I to judge? Clearly, I had too much punch. I don't feel too bad now, but I really am ready to fall asleep.

In the morning, my sister enters my room with orange juice, a bagel with cream cheese, and two Advil. "How are you feeling?"

"Ugh." I say, "Why is it so bright out? I have a headache."

"I figured you might. Take this and make sure to eat; it will help."

"Thanks, Jen. I had so much fun last night. I think I said some weird stuff to Nate, though."

She starts laughing, "Well, I wasn't with you guys much, but you did almost say you loved him."

"I'm glad you find that funny."

"It was pretty funny, the look on your face and how you froze trying to stop yourself from finishing the sentence. 'I loveeee'" she says imitating me. She starts laughing even harder. "I swear, I can still picture it." She is now almost uncontrollably laughing. "I'm so glad I was there for that."

"Thanks a lot!" I say, but now I'm laughing too. I think I'm just laughing at her, though, because her laugh is contagious.

"Well, you two sure sound like you're having a good time," Mom says as she comes into the room. "Breakfast in bed, huh?"

"Yeah, I felt like being a nice sister today," Jen says.

"So, tell me all about last night!" Mom says excitedly, coming into my room. I'm so glad Jen came in early to give me Advil and food. It did help and made it easier to tell mom all the stories from last night. We all sit on the bed and recount stories from the night before. Mom shows me all the pictures of Nate and me that she took before we left for the dance. I have her send them to my phone so I can post them later. I told her all about Nate kissing me on the dance floor, Austin's surprisingly fantastic dance moves, and how the after-party made me feel like such an adult. Jen mostly listened but would add a little comment here and there. After we rehashed the night, they left the room so I could get ready.

It was a good thing mom didn't ask if I drank last night. I'm a terrible liar, so that was lucky. All of a sudden, I'm in a state of panic. The necklace! It isn't on my nightstand where I usually keep it. I don't remember taking off the necklace last night. I reach up and touch my neck. I feel the clover in my hand, and relief washes over me. It would be such a disaster if I ever lost it. I'm going to have to be more careful from now on.

I look at my text messages, and I have one from Nate at 1:20 am.

N: I just got home. I had the best time tonight! Good night Becky, I loveee…☺

Rereading his message, my face turns brighter shades of red, but I also can't stop laughing.

"Jen!" I yell, I have to show her this.

She comes into my room with a towel on her head, wrapped around her wet hair, and her makeup half done. "What?" she asks.

"Look at this text!" I say as I hand her the phone. Immediately, she is hysterically laughing. "I love that he is teasing you about it."

We are both cracking up when Dad walks by, "What is with you two?" He asks, peeking his head in my room.

"Oh, nothing, Dad, it's just an inside joke." We say. He just shrugs and keeps on walking.

It took forever, but I'm finally up and almost done getting ready. The only response I have for Nate is an emoji. He's called me out, and I have nothing else to say.

B: 🖤

N: How are you feeling today?

B: I'm better now. Jen saved me with breakfast and Advil.

N: That's what sisters are for.

B: She's the best! Totally saved me.

N: No kidding. I had a really great time last night.

B: Yeah, me too. Did I say weird stuff to you last night?

N: Maybe…

B: Oh man, sorry?

N: Nah, it was mostly adorable.

B: Whew ☺

N: Talk later? Gotta run some errands for my mom.

B: Okay 😗

It's time for Jen to head back to school, which sucks. It was so fun rehashing all our memories from the night before. I always miss her when she leaves. Thankfully, she got to witness Nate and Stacy last night. Advice from my sister always helps, and having her see things first-hand makes it easier to explain my worries about Nate and Stacy. Jen thinks I'm just being insecure. Once we talked it through, my insecurity had more to do with me over-analyzing everything about Stacy. Still, there is a nagging feeling I have with her. Simply put, she's up to no good. Everything in my body tenses when she talks to Nate. After talking to my sister, I felt better; she focused more on trusting Nate and ignoring Stacy. Jen really likes Nate and told me not to worry. Good advice. Now, I just need to listen to it.

As I walk Jen to her car, she brings it up once more, "Becks, I really don't want these insecurities to get you down. Promise me you won't be jealous when Nate hasn't given you any reason to doubt him. I really like you two together. Stacy can try to win over Nate in any way she wants. Nate loves you, whether he's told you that or not. I saw him with you, and I know it's the truth." She hugs me and gets in her car, leaving me with a good feeling about everything.

Chapter Twelve

Soccer

Regional playoffs for soccer are here, with state finals looming if we win tonight. It's crazy how much pressure the guys are under. It's been a prediction since the start of the season that they'll make it to the state final. They've advanced to the final game for the regional championship. Nate has been tense lately, ever since the start of playoffs. Tonight's game is monumental. Nate, Mark, and the rest of the team have worked so hard this year. All season, they've had huge expectations placed on them, and it's all coming down to the next game.

Ally and I arrived at the game early to get seats and save spots for Trina and Austin. Game time is getting closer, and we have to fight a few people off from stealing our saved seats. Finally, Trina and Austin are in sight, walking towards us. I was worried we were going to lose the seats. The stands are crowded, and we are surrounded by people bustling with excitement. I'm so nervous for Nate. I can hardly stand it. Seriously, I'm almost nauseous thinking about it. Hopefully, once it starts, I will be fine; this anticipation is killing me.

"How do they do this? I'm so nervous about Mark right now. I could be sick!" Ally yells to me over the noise of the crowd.

"I was literally thinking the exact same thing!" We are sitting with all the dance team girls. All the girls have the school mascot, a shimmering silver and blue cougar, temporarily tattooed on their faces. Austin and some of the other guys full-on painted their faces in the school colors. Fanfare is out in full force.

The game starts, and I'm too wrapped up in every play to be nervous anymore. Cheers of excitement roar through the sky with every near miss. Another shot that just misses the goal.

"Ughhh," the crowd collectively groans as the shot goes wide.

They have come so close multiple times, and each time the ball barely missing the net. It seems like all their chances are little wide or too high. Mark takes a shot that looks like it is going in, but the goalie stops it and passes it down the field to his teammate.

"Ugh. Good shot, baby!" Ally yells as the crowd gives a collective sigh of disappointment. Both teams are known as really great defensive teams, so the opportunities for goals are limited. Each time someone gets close, the crowd cheers and moans as it once again doesn't go into the net. The opponent has a few good looks as well, but our goalie is amazing. He's had to make a couple of incredible saves to keep us in the game. Time is flying, and the clock is winding down, but still no score; it's unreal. I feel my blood pressure rise as the stress of the game gets to me. There isn't much time. We need to do something now. Mark intercepts a pass, and Ally grabs my arm and squeezes it so tight, "Ouch!" I yell.

"Sorry." She says absentmindedly while letting go, followed by her yelling, "Come on, Mark!" Nate is running just up ahead, and my heart is thumping as if I'm running a sprint. I realize I'm whispering, "Pass it to Nate. Pass it to Nate," until I finally scream, "Pass it to Nate!!" It was as if Mark heard me because, just as I yell it, he spots Nate. He passes it, catching the defense out of position. Nate is wide open. My heart is going to explode. Oh my god, he could win it. Nate could win it! I'm dying to watch, yet I almost can't stand to look. The crowd is on high alert as Nate takes his shot. The goalie jumps to the left and gets the tip of his fingers on the ball. It redirects the shot, but not enough, and the ball goes into the net. "GOALLL" reverberates in the sky as the crowd loses control. Releasing a huge breath, since apparently I had been holding mine, I raise my arms in pure joy and just scream, "YES!! Nate!!!!"

Everyone around me is jumping up and down, including Ally, who has her death grip on me. It's impossible to stand straight as I'm being pushed in multiple directions, totally at the mercy of the crowd. I have no control. Half the time, the field is out of view because of all the people jumping up and down. I'm in awe. That was incredible. Literally bursting with pride, Nate just won us the game. I'm dying to see him.

"That's our boys! Mark's assist to Nate's goal!" Ally says, beaming. "I am so proud of them. Let's go find them. I can't wait to get my arms around Mark!"

"I know! This is the best night ever!" exclaiming loud enough so I could be heard over the crowd.

"Well, they won't be available until late tonight. They need to celebrate with the boys and do all that guy stuff first. Come on, let's make sure we catch them before they head into the locker room." Ally says as she pulls me through the crowd hurriedly. We push our way through the crowd, repeating, "Excuse me," "coming through," and "sorry." We finally reach the area where the guys will exit the field. Mark and Nate are both clearly hanging back, looking for us. We stand on our tippy toes, waving our hands and yelling, trying to get their attention. Finally, Mark spots us and points us out to Nate. They smile and run over to us.

"Congratulations! I'm so proud of you!" I'm yelling over the crowd as Nate reaches me, immediately picking me up and twirling me around. Pure happiness.

"I can't believe it. I can't believe it!" Nate keeps repeating with the biggest smile I've ever seen. Players run by him, patting him on the back, all complimenting him in different ways. He's on top of the world. "I couldn't wait to see you. I just wanted to celebrate with you. I won't be back until later; the guys will want to hang out for a bit, but could I come over once I'm done? It might be close to curfew." He asks with a mixture of hesitancy and hopefulness. He knows my parents aren't very lenient about curfew.

"Yeah, I'm sure my parents will understand. They're here somewhere. Grandpa and Grandma came too, so I'm sure they aren't even attempting to fight the crowd yet."

"That's so great! Tell them thanks for coming! I guess just shoot me a text once you find out for sure if it's okay?"

"Yeah, I will."

"Did you see my parents by any chance?" He asks while looking at the crowd.

"Yeah, they were sitting at center field with your brother and Leslie. I'm sure they're making their way over here." He keeps getting congratulated by different people as they walk by; some guy from the stands yells, "You're the man, Nate!" Nate just looks in his direction, smiles, and nods to acknowledge him. This must be how it feels to be dating a celebrity. He keeps trying to talk to me but is continually interrupted by words of praise from passers-by; the same is happening to Mark. Nate looks at me and says, "Sorry, I can't seem to get a word in without getting..."

"Great game, Nate," someone yells.

"Thanks!" Nate yells back before looking at me to finish his sentence, "without getting interrupted."

"Nate!" Someone else yells from the crowd, and we both start laughing. He looks at me, smiling and shrugs. No doubt, he's loving all the attention.

Shaking my head in amazement, all I can say is, "Enjoy it. You deserve every bit of this." Honestly, I'm on a high like I've never felt, and I simply can't imagine what it must feel like to be him right now. Nate's family is approaching a little further down and I point them out to him. They're with Mark's family too. He kisses me goodbye, saying, "I'll text you later!" before he runs off with Mark to see their parents.

Turning my attention to Ally as we walk, I say, "Can you believe that game? I feel like I'm on top of the world. I mean, Nate and Mark must feel like..." shaking my head, unable to think of the right word.

"I know. I am so proud of Mark. It's like I'm dating a rock star or something." Ally says with a laugh.

"I feel the exact same way! It's awesome!" I completely agree with her; we are both giddy at the thought of our famous boyfriends.

"Well, we may as well ride this high while it lasts. There's no way we can go home now! Where should we go to celebrate? The boys will be doing their own thing for a while."

"Most people will probably go to Main Street, right? Let's head over to the diner and see what's going on." I suggest, knowing that Rob, the diner owner, and Nate are buddies. I'm sure he'd probably like to hear all about the game.

"Let's do it!" Ally says, and then texts Trina to see where she and Austin ended up. "They are just getting to their car and will head to the diner to get us seats. We'll just meet them there?"

"Yeah, that works. It'll be super crowded in there, so hopefully, they can get us a seat."

"Good thing they are already in the car. I'm sure they'll be able to hold us a spot."

It took Ally and I almost a half-hour just to get out of the parking lot. Thankfully, Trina had texted that they were able to get us a table. By the time we make it to the diner, it's packed, and the energy is off the charts. Every once in a while, someone will start one of our team's chants, and the whole place joins in wholeheartedly. It's packed full of high school students from every grade. Even the popular senior crowd is sitting in the corner. It looks like they are sneaking alcohol into their drinks. Stacy is over there sitting with Blake. He's pouring whatever is in his flask into her drink. She looks smug as if she thinks she's superior because she's sitting with the seniors. It seems to me like they are missing out on the fun. They're basically hiding in the corner as if that somehow makes them cool. Although, the fact that they're here at all shows just how huge this game and win really is. Usually, they would pretend to be disinterested in anything that isn't football since everyone follows Blake's lead on what is considered cool.

"I am dying to see Mark!" Ally interrupts my thoughts, thankfully. I don't want to think about Stacy. The last thing I need is her ruining my night. Tonight is literally the best night ever!

"I know. I can't wait to see Nate, too. I really hope my parents will let him come over."

"When's the next game now?" Austin asks.

"I think it's exactly a week from today, so next Friday," Ally says

"Yeah, I think that's right." I agree.

"Do we know who won the other game?" I ask, wondering who they will play. I know that no matter who they play, it's going to be difficult, but Nate was more worried about playing Central.

"Central won, 2-0," Austin says as he looks at his phone.

"Mark didn't want Central," Ally says, "Oh well, he also said either team would be difficult. Let's worry about that later. We should enjoy this win tonight! I can't wait to be alone with Mark. What is taking them so long?"

My phone vibrates. It's a text from Nate. He is wrapping up with the guys and wants to head over. I haven't asked my parents, but it's not curfew yet. Besides, I know they'll want to see him tonight.

"Hey Ally, did you hear from Mark? Nate just texted that they're almost done, and Mark is going to drop him off at my place."

"Oh, let me look! Yeah, we should head out. Is that okay?" She asks Trina and Austin.

"Yeah, of course, go celebrate with your guys! Tell them congrats from us, too." Trina says. We head up to the register to pay our bill.

"Tell your boys we are so proud of them," Rob says as we pay. "They are really great guys. I'm so happy for them."

"Thanks, Rob." Ally and I both say, "We're going to meet up with them now. We'll make sure to pass on your message."

"Thanks, girls. Have a great night," Rob says and waves as we head out the door.

We pull into the driveway and see Mark's empty car parked on the street. They must be inside talking to my parents. Ally walks inside with me, and we find my parents sitting with Mark and Nate at the dinner table. The boys have plates full of food. I look over at Ally, who shrugs, "He'll always stay for food."

"Hey guys! Looks like you didn't get a chance to eat." I say while sitting by Nate.

"Yeah, your parents are the best Becks!" Mark says as he takes another bite.

"We are starving!" Nate adds, "It's delicious," he says as he looks at mom to acknowledge her cooking.

"They got here before you and were saying how hungry they were. It's nothing. I just heated them up some leftovers. No big deal." Mom says, but I can tell she loves it that they are enjoying her cooking.

"Looks like they're enjoying it. So, how was the team celebration?"

"It was fun; it wasn't really a celebration, but it was more like a motivational speech from the coach. He always picks MVP for the game, which he called a tie between both of us, so that was cool. It really just takes forever to get back and showered, so you guys probably celebrated more than we did, actually." Mark says with a shrug as he continues to eat.

"Congrats on MVP! That's awesome. Also, before I forget, Trina, Austin, and Rob all wanted us to pass along their congrats."

"That's nice," Nate says with a proud smile.

"That game was really amazing. You guys were so close so many times and finally won it at the buzzer!" Dad says in amazement, as he's clearly reliving it.

"I know, it was so close. When the goalie got his fingertips on it, I was so worried. It felt like slow motion, and it was such a relief to see it go into the goal. It felt like an out-of-body experience." Nate says, shaking his head, almost in disbelief.

"Could you hear how loud the crowd was?" Mom asks.

"Oh yeah, it was awesome!" Mark answers, "I'll never forget it."

The boys finish their plates of food and chat a little longer with my parents. Eventually, Mark and Ally say they need to leave. Poor Ally has been dying to be alone with Mark. It was nice of them to stay as long as they did. My parents were enjoying their company. We could have talked about the game all night.

"Can Nate stay a little later?" I ask since it's now past midnight.

"He can stay a little while longer, but not too late. I'm sure his parents want to see him tonight, too." My parents say as they head to the living room to watch some TV. I know they won't go to bed until he leaves, even though they'll probably fall asleep in the living room.

Nate and I head to the basement to watch TV downstairs and finally get a chance to be alone. I tell him once more how proud I am of him. He leans over and starts kissing me. His energy is so intense it felt as if he's passing it to me through our touch. Watching him score the winning goal was such a high. He literally became the hero on the field today. As we kiss, there is a sensation I've never felt before. It was almost as if I can feel what he is feeling. It's never been like this before; it's more passionate, and somehow, it feels like we're totally connected.

His hands start to wander down my body, and I instinctively pull back. "Nate," I say in a whisper, barely getting the word out.

He stops and looks at me with a smirk. "Sorry, I just feel so alive right now. It's like I'm riding a high after winning the game. Really, I didn't mean to make you uncomfortable." I knew he was full of excited energy, but I wasn't expecting this.

"I'm just not ready for..." I start to say, but he interrupts me.

"I wasn't thinking we were, like, going to go all the way or something. I was just feeling, I don't know, it's like my feelings are so intense I couldn't hold myself back. It's hard to explain. You are one of the only people who really understand what this year has been like for me, and it makes me feel so close to you." He says and shrugs, but I knew what he meant because I felt it too.

"I understand, really. I was on top of the world today, too. I'm just not ready for, ummm, you know?" I'm biting my lip now because I'm nervous about this whole conversation. This was the last thing I was expecting to be talking about tonight.

He looks at me calmly and says, "I know, I understand, I really do. Come here. I just want you close to me." He pulls me close to him as we cuddle up, and I rest my head on his chest. The thumping of his heart fills my ears and comforts me. It's such a beautiful sound. "I'm just so happy right now, Becky. I don't think I've ever been this happy. After we won that game, the first person I thought of was you. I wanted to share that moment with you." He squeezes me, leaning down and kissing my forehead. "I think I might be..." his voice trails off, so quietly I can barely make the word out, he says "falling."

I don't ask him to clarify, but I can't help but think he means 'falling in love.' All I say is, "I know the feeling," and look up at him with a smile. He smiles back before kissing me gently. I could have laid in his arms all night. It occurs to me that I now understand what people mean when they say someone 'feels like home.' That's what I have with Nate; it's exactly how I would describe it. The way I feel when I'm with him; Home.

Chapter Thirteen
State Finals

State finals are tomorrow, and the school is in school pride mode. They are offering shuttle buses for students to take to the game since it will be played in a professional stadium. It's an hour and a half away. We even have a half-day of school tomorrow just because of the game so that everyone can go and cheer on the team. Actually, it's a half-day of school plus a pep rally. Tonight, the dance and cheer teams are decorating the buses so they'll be full of school pride as they drive to the stadium.

Trina, Ally and I arrive at the school's garage, where all the buses are parked. We brought paint to paint the windows, and the other girls brought different types of streamers and decorations to hang out of the windows. The excitement in the air is palpable. I'm so proud of Nate. It's unbelievable that I'm his girlfriend. Literally, the luckiest girl in the world is no exaggeration. I'm already starting to get nervous for him. It's so much pressure. The entire school will be watching tomorrow.

"How has Mark been this week?" I ask Ally as we carry the paint over to the bus. It's so helpful to be able to talk to her. Nate has been really distant all week. I know she's going through the same things with Mark.

"He's been the worst!" Ally says with a sigh and continues, "I know he is just focused on the game and is probably nervous. But, man, he has been so grumpy all week!"

"Oh good! That makes me feel so much better!" We laugh at that since we are dealing with the same issues. "Nate has been super distant this week. I was hoping it was just the pressure of the game." I'm so grateful Ally is here to lean on to get through the playoffs.

Nate being this stressed out is new to me, and I completely underestimated how much it affects his mood.

"Oh, that's what it is, for sure! It's totally because of the game. They have such high expectations to live up to! Oh well, we'll probably be horrible to them around our regional dance competition, too." She says with a laugh. I wonder if she's right? We will be under a ton of pressure to perform. All this pressure is stressing me out. It makes me instinctively grab my necklace, letting out a sigh of relief at the touch.

Ally and I grab some blue paint and pick windows on the bus next to each other to start painting. On the windows we start painting 'Nate #9' and 'Mark #21' with a couple of hearts. We try not to make it too cutesy for them though. Trina is the 'go-to' for drawing the mascot. She is busy painting a huge cougar on the back of the bus. Once we are satisfied with the boy's windows, we head over to look at Trina's drawing. Everyone else is done, and they're all gathered around her as she puts on the finishing touches. It looks amazing; she is finishing the claws of the cougar. She stands back to give it one more look, turns around and proclaims, "Finished!"

"That looks amazing!" Ally says in awe, which is followed by a multitude of compliments from everyone who is watching.

"I can't believe we are going to State!" one of the football cheerleaders says, followed by someone's reply, "I'm just excited we get a half-day on Friday!" Looking over at Ally, I'm somewhat annoyed, but she just shrugs it off. We both know how important tomorrow is for Nate and Mark. At the same time, we can't fault someone for just being happy to have a half-day. Honestly, it would be nice to just enjoy the half-day off instead of being stressed out over the game.

The busses are decked out, just like the school, which has been draped in blue and silver all week. There's no way you could forget about the looming game while at school. Everywhere you look, there are signs, streamers, and balloons. Looking over at Nate during history class, I can tell he isn't paying attention. He is staring in the direction of Mr. Whitman, but his leg is shaking as he keeps tapping his pen on his desk. Nervous energy surrounds him. I wish I could calm him and instinctively touch my necklace as if maybe it could somehow help him, too. He looks over at me, and I smile at him reassuringly. He gives me a half smile, seeming unsure; I've never seen him like this. Before the regional championship, he wasn't this anxious.

At lunch, Mark and Nate sit next to each other while Ally and I sit across from them. We never sit like this, but they're both lost in their own thoughts. Eating in nearly complete silence, only speaking to each other once in a while, with some soccer epiphany, like "They're going to try to tire us out. We can't let our guard down. That's when they'll score." Mark says to Nate, who just nods before adding, "I know." It's odd to see them like this when normally they're so full of life and carefree. Usually, they're joking around at lunch. Their intensity is making the vibe of the whole lunch table feel off.

I look over at Ally, who just shrugs. "Game day," is all she says. It really is that simple.

"Are you nervous?" I whisper to her, not wanting Nate or Mark to hear. They'd probably be so annoyed that we're nervous. After all, we aren't even playing.

"Yeah, I always am before big games." She whispers back, and I nod in agreement.

"Are you guys ready for the rally?" Austin asks, breaking the unusual quiet surrounding the lunch table.

"Yeah! I always love performing with the competitive team." I say happily, trying to improve the mood. Plus, I am really excited. There are limited opportunities for us to perform in front of a crowd, and it's so much fun.

"I wish they weren't doing all this stuff before the game. It's too much hype. They should wait until after the game." Mark says in a grumpy tone, and I look at Ally.

She leans over and whispers, "I told you, he's been grumpy all week." She's not kidding, but it makes me laugh to myself.

"I'm glad you guys are performing," Nate says, but it sounds distant as if his mind is somewhere else entirely. "You know we won't get to see it, though, right? You guys perform before we're announced, so we'll be in the cafeteria."

"Yeah, it's too bad. I'd love for you to watch." I say, even though I know he wouldn't be paying much attention today.

After lunch, everyone files into the gym for the pep rally. The football cheerleaders lead some of the more generic cheers. We hear the chants of "Let's Go Cougars!" as we wait in the hall before being announced.

The chanting stops and is replaced with someone speaking on the loudspeaker. As always, the announcement is my cue to grab the necklace, think to myself, 'Thank you,' and place it safely under my uniform. Coach starts waving us over, our sign to enter the gym, and we run into position. The music starts, and I lose myself in the dance. I love how it takes away all my nerves once my body starts to move with the beats. It's peaceful, and dancing makes it impossible to worry about Nate or the game. It brings me a moment of freedom. The music stops, and we are all in position except Kelly, who is a little too far to the left. She must have drifted during the routine. Slowly, she's trying to make her way back into position without being noticed, but it doesn't work. Little mistakes like that are all it would take to become an alternate since we are all great dancers. The crowd is cheering for us, and I know we did well. Even if there were some kinks in the routine we still need to iron out.

We line up alongside the cheerleaders to form a tunnel for the players to run through. The soccer coach announces the team, and they run by us; Nate doesn't even acknowledge me. I don't know why, but it bothers me. Even though I know he is just focused on the game, it still makes me a little sad. Honestly, he didn't even look in my direction. Mark does a little head nod to Ally as he runs by, and it makes my heartache. Aching for acknowledgment from Nate, I do the only thing that may help, and I reach for my necklace.

The team's coach gives a motivational speech to get the crowd pumped before yelling, "Let's go win the State Championship, boys!" Everyone cheers as the guys run out of the gym. I know they're running to grab their bags from the locker room and then jumping on the bus. The pep rally will continue a little longer before we can board the busses ourselves. Ally and I sneak out of the rally, wanting to find the guys and wish them luck before they leave.

As we stand outside the locker room, waiting for Mark and Nate to exit the locker room, I'm anxious. Nate may not want to see me, judging from how distant he's been. Finally, their coach comes out with the captain, followed by Mark exiting the locker room. He smiles when he sees Ally and hugs her right away. He is saying something in her ear, and they're kissing when Nate walks out of the locker room door. I have nervous energy as I see him; he's been so different this week, and I hope I'm doing the right thing by being here. I don't want to be distracting for him before he heads to the game. When he sees me, he smiles, and my worry immediately disappears.

"I was hoping to see you before we left. I'm sorry I've been so distracted lately. Come here." He says, reaching out for a hug. I'm so comforted and relieved to be in his arms. Everything is fine now, and I'm so glad I came here to say goodbye.

"I'm so proud of you," I say, and he gives me a squeeze in response. Clearly, he's still not in the mood for talking.

"Alright, guys, time to go!" Someone yells down to us.

"Guess it's that time," Nate says as he gives me a quick kiss goodbye; another person yells down the stairs that it's time to leave. He shoots me that smile of his, and for the first time in a long time, he shows his excitement. "Gotta go, wish me luck!" He says as he turns to run up the stairs and to the bus. He stops once more, looks back and waves before disappearing upstairs.

As he leaves, I'm smiling ear to ear, appreciating the moment. Seeing Nate happy and excited has made my day. It was so strange seeing him full of anxiety and moodiness. It makes me wonder if other people picked up on it; my guess is they haven't. One thing about him is that he hides his true feelings from most people. Thinking back, before I really knew him, I always thought his life was perfect and that he was always happy. It's the first time I really got a glimpse into what he's like when he's troubled. All his struggles over the summer are even more vivid to me now. As the varsity players were resentful towards him, I can easily picture him acting as if everything was great. In reality, he was struggling. This week, moodiness and all, he was his true self with me, and it only brings us closer.

"I'm so glad we came down here to say goodbye," I say to Ally, who is also smiling genuinely for the first time today.

"Me too! Mark apologized for being such a grump all week." She says, smiling.

"Nate, too!" We both laugh at that, relieved.

Students are exiting the gym now. The pep rally must have ended. We have plans to meet Trina and Austin on the first bus, so we head there to grab seats. Once on the bus, we find the windows we painted with Nate and Mark's names and sit there. We were the first to arrive on the bus since we were already in the hall. It gave us a head start. We saved Austin and Trina's seats in front of us so we could talk easily. As the bus pulls out of the drive, excited energy with chanting and singing starts, and it lasts the whole way. It was so much fun! As the bus pulls up to the stadium, my heart leaps to my throat, and the weight of the game hits me again. Glancing at Ally, it's obvious she's anxious too. We smile uncertainly at each other, "Here we go" she says nervously as she stands up to get off the bus.

The stadium is big, and the crowds don't fill it. It doesn't matter; the crowd is still loud, and as the game starts, so do the chants for both teams. My eyes are fixed on Nate and sometimes Mark. Please have a good game; that's all I want. Central is a very competitive team, and they have more seniors with experience in championship games. They're known for their offense, but their goalie is a senior who is also well-known for making key saves. Tonight is no different. We have already had five really good attempts on goal, and he has stopped them all. The crowd is energized as Mark gets the ball and passes it to Nate. "Go, Nate, Go!" I'm screaming in anticipation with the rest of the fans. It's a replay of how they won regionals, except the goalie stops it once again. A collective groan follows from our side of the field while the opposite side is full of cheers of joy. It's clear the guys are getting frustrated. It's our goalie's turn to make a huge stop, and the crowd explodes with cheers. Despite the 0-0 score, the game has been exciting, with multiple close calls for both teams.

Suddenly, I see someone steal the ball from Mark. Oh no, this is bad. They're running back toward our goalie and are alone. It caught our defense too far back, so nobody can catch him. Mark is the closest and is doing his best to defend him, but he's too slow. The opponent shoots, and our goalie dives to catch it, but the ball goes just over his hands and into the net. Our stands are silent. Only one side of the stadium is cheering now. Instinctively, my eyes look for Nate and find him yelling something over to Mark, who nods as the play begins. They look like it's all business on the field. Leaning over to Ally, I tell her, "It's okay; there is still a ton of time." It isn't really true; time is running out fast. She nods, but worry is all over her face. I know all she cares about is Mark having a good game, and he just messed up big time.

The game is played in the middle of the field for a while, with both defenses stopping any real movement. Nate gets the ball and creates an opening. My nerves shoot through the roof. Mark is open, he passes the ball to him, and he wastes no time getting the ball on goal. Ally is screaming and gripping my arm with her painful death grip. As if in slow motion, we watch as the goalie looks like he's going to stop it. Somehow, he just misses it.

"GOAL!" is yelled over the loudspeaker. Ally still has her death grip on me as we jump up and down.

"I'm so happy! I'm so happy!" She exclaims repeatedly.

As we keep reliving the goal, another Nate and Mark play, we are amazed at their chemistry on the field. We're admiring how good they are, and they seem to know how to find each other at the perfect moment. We are talking so excitedly we aren't paying close enough attention. Out of nowhere, we hear the concern in the crowd around us. Looking up just in time, Central's star player has the ball while our captain is defending him. Just as Mark predicted, you can see he's losing the battle, and the opponent is just faster than him at this point in the game. Central has tired us out. He has a leg up on us and shoots. The crowd is at a standstill. The entire stadium is holding its breath. It's up to our goalie now; the shot is on goal, and it's just wide of the goalie's outstretched arms as he leaps. It goes in the net. Once again, half the stadium erupts in cheers while our side of the stadium is stunned to silence.

"Let's go, guys! You've got time!" Ally yelled, and I realize just how silent the stands are; she was the only one yelling anything. It helped, though. She woke up the crowd as someone started chanting, "Let's go cou-gars!"

Time is running low, and I know we need to score soon to tie it up. Nate has the ball, and I'm holding my breath. I can't stand it. I'm so enthralled by the game, but when Nate has the ball, it's almost unwatchable. My nerves are shot. He passes the ball to the captain, who takes a shot, but the goalie stops it once more. The crowd collectively sighs again, and as I look at the clock, I know they don't have enough time left to win. The clock runs out, and the fans from Central storm the field. Tears swell up in my eyes, not because we lost, but because I know what this means to Nate. I feel so bad for him. Looking over at Ally, she is teary-eyed as well.

"We can't cry. We have to talk to them." Ally says, but this isn't a high school where we can just wait outside the locker room. They exited into a tunnel, and this time, they didn't wait for us. Instead, we find their parents, who were also trying to get a word into the boys before they left.

"This is going to be a tough one for them," Nate's dad says. He has his arm around his mom. She looks like Ally and me, trying to hide her emotions, but her tear-stained eyes are giving her away.

"It was a good game with a tough opponent. Mark is never going to let himself live down that turnover." Mark's dad says, and we all know he's right. Mark is easy going, fun, and goofy by nature, but when it comes to soccer, he's a perfectionist.

Mark and Nate were right to be worried about Central. Ultimately, they were the better team, and they ended up beating us 2-1. My heart wants to text Nate, but I don't know what to say. Everything seems to come up short. I decide to ask him if he wants to come over, knowing all I want is to give him a hug.

B: Want to come over? Or, talk later?

N: Maybe tomorrow? I'm not up for it now.

B: Okay, ♥

Feeling his pain and still not knowing what else to say, that's all I could text, hoping it was enough.

Ally and I decide to ride home with my parents. We don't feel like sitting on the bus with all the disappointed fans.

"It was a good game, and they should be so proud of themselves for making it this far. It's a really amazing accomplishment." My mom says, and dad agrees.

"I know, but you know Nate, he puts so much pressure on himself. He's not going to be happy." I say.

"At least Nate didn't give the ball away. Mark is going to be distraught, and I thought he was grumpy *this* week!" Ally says, exasperated. We all know she is serious, but the tone of her voice is so funny we all start to laugh.

"Thanks, Ally, I really needed that laugh," I say.

"Yeah, Ally, we all needed a good laugh." Mom adds.

Ally is smiling now, too. Mark is going to be a handful, but she also knows it'll be short-lived. "Let's hope it's only one more week of grumpy Mark. I can't handle too much more of this."

"No kidding! Nate, too." I am also imagining what kind of attitude Nate will have next week.

"We should keep them busy so they don't have time to mope around," Ally says, and for the rest of the car ride, we all come up with ideas to keep them busy every night next week. They'll have a couple of weeks off before their indoor soccer league starts, so they'll have too much time on their hands after this crushing loss.

"Think they would want to help me paint the basement office?" Dad asks jokingly, but we put it on the list.

"We'll ask them!" Ally and I say in unison, which makes us laugh. The ride back didn't end up being as depressing as I thought since we gave ourselves the challenge of keeping the guys busy.

I slept in, and it wasn't until the afternoon that Nate finally called. As it rang, I dove for my phone, answering with a too-cheerful "Hey!"

"Hey, sorry I didn't call last night." He says, his voice sounding depressed.

"No worries, I totally understand. Do you want to get out of the house today?"

"No, honestly, I don't want to see anyone. I know seeing you might make me feel better, but I'm in such a bad mood. I really want to stay in this weekend. Is that okay?" He asks.

"Of course, that's okay."

"Well, I'll text you later. I'm sorry, but I just don't feel like talking, and I'm no fun to be around. I'll see you Monday, okay?"

"So, I won't talk to you tomorrow, either?"

"Just give me until Monday, sorry, Becky. You know this has nothing to do with you, right?"

"Yeah, I understand." It's true, I do understand, but I just ache to hug him. I don't need to talk to him, but I really want to be near him.

"Okay, bye Becky, I'll text you later." The sadness in his voice is unmistakable, and I know I need to give him space.

"Bye, Nate."

Monday came around, and both Nate and Mark are not acting like themselves. We all understood after the crushing loss in the state finals. Nate was very gracious and handled everyone's supportive comments very well. I know how much he hated it, though. He didn't like all the reminders of the game they lost. He also understood people meant well, but his true feelings would come out around his closest friends. He and Mark both had short fuses, and none of us dared bring up the game. They didn't want any words of encouragement from us. It was the first time I saw Nate discouraged. It's amazing how well he could hide that side of himself from others. He only opens up to a select few people about how upset he really was over the loss. Realizing how special it was that he shared his true self with me made it easier to handle his moods. Oddly, it feels like Nate and I are stronger and closer than ever as he goes through this.

Ally and I tried our best to get their minds off it by keeping them busy after school by going to a movie, but they were seriously no fun to be around. Agreeing to help my dad paint the office turned out to be a godsend, and it became the perfect distraction.

After school, the boys head to my house, which has become the new regular this week; they've been painting with my dad since Tuesday. As we near the end of the week, they are getting closer to completing the painting. They blast rock music as they paint alongside my dad. I bring them some drinks, and when I walk in the office door, they all have smiles on their faces. Smiles! I don't know what they were talking about, but I was so appreciative of seeing them acting more like themselves. They each grab a drink and are grateful.

"I was so thirsty. Thanks, Becks! This hits the spot." Mark says in his usual gracious way.

"Thanks, babe," Nate says quietly.

"Thanks, Becks. I was just telling the boys my newest joke." Dad says proudly. I guess they were smiling at that.

I look over at Nate, who gives me a smile and a nod.

"Oh yeah, what joke is that?" I ask, knowing I've probably heard it before.

"Have I told you the one about the cop and..." Dad starts, and I know the joke.

"...the husband getting pulled over....yeah. That's a good one." I interrupt, knowing exactly which joke it is. As I look at the guys smiling and drinking their soda, I'm full of happiness seeing their funk is finally leaving them behind.

"How's it going down there?" Mom asks when I return with empty cans.

"They were all smiling! I guess dad is telling his jokes." I say with a laugh.

"They like dad's jokes?" Mom asks with a laugh and a shake of her head. We hear his jokes every time he tells someone new, so we know them all.

"Well, you know, sometimes it's dad's delivery that's funny," I say because sometimes he makes me laugh, mostly because he finds his jokes so funny.

"Yeah, that's true. I'm glad to hear the guys are having a good time down there, and I'm excited to see the office once it's painted!"

Around dinner time, the guys come back upstairs, and Nate decides to stay for dinner. This makes me so happy. All week, he has gone home. He is finally ready for some company and seems like his usual self. Its perfect, just in time for the weekend. I lean over and ask Nate, "Want to do something tomorrow?"

"Yeah, let's go out. Dinner?" He asks with a smile, and I know he is back to himself. He just needed a little time.

Chapter Twelve
Birthday Party

November is here! November means Nate is getting his license. We can finally go out on our own without finding someone to give us a ride. It comes at a perfect time. It's part of what snapped him out of his funk. The school has been buzzing non-stop about his birthday party. It's the next big thing. Everyone is invited; his parents are ordering a huge tent for their backyard. It's a huge bash this weekend. The McNeil's are going all out. Between Nate's popularity and his brother inviting his friends, it seems like the whole town will be there. Even my sister is coming home for his birthday. This birthday bash became much bigger than initially planned.

Nate's parents made sure they invited all the Sophomores, which, unfortunately, includes Stacy. She will probably be there unless Blake decides he's too cool for Nate's party. That's doubtful, though, because everyone is going. Just the thought of Stacy being at the party brings me anxiety. It floods me with memories of her snootiness at homecoming. Maybe it won't be that bad. We will be at Nate's house, so hopefully, she won't be hanging all over Nate. That would be a little rude, even for her. All I have to do is avoid her typical offensive comments. One thing is for sure: no drinking for me at this party. That certainly didn't help with Stacy last time and almost got me in a load of trouble. Lesson learned! Plus, if I get caught, I'd be suspended from the dance team. Ally catches me on my way to lunch and gives me the news.

"Well, I heard for sure, Stacy is coming. Blake was talking to Mark about it." Ally says to me apologetically.

"Great," I say sarcastically. "I figured as much. It'd be fine if she just stayed by her boyfriend and left Nate alone. It just seems like she makes a point to find Nate. I don't understand why she's always pulling him aside."

"Yeah, she's just so insecure lately. That would never work on Nate. I do wonder what her deal is with him, though. Does he ever say why she always needs to talk to him?" Ally asks.

"All he says is that she's having issues with Blake. Apparently, Nate's the only person who can give her advice. I don't know. It seems like she's making excuses to try to reconnect with Nate." I'm annoyed as I explain it, and just the idea of her being at Nate's party gets to me. "I don't want her ruining our good time. You know?"

"She won't! Promise!" Ally says with a huge smile. My insecurity about Stacy is bubbling over, and I reach for the necklace to get some comfort. It's the reminder I needed, realizing I have nothing to worry about. Luck is on my side, after all.

"It's so awesome that Nate will finally be able to drive!" Changing the subject, I start focusing on the good stuff. "I can hardly believe we won't have to beg for rides anymore!"

"It'll be so nice! You guys can go on dates alone now!" Ally says excitedly.

When we reach our lunch table, everyone is talking about Nate's big bash. Except for Nate, he's telling Mark about the car he picked out; I'm pretty sure it will be his birthday present. It's not new, but it's a nice car. He picked an older Jeep Cherokee. Those McNeil boys like their Jeeps. He's following in his brother's footsteps.

"Hey, I heard Stacy is coming," I tell Nate as I sit down.

"You always knew she was going to, try not to be so hard on her. She's had it rough lately." Nate says, seeming sincere. For a minute, I start to feel bad for her, but then I wonder if she is just manipulating him. It's hard to know. He never explains the problems she is having. For now, I give them the benefit of the doubt.

"I'm sorry. I'll try to be nice. It feels like she purposely tries to get under my skin."

"Well, don't let her," Nate says, and I know he's right.

"You're right. I just needed the reminder." I say and kiss him on the cheek. He gives me a grateful smile. It's true. I don't want to give her the power to get under my skin. The truth is ever since homecoming, she has been cornering Nate to talk to him. From my vantage point, it looks like she's really just flirting with him. It puts him, and me, in the most awkward position. Often times, it's pretty obvious he is trying to get away from her, but she's persistent. Ugh, the thought of it makes me instinctively grab my necklace. Again, it reminds me that no matter what she does, it won't matter. Tomorrow is Nate's birthday, and I'm determined to make sure it's perfect.

Saturday morning, I wake up extra happy. It's Nate's birthday, and tonight will be amazing. My goal is to finish homework before his party, so I'm reading for my English class to kill time before I can get ready. Stevie is going crazy, and I look out my window. It's a black Jeep Grand Cherokee. Nate! I run downstairs as I hear my mom yell, "Becky, Nate's here."

"Happy Birthday!" I yell and jump into his arms. "What a nice surprise!"

"I had to bring you along on my first ride in my new wheels." He says with a huge smile.

"Happy Birthday, Nate! Sorry, we can't make it to your party tonight." My mom says as she gives him a hug. "Do you want to stay for lunch?" My mom asks. My parents were invited to his party but had their annual dinner with long-time friends tonight. They plan it literally a year in advance, so don't want to miss it.

"I was hoping I could take Becky out for lunch today."

I look at my mom, who smiles and nods, giving her approval.

"Let's go!" I say and excitedly grab my coat.

"I just wanted to take a short drive before I have to get ready for the party. Actually, want to go to our spot by the river for a minute and then go for some pizza?"

"Sounds perfect."

It's beyond exciting to be going somewhere with Nate alone. His new ride is super nice. I'm impressed. Even though it's older, it's an upgraded model. The leather seats are so nice, and I notice the butt warmer button and immediately push it, making Nate laugh.

"It's not that cold out." He says, shaking his head in amusement.

"I know. But, still, I love the warmth. Besides, I have to test it out!" I say, looking over at him. He's still shaking his head at me. "How do you like your new ride?" I ask, changing the subject.

"I love it! It's so awesome to finally be able to just drive somewhere. Life is going to be so much easier. Now I can bring you on real dates, too!" He says with a proud smile.

"I can't wait. It almost feels like it's my birthday!" I say, and we both laugh at that. "I have part of your birthday present with me. It's in my coat pocket, but it isn't wrapped yet. I could still give it to you if you don't mind?"

"Yeah! I don't care if it's wrapped. I'll open it at the tree, how about that?"

"It's beyond perfect," I say, knowing this is working out better than I ever could have planned. Nate parks along the street near the park, and we walk over to our spot.

"It's so nice outside, and it's my own tradition. Ever since I was old enough, I come here around my birthday. Sometimes, I have to wait until the nicest day outside and walk here myself." He says with a smile. "It just felt right to bring you with me today. For the first time, I didn't want to come here alone. Someday, I'm going to carve my initials in that tree with the woman I love." He says, eyeing me intently, and a part of me wonders if this is his way of telling me he loves me.

"Yeah, I know you will. It's a beautiful tradition." The thought of our initials on the tree makes me smile ear to ear. He makes my heart beat so fast.

"Well, maybe it will be our initials on that tree." He says, spinning me around so that he can kiss me. My heart is racing; all I feel is pure happiness. He stops kissing me, looks me in the eyes, and for a second, I think he is going to tell me he loves me. Instead, he just pulls me in for a hug.

"Speaking of this tree, do you want to see your present?" I ask.

"Of course! I can't wait." He says, and we sit down on the ground. He didn't bring a blanket, but the ground is dry, and we won't be staying long. I reach into my pocket, pull out a little box, and hand it to him.

"Sorry, it isn't wrapped. I just got it and haven't had time to wrap it yet."

"No worries," he says and kisses my cheek. He opens the box, and his expression was exactly what I had been hoping for; it was like he had just opened a gift that touched his heart.

"Becky, it's amazing. Where did you find this?"

"I found it online, on Etsy. I had someone make it, and it just came in the mail yesterday." It was a small silver keychain in the shape of a tree trunk with our initials carved into it. "I know we can't carve them in the real tree, but I hoped this was the next best thing."

"I absolutely love it." He says, pulling me in for a kiss. "I'm putting it on my keyring right now. Thank you." His face still looks astonished as he looks at it intently. "It's the most thoughtful gift I've ever been given."

All I can do is smile and snuggle up in his arms. We haven't said anything for a while. We don't need any words. Instead, we sit in peaceful quiet, listening to the river rushing over the boulders and the soft rustling of the leaves in the fall breeze. It's perfect just being together.

Nate drops me off at home after spending the day together. Now I don't have much time to get ready. I'm hitching a ride with Ally and Mark. They arrive at my house just as I finished up. Whew, I made it just in time. Stevie is barking as I hear them say hi to mom and dad. Once I meet them in the entryway, my parents remind them of my curfew. As always, that's followed by dad saying, "Nothing good happens after midnight!"

"Don't worry, Austin will bring her home in time. Trina needs to be home by midnight, too." Mark says, passing the responsibility to Austin.

"Have fun, guys," both my parents say as they watch us get into the car from the porch.

"We will!" we yell back and wave.

We arrive at Nate's at the exact same time as Blake and Stacy, who are walking up the drive. I'm immediately annoyed when I see them. Stacy turns, sees us, and waves. We all wave back. She is wearing a tiny red dress that doesn't match the cold nights of November. Here we go again. I'm sure she picked that dress to get Nate's attention. Reaching for my necklace, I remember she is here with her current boyfriend, and it helps me let go of the annoying feeling that's been following me. Tonight is Nate's night, and nothing, including Stacy, will ruin it.

Nate is greeting everyone as they walk in; he's hugging Stacy, and she lingers too close to him. He looks uncomfortable, turns away from her, and sees me. Immediately, his face lights up, and he leaves her behind and heads straight towards me. Once he reaches me, he wraps his arms around me, giving me the biggest hug.

"Happy Birthday, Babe." I say to him as he squeezes me once more before letting me go.

"I've missed you. When I got home, I showed my mom your gift, and she was teary-eyed." He says, smiling like that was an accomplishment.

"Is that a good thing?"

"Yeah, I think it made her reminisce about dating my dad."

"Aw, that's really sweet."

"Happy Birthday, my man," Mark says, and they do their guy handshake thing.

"Happy Birthday, Nate," Ally says while giving him a hug. "Your parents really went all out."

"I know. They're crazy. They have a bunch of friends here, too. Come here," he says as he grabs my hand, leading me to the tent entrance. Ally and Mark followed us, and Nate points out a couple of reserved tables near the entrance and bar. "Those are for us. Our group."

"I take it you're not drinking tonight? After your homecoming dance experience?" Mark asks me, laughing, as he follows my gaze towards the bar. He had texted Nate the night of homecoming, asking if they should meet us, but I was already too drunk by the time he asked. Mark loves teasing me about it. Anytime there is alcohol anywhere in the vicinity, he brings it up.

"Very funny, Mark. I'm never drinking again." I say, partially being sarcastic and partially meaning it. Definitely not touching alcohol, at least not for a while; that next day was rough.

"We'll see about that!" Mark says, laughing, before adding, "You shouldn't tonight, though, seriously."

"I won't, don't worry." Now I'm laughing and shaking my head. Does he actually think he has to worry about that? I thought he knew me better by now.

"Technically, the alcohol is for my parent's friends and some of my brother's older friends. The bartender was told to ID everyone, but I'm sure some of the high school kids will still manage to get some drinks if they really want it." Nate added with a shrug.

"Dude, look at the food!" Mark says, noticing the appetizers, and he's off. He makes me laugh. You'd never know it from his size, but he is a bottomless pit.

"Mark and his food," Ally says, shaking her head. Once again, Nate is entertaining more guests who have just arrived. They look older and must be family friends. "We should eat. Let me ask Nate if he wants me to make him a plate."

Quietly, without trying not to interrupt too much, I ask him if he wants me to make him a plate. He looks at me with a grateful nod as he continues to talk with his guests. Ally and I head over to get some food. It's a buffet with a mixture of appetizers, and Mark walks by carrying two plates full. "Oh, did you make a plate for Nate?" I ask.

"What? No! These little plates? I needed two!" He says, laughing as he heads back to sit down. The plates were small, I'll give him that. Nobody was expecting food. Appetizers are a nice touch.

I'm in line making two plates and hear, "Somebody sure is hungry." Turning around to see who it is, and of course, it's Stacy. Her judgmental eyes staring at my two plates of food.

"Oh, ha ha, I'm grabbing Nate some food," I say, trying to be nice, but am aware my laugh sounded completely fake.

"Yeah, the poor guy seems like he needs rescuing from the front door. He's going to be stuck there all night. By the way, I heard about your gift for Nate. I remember when he took me to that spot by the tree. It was such a special time for us. Well, since your hands are full, I'll make sure he has a chance to get away from the front door." She says in her fakest sweet voice and starts walking towards Nate. Anytime she mentions it, I can't believe he took her to that spot; it doesn't make sense. She just loves rubbing it in my face that he brought her there, too. Tonight is about Nate. I'm not going to let it bother me. Although, I am going to ask Nate about it some other time. Just like Leslie said at homecoming, there's probably more to that story.

Catching Ally's eye, she has an exasperated expression and just shakes her head. "She's here with Blake. She needs to leave Nate alone." Even sweet Ally sounds annoyed.

"I know. Nate needs to put his foot down, too." It's hard to look over at them as they are talking and smiling. Stacy reaches for his hand, and he's trying to protest. She wins. Watching him give up and follow her to the dance floor makes my heart sink. Just when they reach the dance floor, it switches to a slow song, of course, great timing. Nate is looking around for me as I'm standing here with two plates of food. Stacy wraps her arms around him, and they start slowly dancing. Looking at the crowd, I spot Blake, he is staring at her and his facial expression looks angry. He walks over and cuts in. Thank you, Blake.

Finally, I make it to my seat with my two plates and drop off the food. Time to go find Nate.

"Hey, you want to dance?"

"Only if it's with you." He says. He grabs my hand and leads me to the dance floor.

"I think most people are here now, so I won't have front door duty anymore. Now it's time for fun." Sadly, the slow song ends. I could stay in his arms forever. As the dance floor gets crowded, we start dancing with a group of people near us. It's so much fun. We're having a blast until Stacy ends up right next to Nate again. Blake is across the way, and it's obvious he is angry; maybe they are fighting? Or maybe she's using Nate to make Blake jealous? I don't know what's going on, but something's up.

"Hey, are you hungry?" I ask Nate.

"Yeah, let's go eat!" He says, and we head off the dance floor, escaping Stacy. Mark and Ally are still at our reserved table, and I grab a seat next to Ally. Suddenly, I'm so hungry.

"Have you been watching this?" Ally asks.

"What? Stacy?" I ask.

"Yeah, she and Blake are fighting."

"Oh, great," I say sarcastically. "If she's single, poor Nate will never get a break from her."

Ally laughs at that, "True!" She adds, looking almost concerned, "It looks pretty bad when they're arguing, though."

"What's so funny?" The guys ask, completely distracted by their food.

"Oh nothing, let's just make it a fun night!" I say and mean it: whatever is going on with Stacy can wait until after Nate's birthday.

"I second that!" Nate says, and adds, "Let's dance."

We all get to the dance floor and are met out there by Trina and Austin, who had to come late because of a family thing. It reminds me of homecoming, with our group dancing all night and having a great time. Stacy keeps coming around, but I have no worries about her. I'm with my friends on Nate's birthday, and nothing is ruining my night. Just as I think this, Nate takes my hand and spins me around on the dance floor. Tonight is so perfect.

"I have to go to the bathroom," I tell Nate and head inside. There is a line, so I go to the bathroom upstairs that's connected to Nate's room. Nobody else is up here, so I miss the line. On my way back out to the dance floor, I hear my name from behind.

"Becky." I hear and turn around. I'm just inside the tent, making my way to the dance floor, when Nate's mom stops me.

"Oh, hi, Kristine. This has been such a wonderful party, and Nate is having so much fun!" I say once I realize it's Nate's mom calling for me. She is all dressed up and looks stunning. I've never seen her dressed up before. This is her element. She really enjoys throwing a party. I'm convinced it's where Nate gets his friendly openness.

"Becky, I just wanted to say what a wonderful gift you gave Nate. It brought back so many memories of when I was dating his dad. I'm surprised Nate shared the story of that place with you; it's a big deal for the family."

"Oh, yeah, it's beautiful and moving story. He loves it there."

"Well, yes, it's a special place to all of us. That was such a meaningful gift. What a great way to share that tradition without making it...permanent." She says. Something in the way she says it makes me unsure of how to take it. My guess is she means we aren't ready to carve our initials into that tree. I'm not sure if this is a compliment or a warning. She certainly doesn't want us carving our initials in the tree from her tone. That much is clear.

"That's what I thought. I just wanted a way for us to share that special place."

"By the way, who is the girl in the red dress?" She asks, changing the subject as someone catches her eye. I know, without looking, who it is. Stacy.

"Stacy, you've never met her?" I ask, surprised. I guess Nate never introduced Stacy to his mom when they were together over the summer.

"No, is she in your grade?" His mom asks. Really? It's unbelievable she knows nothing about Stacy. Well, Nate must not have been serious about her. It's pretty obvious he didn't tell his mom anything about her. It may be petty, but it makes me feel better.

"Yeah, she's a sophomore. I'm pretty sure she has a thing for Nate." I say with a laugh since, once again, she is slow dancing with him.

"Hm, well, hurry up and get back out there." His mom says, pushing me towards the dance floor. She was kidding, but I could sense there was also truth in it. They were just dancing, but I knew she didn't like what she was seeing.

I make my way over to Nate and cut in. "Do you have to?" Stacy says, slurring her words and pouting.

"Yeah, I do. Are you okay? Want me to get Blake?" It starts making more sense. She's drunk. It doesn't take long for me to realize it's the main reason she's hanging on Nate. He's literally the only thing keeping her upright.

"Ugh, Blake. He's mean and worthless." She says.

I look at Nate, and he nods his head in the direction of Blake. Following his gaze, it's obvious Blake also looks drunk. He is slouched in his chair.

"Want me to get Chris?" I ask Nate, who is stuck since he is holding up Stacy. Literally, he can't do anything, or she'll fall.

"Yeah, just tell him what's going on, and he'll know what to do." I head over to the table where Chris is sitting and see my sister talking with Leslie. At least this time I'm not the one needing help.

"Hey! I haven't had a chance to talk to you all night!" Jen says as she stands up to give me a hug. "I've seen you, though. You and Nate look great dancing together. I really like your friends, too."

"Well, unfortunately, I'm here because we need help with..."

"Stacy?" Jen raises her eyebrows while finishing my sentence. "We've been watching her, and poor Nate has been trying to get her to sit down for a while now. Where were you?"

"Bathroom, and then I ran into Nate's mom. Blake is also drunk," I say as I turn my head in his direction. Now he is sitting at a table with his head down, possibly passed out, I'm not sure.

Jen sighs, "Here we go again. These high school kids can't handle their liquor."

"At least it's not me this time!" I say, trying to get a laugh out of her, which doesn't work. "Nate doesn't know how to move her without making a scene."

"Next fast song, we will all go out there and dance. We'll make sure to surround them and then take her out of here through the side entrance of the tent. Hopefully, without it being too noticeable."

"I'll tell Chris," Leslie says as she gets up. She stops when she's next to me, "I heard about your gift. That was really special." She gives me a smile and tap on the shoulder. "Now, let's handle this mess."

The next song is upbeat, and all my sister's friends hit the dance floor with purpose. They surround Nate, so the parents can't see the protest Stacy is putting on. "Let go. We have to go!" Ally is saying to her with no luck.

"It's time to leave. Now, Stacy!" Chris yells at her with a commanding voice that seems to snap her out of it.

"Okay," she agrees meekly and finally lets go of Nate. Now Chris has her and takes her out the side door with the help of Jen and Leslie. As far as I can tell, not many people notice, but I do see Nate's mom keenly watching the situation. We still have Blake to deal with, but at least he is sitting and not causing a scene.

A few minutes later, Jen comes back and says, "They're driving her home. Chris thinks you should just have Blake stay the night here. He's too big to move, and he can get suspended from football if we aren't careful moving him. Let's try to just enjoy the rest of the night."

"Okay, he can stay in the guest room. Thank you so much for your help. I feel bad for her, but she was so drunk. I felt like I was literally stuck holding her up." Nate says and looks relieved.

I give him a peck on the cheek, "Well, it's done now. Happy Birthday, Babe. Let's celebrate!"

"Thanks," He says and spins me around on the dance floor.

A few minutes later, Chris is back at the party, and we're told Stacy is home safe. The guys were able to make sure Blake sobered up enough to make it to the guest room, where he was passed out for the night. The rest of us, the true friends and family, were the only ones left. The DJ would play for another hour. It's the most fun we've had all night. Nate slow danced with my sister while I slow danced with Chris. It was nice to get a little extra time to chat with each other's siblings. We all get along so well. An upbeat song comes on and we all start laughing at Mark, who was doing the worm. My phone is across the room. I wish it was with me so I could capture it on video. It's so hilarious!

"Alright, party people, it's the last song of the night. Happy Birthday, Nate! Grab someone you love and sing along for this last one." The DJ says and plays Billy Joel's Piano Man as he packs up his equipment.

Everyone who is still at the party sings along. We link arms in a circle and begin to sway from side to side. Looking around, it's all the people we love. Nate's family, our closest friends, and my sister are all dancing together. The only ones missing are my parents and grandparents. Other than that, it's close to perfect — what an unforgettable night.

Chapter Fifteen

Lost

All the school gossip is focused on rumors of Stacy and Blake's break up at Nate's party. Apparently, Blake noticed her flirting with Nate as well, and I hate that everyone is wondering if there was something going on between Nate and Stacy. Now that she is single, she's even more blatantly after Nate's attention. I think back to how I used to admire Stacy, the way she could command a crowd, and how fun she seemed. I don't admire her anymore, it's like she's a totally different person. She's lost all of that. Now, she hardly ever hangs out with any of her old friends. She was always with Blake and his friends. I don't know who she will hang out with now that they broke up. Nate is trying to be nice to her without leading her on, and it constantly makes for awkward situations. He keeps acknowledging that I'm so understanding and that he appreciates my patience.

The problem is, deep down, I'm not sure how I really feel about it. I'm so conflicted. Do I trust him, or do I trust the power of the necklace? Is it all the same? If I didn't have the necklace, would I be as understanding? Every once in a while, I wonder if Nate is with me only because I have this necklace. Anytime that self-doubt creeps in, I hate it, but all it takes is a touch of the necklace for it to go away. One thing's for sure: I'm never going to know if he likes me for me or if it's the power of the necklace. I'm definitely not going to take it off to find out. That much I know for sure.

The school year has been flying by; in the blink of an eye, Thanksgiving is over, and Christmas break is quickly approaching. We have to finalize our routine for the competition, which is right at the start of Christmas break. The coaches still have to announce who will be dancing at the competition. Rumors are flying around like crazy about who will be dancing in the regional finals and who will be the alternates. Everyone on our team is so talented that it seems like an impossible decision. Being a sophomore seems like a disadvantage, except for the fact that I have my lucky charm, which changes everything. I believe it gives me an edge over the competition. Everything keeps falling into place for me, so it's hard for me to imagine being an alternate. I have so much more self-confidence then I have ever had in my life, knowing that I have my lucky charm on my side.

Tonight is the last time the competitive team will do the routine in front of an audience before the actual competition. It's the night that will determine who will be dancing in the competition and who will be sitting on the sidelines as an alternate. We are performing for the varsity basketball team's halftime show. It will be a big crowd. We are playing a rival team, and we have an undefeated record so far this season. The dance team is waiting in the cafeteria before our final walk out to the gym. I'm touching my necklace a lot tonight to calm my nerves. My tradition before any performance is after we are announced, right before we walk out to perform, I touch it one last time. Before I run out to the crowd I tuck it safely under my uniform.

We're told to head to the gym and start walking to the entrance to wait until we are announced. Usually, we have more time, but just as we get in the hall, our team is being announced. Coach is waving us into the gym, yelling, "Go, go, go." We immediately run out to our spots. It happens so quickly, much quicker than usual. I didn't get a chance to tuck my necklace back into my uniform. Once we get into position, I reach up for the necklace to tuck it in quickly before the music starts. My heart starts racing. It's not there! Panic, I'm in sheer panic. No, no, no! This can't be happening! I look down where I'm standing but don't see it. I repeatedly feel around my neck, but it is not there. Looking around the floor, I'm trying to spot it, and nothing. My mind is racing. I'm totally distracted and realize all the girls are on the ground for the beginning six-count, and I am just standing there. It's as though everything is happening in slow motion with a spotlight shining directly on me. I'm temporarily paralyzed, mortified, and feel tears coming.

The six-count on the ground happens really quickly, but when you are the only one on the team standing, it feels like an eternity. I'm completely exposed. The team pops back up, and somehow, I manage to find my place in the formation. Suddenly, with the team surrounding me, I knew I could finish the routine. Once I catch the beat, it's easy to lose myself in the music. Miraculously, I finish the routine without any more errors. Managing to finish the dance is the least of my worries. I'm totally distraught. This wasn't a small mistake; the entire crowd knew I had messed up. My anxiety is palpable. Where is my necklace? My lucky necklace? I have to find it! We finish and run off the court to the hallway. All I can think about is finding my necklace. It's impossible to look for it on the basketball court. The second half of the game is starting. For the first time this year, I was without the necklace and completely humiliated myself in front of everyone. My luck has run out, unless I find it. The panic actually helps. I'm too worried to cry or focus on what anyone else is saying about me. All my energy is focused on finding the necklace. Nate is running down the hall towards me looking concerned.

"Hey, what happened out there?" Nate asks in his most comforting voice, wrapping his arms around me. "I was hoping to find you before you went into the locker room."

"I lost my necklace. I have to find it. I was distracted looking for it. It must have fallen off when I ran out there. I can't believe I missed the start of the routine. I have to find it, Nate." My thoughts are all over the place, while in Nate's arms, the tears start to well up in my eyes. All I can think about is that I have to find my necklace.

Nate leans back to look at me, sees I'm trying to hold back tears, and pulls me in close for another hug. "It's okay, Becky. We'll find the necklace, and everything will be fine. It's just a necklace, and it wasn't that bad; you were amazing for the rest of the dance." He says, trying to comfort me.

People are looking at me in the hall and laughing with each other. I'm positive they're laughing at me, probably mocking me. Stacy's walking towards me. Ugh, not now. She's the last person I want to see right now. Now that she isn't the most popular girl in our class, she sure is mean.

"Nice job, Becks," Stacy says in a mocking tone as she walks past and shoots me a spiteful smile. Ignoring her is all I can do, because I can't deal with her right now.

"Becky, come on!" Trina is yelling at me to get in the locker room.

"I need to go. I'm sure I'm going to get yelled at," I say to Nate as I head over to Trina. Nate calmed me down, but now I want to burst into tears. She's holding the locker room door open for me, and she just gives me a sympathetic look. We both know I'm in trouble.

Everything amazing that has happened to me this year could disappear if I can't find that necklace. All my dreams could come crashing down. No more Nate, no more dance competition, no more friends. Living an invisible life now seems impossible. I need to stop it, these thoughts are not helping. My hands are sweating, my breathing is short and rapid. Walking into the locker room full of stares from all the girls, a mixture of different emotions on their faces, ranging from disappointment to anger. All except Kelly, the one happy face in the crowd. Most likely, she thinks she will be performing in the competition now. It was rumored Kelly would be an alternate, and after my performance, we both know coach will choose me to sit out the competition. Her chances of performing went way up now that it's practically guaranteed that I'll be an alternate.

"Well, team, we have a decision to make over the weekend. We will carefully consider everything we've seen this year and will make the best decision for the team. Tonight wasn't perfect, but the end of tonight's performance was terrific. Obviously there were some hiccups early on, but we are a team, and we will work through those as a team. That's all for now. Try to enjoy the rest of your weekend, and we will give you our decision at practice on Monday." Coach is walking towards her office, and I'm standing in the very back since I was the last person in the room. As she passes me, she says, "Becky, let's have a chat in my office."

Nodding in agreement, knowing we need to talk, but unable to speak. My nerves are shot, following coach to her office in the back corner of the locker room feels like the longest walk of my life. Once inside, she closes the door behind me.

"Have a seat." She says as she points to the chair. "What happened out there today?" She asks, sounding unexpectedly calm and not angry. Her tone is kind and concerned, and it just makes me feel even worse that I let her down. Fighting back tears, all I can do at the moment is shrug my shoulders. If I start talking, I'm worried I'll start bawling.

"Now, Becky, I've watched you at practice and during live performances. One thing I know is that you are talented. In fact, you are much more talented than you give yourself credit. I want you to dance with us at the competition, but I need to understand what happened."

Tears start to fall down my face, and I look up at her. "I don't think you'll understand." I take a deep breath, trying to gain my composure, and continue "I lost my necklace right as the music started."

"Necklace? You aren't supposed to wear any jewelry for exactly that reason. It can be very distracting."

"I know. But, it's a good luck charm. It's really special to me because it was given to me by my grandpa. It helps calm my nerves, which I know sounds stupid, but it really helps. I have to find it!" I say and start crying, so much for gaining my composure.

"Becky, you did the whole routine flawlessly once you got back with the music. You did that without the necklace and in a very high-pressure situation. Honestly, I was quite impressed with the recovery you made after the start of the routine. But, I can't have you competing if you doubt yourself."

"I understand," I agree, meekly, convinced she is going to tell me that I am an alternate.

"Do you? I think we may pick three girls as potential alternates and have you all learn different spots in the formation. It will give you a couple more practices to get your confidence back up. We'll make our final decision on the two who will not be dancing after a couple more practices. I want you out there with us at the competition. I really do." Coach says earnestly, and I realize she really believes in me. How do I know if I'm as good as she thinks I am though? All year, I've never danced without the necklace.

"Thanks, Coach," I say, hoping I'll find the necklace tonight so it won't be an issue by Monday.

"Now, try not to get in your head about this. You had one bad night, but a whole season of great performances. Put this one behind you, okay?" Coach says as she touches my shoulder encouragingly. She walks with me to the door of the locker room, looking at me for some sort of response.

"Okay" is all I manage to say. She doesn't understand the power of my lucky charm; how could she? My whole year has been astounding, since the necklace, everything just kept falling into place. Now, how do I know if I'm any good without the necklace? How can I get my confidence back? And, my biggest fear, will Nate still feel the same about me? My heart is beating so fast, and I'm so heartbroken. I have to find that necklace. Retracing my steps leads me back up to the cafeteria, where Nate finds me looking around urgently.

"Hey, looking for your necklace?"

"Yeah, I really have to find it, Nate. It's really important. My grandpa gave it to me." I say.

"Okay, I know it's important. I'll help you look."

"Yeah, thanks. I know it sounds stupid, but it was my lucky charm. It always worked for me."

"I understand. Don't tell anybody, but I have lucky underwear I make my mom wash before every soccer game." He says with an embarrassed chuckle. It's sweet he is trying to cheer me up, but superstitions with underwear just aren't the same. There is no way he can understand the real power of my necklace.

"Oh, Nate, what am I going to do?" Hugging him for reassurance, now that the necklace is gone, I need the comfort of his arms. It's impossible to keep fighting the tears, so I give up, allowing the flood gates open as I start to cry.

"Hey, it'll be okay. We'll find it. We will." He says as he starts wiping away my tears. He gives me a sweet kiss on my forehead and says, "Let's get to work, where were you standing when you were in here?" On his hands and knees, he's scouring the floor with his phone flashlight. Watching him crawling around, urgently looking for my necklace, makes me fall even more in love with him. Please, God, don't let me lose you too.

Luck wasn't on my side, and it was a hopeless endeavor to find the necklace. Totally distraught, I spent the entire weekend in my room. The only time I left my room was when my mom made me. Grandpa and Grandma stopped by, even they couldn't cheer me up, which is very unusual. Nate checked in a couple of times, but I couldn't face talking to him. Everyone just kept saying it would be alright, but none of them really understood. How could they? All my growth and good things that happened this year were because of the necklace, but they couldn't understand that. My lucky charm is gone, along with my confidence. All that's left is self-doubt. Questioning everything, my mind continues with the worst-case scenarios. Does Nate really like me? Do I even belong on the competitive stage? What if I single-handedly ruin our chances at winning regionals? Ugh, I just don't know about anything anymore.

Three weeks is all I have left to either find the necklace or prove, on my own, that I shouldn't be an alternate. The problem is, I don't believe that I'm the best person to perform anymore. Missing steps in practice is my new normal, even though coach keeps trying to get my confidence back. It's just not happening. Things with Nate aren't any better since Stacy has been on a full-fledged attack of my self-doubt. She's relentless, flirting with him any chance she gets. Even though I know he wouldn't do anything malicious, I'm not that fun to be around anymore.

"How serious were you and Stacy over the summer?" I ask Nate after seeing them talking over by the drinking fountain. Insecurity takes over all my thoughts without the confidence of the necklace. Reaching up out of habit, feeling an emptiness where the necklace once laid, it crushes my confidence.

"What? Why are you asking me that now? We weren't serious, you know that." Nate says, sounding genuinely confused.

"Then why did you bring her to the tree?" I have wanted an answer to this for a while now, and sound upset. More than anything, I wish I could simply reach up for the necklace to calm me. Before, it was easy to believe that Stacy didn't matter; with luck on my side, I truly believed she wasn't a threat. Without the necklace I feel like a fraud, and it makes me want to push Nate away. Maybe Stacy's right, I'm just not 'on his level.'

"Why did I bring her to the tree?" Nate repeats, confused, before adding "I didn't, not really."

"What do you mean, you didn't? She told me how special it was when you brought her there!" Now, I sound genuinely confused and angry.

"Honestly, Becky, it wasn't special with her. Where is all this coming from? You know she's had a tough time, and I'm just trying to be nice. She might still have feelings towards me, but I promise you, I'm not interested in Stacy. This is what she wants. She wants us to fight. I only want to be with you, Becky. Can't you see that? She's just trying to make trouble between us so we'll break up!" He says exasperated.

"What? Are you thinking we should break up?!" All I heard was 'break up,' and tears start welling up in my eyes. I knew it! I knew everything would fall apart without the necklace.

"No! Good Lord, no, that is not what I'm saying! I feel like we can't even talk anymore. I don't understand what is happening!" He looks so sad and frustrated.

"I'll tell you what's wrong! I lost the necklace, and now everything is falling apart!" I yell while running away toward the bathroom, wanting to hide behind a stall as the tears start falling.

"Becky...I never brought her there!" Nate calls after me desperately, but I can't look at him right now. All I want is privacy so I can stop fighting my tears.

I heard what he said, but it still doesn't make any sense. They were at the tree together. He even admitted that in the past, we talked about it multiple times! Why would he even try to say he never brought her there? He's lying!

Nate keeps trying, but I don't know why. He still sits by me in History and tries to cheer me up with notes during class, or by mocking Mr. Whitman. Nothing works. I feel so lost. My world has gone from the ultimate high to an abyss of self-doubt. Thankfully, I'm still doing fine in school. I've always been a good student, and I know that has nothing to do with the necklace. Two things that I wanted most this year: the dance team and Nate. Those two things are now steeped in uncertainty. My dancing has deteriorated, and my relationship with Nate is practically non-existent. Honestly, I'm not even sure if we're still together or if that fight was the end of us. No point in asking; if it wasn't that fight, it'll be something else.

Lunchtime is interesting, and even though I'm not really engaged with our group, I still sit by them. They all try to cheer me up, but I feel like an outsider. Trina and Ally offered to practice the routine with me over the weekend, but I'm afraid I'll freeze on stage now. Someone else should perform; that's what's best for the team. It would break my heart if I was the reason we didn't win. It's similar to how I feel about Nate. He shouldn't wait around for me, either. Before, it was my confidence and self-assuredness that he loved. The thing he didn't know was those qualities actually came from the magic of my necklace. Now, I'm the opposite of that girl, and I am positive he doesn't like this insecure version of me.

"Nate," I say after thinking that last thought. He's sitting next to me at the lunch table. Usually, I sit quietly at lunch. Today, we need to clear things up, and I feel an urge to say this to him, no matter how much it'll break my heart.

"Yeah," he says, giving me his full attention.

"Nate, do you think we should just call it quits? I mean, I'm not myself, and I don't know if I ever will be. That's not fair to you." It's the right thing, knowing if I don't find the necklace, I may never be the same. He shouldn't wait for me.

"Becky, no, don't give up on yourself like this. Don't give up on us! It was just a stupid necklace. It doesn't really have superpowers." He is pleading, his bright blue eyes looking into mine urgently searching for answers...

"Nate, I can't." After that, I walk away, assuming it's over between us. Needing to get away from him before I take it all back, I leave and don't look back. I love him, and he deserves someone amazing. Right now, that's not me. Even though I never told him that I love him, it's true, and sometimes when you love someone, you need to let them go. It's what's best for him, and I don't want to hold him back.

At home, I'm laying down in my bedroom, when Stevie nudges my door open with his nose. He jumps up on the bed to snuggle with me. He is comforting. Lately, he seems to know I need some love. He's been hanging out in my room with me every day when I get home as if he senses my sadness. Remembering what Grandpa told me about going for it when it comes to love, I know he was right. Even though I am brokenhearted, and miss Nate terribly, I would absolutely choose to do it all over again. The good times with

Nate were the best in my whole life and were worth this heartache. Memories that will be with me the rest of my life were created this year. Tears start to fall down my cheek, as those memories flood my mind. Those perfect times are now gone. Stevie climbs up and starts licking my tears until I start laughing. His tongue tickles my face. Nothing heals a broken heart like the love of a dog. Deciding it's my turn to make him happy, I ask him if he wants to go outside, which results in him doing twirls of excitement.

Chapter Sixteen

Regionals

My heart is racing as it's the day of the regional dance competition. Even though I will be sitting on the sidelines, my nerves are working overtime. Coach decided after the extra weeks of practice that my performance was less than stellar. Interestingly, once the decision was made, my mojo came back. My dancing hit a new stride, and I was performing better than I had in weeks.

"Looks like once the pressure was off, you found your confidence again. That's a good sign for next year." Coach says with a smile while we run through the routine as a team. She was right; I did feel more like myself.

Nate and I really didn't talk since that last conversation at lunch. Every once in a while, I see him talking with Stacy. Sometimes, she puts her arms around him, but it looks forced. It's obvious he isn't interested. Gratification sets in any time I see him squirm away from her. Even without the necklace, at least he isn't interested in her. Here I am before the biggest competition of my life, and I'm thinking about Nate. I miss him.

At the venue, we ran through the routine a few times with the entire team, including alternates. Our final team roster will do one run-through on the stage without the alternates in the early afternoon. It'll be my first time sitting out. It's a long day, with plenty of downtime until we come back to the main stage for the final performance this evening. ESPN 2 will be covering the competition, so people can watch it nationally. The winning team will be the regional champions and will head to Orlando for the Nationals. Talk about a dream come true. That would be the most incredible experience.

It's time for our team to run through the routine on the main stage. I'll be watching from backstage, along with Kelly, since we are the two alternates. Ironic, since she looked so smug in the locker room the night I screwed up. My failure didn't work out in her favor, after all. Beats of our music blast through the speakers, automatically causing me to perform the movements in my head. Suddenly, the music stops. Halfway through, it's silent, except for screaming. I wonder what happened. Someone is in pain. Instinctively, I jump up and run onto the stage, I knew something bad happened. Reaching the stage, the girls were standing around someone with concerned looks. Oh no, who is hurt? Walking closer, I finally see who is lying on the floor: It's Ally, holding her leg and rolling around in agony. My heart sinks. Not Ally! Running over to her, I bend down to hold her hand, as she is moaning in pain. The girls are just standing around in complete shock.

"Is it a sprain? Can she still perform?" The coach urgently asks the doctor who is examining her ankle.

"No, she won't be able to perform, not tonight anyway." She tells the coach and then looks at Ally, "I'm sorry, honey. We need to get you in a brace right away."

Looking around at all the worried faces of the girls, suddenly, I notice Kelly. Unbelievable. She has that same smug grin she gave me when I messed up. I can't help myself; that's it! Jumping up, I head straight over to her, yelling, "What are you smiling about!?! Do you have no compassion for your own teammate? If you want to win, you should feel horrible that we just lost one of our best dancers!" I don't wait for a response and storm off the stage to regain my composure. I'm in the hallway, taking deep breaths, trying to calm myself down before attempting to return to the team. Someone followed me into the hall, I hear the door creak as its opened. Expecting to see Trina when I turn around, it surprises me to see the coach walking towards me.

"Becky, we need you," Coach says urgently.

"Me? Are you sure?" There's no hiding the surprise in my voice.

"Becky, Ally has a big role in the front, and Kelly never even practiced it. Plus, I've seen you dance. Your confidence is back. You've been dancing perfectly. All you have to do is believe in yourself."

"Okay." Nodding to myself, followed by a forced, "I can do this." All I'm focused on at the moment is the team, they need me right now — no time for self-doubt.

"Let's run through rehearsal," Coach says.

"Okay," I say, nodding to the coach as I head towards the big stage. Deep breath, you got this. You can do this.

"Becks, you got this. You've been dancing so well lately. Just lose yourself in the music, and you'll be fine." Trina says, giving me an encouraging tap on the back.

One more deep breath, the music starts, and all I can do is dance my heart out. It feels good, but one part is a little different for me since it's Ally's part. I missed a couple of steps, which wouldn't be noticeable to the crowd, but it would be noticeable to the judges.

"You did great!" Trina says excitedly.

"I missed a couple of steps. I'm not used to Ally's part." My voice sounds concerned.

"Maybe we could switch, I know it. I'll talk to Coach, okay?"

"Yes, thanks, Trina." Relieved, I know Trina's part as well as my usual spot.

Trina disappears as she talks to the coach. Reaching my phone, I text Mom to tell her the news.

B: Hey, mom, I'm dancing tonight. Ally was hurt in rehearsal.

M: You'll be great, honey. Tell Ally we're thinking about her.

B: Thanks, mom. Wish me luck.

M: Good luck. You don't need it, though. You'll be great.

M: How can I see you before you perform?

B: There is a holding area. Ask at the reception. Tell them you're family, and they'll direct you.

M: We'll be there and will try to see you before. Good luck, Sweetie! You deserve to dance. I'm sorry about Ally, though.

Trina comes back, "Coach agrees. You and I have the same part, so nothing will be different for you. Well, except you'll be on the left side of the formation. You've done that before so it shouldn't be a problem, right? And I'll do Ally's part."

"Yes, I know your spot! Thank you so much. I'm much more comfortable with your part. Do you want to run through Ally's part a few times, and I'll follow you on the left side?"

"Yes, definitely! I'll feel much better about it." Trina says.

We run through the routine a few times, and I'm actually feeling good. Music is blasting in the background, the competition has started, and all I want is to text Nate. I want him to be here, even though I don't know how he would feel about it. Once again, I pick up my phone and start to text him. Losing my courage, I put my phone down, stopping myself from hitting send. If he doesn't text me back, I will be upset and distracted. For the team, I can't afford any distractions. I wish my family was here to get my mind off Nate.

Where is my mom? She should be here by now. Just as I think this Grandpa peeks his head into the holding area, looking for me. Waving to him to get his attention, I run over, "Hi Grandpa! Where's mom?"

"Oh, hi, honey! I told your mom I wanted to talk with you alone. How are you feeling? Are you ready?" He asks and looks as if he is assessing my attitude.

"I was dancing really well earlier, but the closer it gets to the performance, the more nervous I get. I wish I had my lucky necklace, Grandpa."

"Well, Becks, that's what I wanted to talk to you about. People always say how lucky I am, you know?" He asks, proudly.

"Yes, Grandpa, I know! That's because you are really lucky!" There is no denying it, he's always had luck on his side.

He laughs his good-hearted laugh but then becomes serious. "You know, Becks, there is a trick to it. The trick is I learned to believe in myself. All of a sudden, a bunch of amazing things started happening to me. The truth is, your belief in the necklace was helping you believe in yourself. You deserve whatever it is that makes you happy, and you need to believe that. Think of everything you achieved this year: in dance, the friends you've made, and your relationship with Nate; all of that happened because of you. It didn't happen because of the necklace. The necklace helped you find the confidence you needed, but you don't need the necklace to have that confidence. Does that make sense?" He is looking at me, trying to see if I understand what he is saying.

"But, you were the one who told me it was lucky! You even gave me $50 because it helped you win the lottery. Remember?" I say as proof that the necklace was magical. Grandpa smiles and laughs.

"Alright, I shouldn't have done that, but I knew you needed a boost of self-confidence. All I wanted was for you to see yourself the way that I see you. When I look at you, I see a beautiful, talented, amazing young lady who can achieve anything. She just needs to believe in herself. I knew you were struggling with confidence last year at school. It was awfully lucky to find that necklace, and I couldn't help it. I thought it might help you see things differently. The thing is, it's not the necklace that was bringing you luck, Becks. It was you. You are the good luck charm. What you believed to be luck is really all because you believed in yourself." He says with a grin and wink. "What did you do with the necklace when you felt you needed it's luck?" He asks.

"I would touch it to calm my nerves, often thinking 'thank you.' It always made me feel better." I admit, feeling a little self conscious.

"Well, you can still do something similar. You could touch your heart or where the necklace once was and say thank you. Believe in you, not in an object. You are the good luck charm. All the necklace did was remind you to have self-confidence and trust in yourself. That's why it calmed you. Do you believe that?"

"Yeah, I think I do now." Tears are welling up. I don't know why I'm emotional. Somewhere deep down, I know he's right; it was always within me. All I have to do is trust in myself, and I'll be able to dance. Nate, this includes him, too. I wish I had never pushed him away, and I know I need to fix things between us. "Thanks, grandpa. I love you!"

"I love you too, Becks. Now go get 'em! We'll be cheering you on!" He says and nudges my arm the way he does when he wants to lighten the mood. Hugging him makes my heart feel full and happy again. Back in the holding area, I pick up my phone once again and send my text to Nate.

B: Hey, I just wanted you to know I'm dancing tonight. Ally was injured, so I'll be filling in for her. I'd love it if you could come. Understand either way. ♥

No response. Okay, now I just have to promise myself not to look at my phone again until after I perform. He can't be on my mind when I dance, and I know it doesn't matter. All that matters is my belief that I am good enough for Nate, with or without that necklace. Begging him for forgiveness might be in my future after pushing him away, but I can't worry about that right now. First, my focus is on being ready to put on the best dance performance of my life.

"It's time! Let's go, let's go, let's go," Coach says as she waves us out of the holding room.

Backstage, it hits me, and my nerves start to overwhelm me. Reaching up, I want to grab my necklace, but get reminded it isn't there. Remembering Grandpa, the next best thing is to touch my heart, take a breath, and think 'thank you.' This time, I don't know who I am thanking. Before, I was thanking the charm, but now it feels like I'm thanking something much bigger. Like magic, it immediately calms me. Suddenly, I know I'll be okay. This is my chance!

Trina turns to me, "Are you ready? Left side!"

"I am," I say, giving her a genuine smile for the first time in weeks.

"You got this. Let's kill it!" She gives me a high five and a nod as we hear them announcing us.

Walking out on the big stage was surreal. Once in formation, I'm on the left side, in Trina's place. As the curtain is pulled back, I take a deep breath, and the music starts. Dropping to the floor for the dramatic beginning, and feeling the music, I feel my confidence grow. Halfway through, I haven't missed a step and am one with the music. I've found myself again. I'm back.

Posing in the perfect position for the final beat, the music stops, admiration and applause filled the room. Looking out to the crowd, there is a standing ovation. It's a dream come true, even better than I had imagined. The judges look stern, but that is how they always look. We start jumping up and down before running backstage. Coach comes over to me and gives me a hug. "I'm so proud of you!"

She lets me go and gives the team a pep talk for the ages. She is so passionate and sincere when she tells us how proud she is of us. Even though she believes we deserve to win, if we don't, we are all winners in her eyes. As we head back to the holding area, we find Ally hobbling down the hallway with Mark...and Nate. My heart stopped before an explosion of excitement and nerves hit me. The sight of him makes me catch my breath. I need to talk to him — it is time to fix all my mistakes.

"Great job, Becks, you were amazing! And Trina, you were incredible. Austin is still in the auditorium, but he said to tell you he's on his way. He's so proud of you. You should have seen his face as he watched you perform. It was adorable!" Trina looks so happy and gives Ally a hug.

"Thanks, Ally," I say distractedly as she hugs Trina. My eyes are focused on one thing right now. Nate. Determined to smooth things over, I head straight to him.

"Becky, you were amazing tonight! It was so awesome to see you dancing like that." Nate says, as he reaches for me, unsure, and gives me an awkward half hug. Not accepting a little hug from him, I wrap my arms around him in a bear hug. It reminds me of all the bear hugs he used to give me. Squeezing me back, he holds me tight, and it's perfect. Engulfed in Nate's arms is exactly where I belong.

"Nate, can we talk?" Finally getting the nerve to ask as I let him go.

"Yeah, of course." He says, with a look of uncertainty. We walk over to a bench further down the hall, away from the crowd, for privacy. Sitting next to him reminds me of our first date. Ahh, I've missed him so much.

"Thank you so much for being here. I was hoping you would come." Off to a shy start, nervously looking down before admitting, "I miss you, Nate." Getting the courage to look up, needing to read his expression, I see his kind eyes brighten. He smiles at my admission. So far, so good; continuing, I add, "I need to explain what has been going on with me lately, you know, since I lost the necklace." Trying to find the words to explain how I have been feeling is difficult. Nothing quite fits.

"It's hard to know where to start. I've been pushing you away for all the wrong reasons. The truth is, I lost all my confidence when I lost that necklace. It felt like I wasn't the same girl that you met when we were first dating. I was convinced you wouldn't like the person I was without the necklace. This year has been incredible, and I've grown so much. For the first time, I was self-assured and had confidence in myself that I had never experienced before. I really believed that the necklace was lucky, and it was the only reason all these amazing things were happening. Once I lost the necklace, I just assumed I'd lose everything good that came to me this year. Including you." Looking at Nate, I shrug sheepishly. "It felt like I didn't just lose a necklace; it felt like I lost myself." Pausing to wait for a reaction from Nate, but all I get is a nod. He's looking at me as if I should continue, so I try to explain it further. It's hard to convey to someone just how lost I was, and the words sound too small for the emotions I was feeling.

I continued trying to find the words to help him understand. "I was miserable, doubting myself in every moment. It didn't feel right to make you stay with me when I didn't know if I would ever find myself again. I was afraid. I thought I wasn't good enough for you."

"Becky, you are perfect for me! I have never been able to open up to anyone the way I can with you. I hate that you felt like you couldn't share this with me. I wish I knew how to be there for you, but it just seemed like the best thing I could do was give you space." Nate says, looking unsure. "I don't know if that was the right thing to do."

"It was, Nate. I had to figure this out on my own. It was never the necklace. I finally realized that. All the good that was going on in my life happened because of me. The necklace just gave me the courage I needed. I just needed to learn to believe in myself." Grandpa's voice is in the back of my mind, and it makes me smile. Tentatively, looking up to search Nate's face, hoping for a reassuring smile. He looks thoughtful, not happy or mad. Unsure what to think. My only hope is that I explained it well enough so he can find a way to understand and forgive me.

After what feels like an eternity, he looks up at me and says, "I always knew that, Becky. I knew the necklace wasn't why you made the team. I also understand that belief and how strong it can be. I told you about my weird soccer superstitions. I knew you'd figure it out in your own time. At least, I hoped you would. I just thought you needed the necklace for dance. It never occurred to me that you thought the necklace brought us together as well. Necklace or not, I want to be with you. Only you. If you're going through a hard time, I want to be there for you. We can get through it together." His deep blue eyes gaze into mine, and relief washes over me.

"I hope you can understand and find a way to forgive me. I'm so sorry I pushed you away. All of a sudden, I was questioning everything, even you. I worried that when I lost the necklace, I would lose you, too. I thought it would hurt less if I pushed you away. I'm sure it sounds stupid, but honestly, I was just afraid. I'm really sorry." That really was my biggest fear. Without the necklace, Nate would see me differently and realize he never really liked me. The mask was off. I felt exposed.

"And, what do you think now?" He asks.

"I'm still not sure how you feel, but I've missed you so much. I'm sorry it took me so long to find myself again. Please forgive me, Nate." I'm desperate for his forgiveness.

"Of course I forgive you! Honestly, Becky, you don't need my forgiveness. I was never upset with you. All I wanted was to help you, but I didn't know how. I'm just so happy you found your way back to me." He says as he wraps his arms around me. "I missed you so much, Becky."

An overwhelming rush of emotion fills me; without a doubt, I love him. More importantly, I love myself now, too. Time to take my grandpa's advice and go for it. Deep breath, calm down. Searching for the courage to say the thing I've been wanting to say.

"I love you, Nate." My head is on his chest, and he can't see my face. Terrified to look up at him, I keep talking, unsure of his reaction. "I know that might be too much for you to hear, but I need to be honest. I believe in us. And, I just want…" he pulls away from our hug, interrupting me.

"Becky, look at me." He says, forcing me to look at him. I've been looking down, avoiding eye contact, feeling unsure. At least I told him the truth. Finally, I find the nerve to look him in the eye. He says nothing. Instead pulls me close and starts kissing me with a sweetness I haven't experienced before. Slowly pulling away, he says, "I love you, too, Becky. I missed you so much."

"I missed me too!" I say, with a little chuckle and sheepish smile, "So, you'll give me another chance?"

"Another chance?" He laughs, "Did we break up? Contrary to what you may think, I've always been your boyfriend. I knew you'd find your way back." He says, happily wrapping his arm around me. As I rest my head on his chest, he leans down and gives me a little kiss on my forehead.

"I'm so happy." I say and secretly touch my heart near where the necklace used to hang and think 'thank you.'

During an intermission, my family came down to see me. Mom and dad brought me flowers and showered me with hugs and kisses on the cheek. "Congratulations, honey," they say at the same time.

My parents notice Nate by my side and raise their eyebrows at each other. My dad has a big smile on his face. I know he really likes Nate, even if he does always remind him of the rules. They bonded quite a bit while painting the office. Mom turns to Nate and says, "It's so good to see you, Nate. We've missed you around the house."

He smiles at that and says, "I'll be around much more from now on." If my mom was trying to figure out what was going on with us, he answered that question for her. He puts his arm around me casually, adding, "Right, Becky?"

Smiling from ear to ear, I agree, "That's right!"

My parents are beaming. They seem so happy we worked things out. Mom is looking down the hall, and following her gaze, I notice she is looking at three people walking down the hallway. As they get closer, it's grandma and grandpa walking at their slower pace with Jen beside them. Jen's here!

"Jen!" I yelled as I run towards her and my grandparents.

"She wanted to surprise you," Mom says loud enough so I can hear even as I run down the hall. Mom is beaming with pride at her girls. I'm so happy. It warms my heart to see everyone who came to support me.

"I wanted it to be a surprise. The minute mom texted that you would be dancing, I jumped in my car and drove over." Reaching her, I throw my arms around her, giving her the biggest bear hug.

"Thank you so much!! You're the greatest big sister!!"

"You were awesome tonight, Becks, really. You could really make a career out of dance." She says, and she means it. That's quite impressive since she's usually the one bringing me down to earth and reminding me to be more practical. "Did you see Nate?" she asks, sounding hopeful.

"Yeah, I did. Oh, Jen, I love him!" I've been dying to tell her. I'm so happy.

"I know you do. He loves you, too, you know?"

"In fact, I do! He just told me about 10 minutes ago." I say with a huge, proud smile.

Jen hugs me and says, "I'm so happy you two figured things out. I really like Nate."

"What's this I hear?" Grandpa chimes in. "Something about love birds?" he says with a teasing grin.

"What can I say? Nate's a pretty lovable guy." I say with a laugh.

"Oh, that Nate character again, huh? Yeah, I guess he'll do." He says with a wink. He gives me a hug and says, "I'm so proud of you, my precious granddaughter," and he squeezes me tight.

"Oh, Becky, you were magnificent out there. Just beautiful. I hope you guys win!" Grandma says. Somehow, I had forgotten about winning. Probably because after everything that happened today, I felt like I already won.

"Me too, Grandma! We'll find out soon. Only two teams left to dance." I say.

Everyone is surrounding the team, and I finally get a chance to talk to Ally. I was glad to be able to redeem myself today but hated the reason I had to dance. Feeling really awful about her injury, I go check on her. "Hey, how are you feeling?"

"Oh, I'm okay. The brace helps, and they say I'll be okay in a month, which isn't too bad."

"I'm so sorry this happened today. We could have really used you out there."

"I wish I could have danced too. But, honestly, seeing you dance and be happy again is really special. If I couldn't dance, at least I know it gave you the chance to shine again."

I hug her, "Ally, you are such an amazing friend. I can't believe you would think of me in a moment like this."

"I hated seeing you doubt yourself and lose your fun-loving side. I would have done anything to have my Becks back. Even if I could have changed it, I wouldn't change a thing, knowing it has helped you this much. We all missed you, Becks." She says, and her words stick with me. She would have given up dancing in the competition just to help me. I'm overwhelmed with emotion.

"Love you, Ally, you're the best. I'm sorry it took me so long to find my way back." Giving her another hug. It's amazing to find another friend who's as close to me as Trina and to think how lucky I am. How lucky the three of us are, really.

"Love you too, Becks. I can't tell you how glad I am that you're back to yourself now. That's all that matters." She says as she hugs me back.

Coach interrupts everyone, letting us know it's time. Judges are about to announce the winners, and everyone needs to head back to their seats. All the teams are back on stage when the presentation starts. Looking around at the teams gathered on the main stage, it is humbling to see all this talent sitting in one area. It hits me. Suddenly, it became very real to me that I was at the regionals, and the results are about to be announced. I've always dreamt of winning, but at this moment, looking around at the competition, it would be satisfying just to place in the top three. As the head judge starts to announce the third-place team, my heart leaps into my throat. It's not us. Third place goes to a team from Chicago, which was in contention to win. Anxiety consumes me. Were we better than them? They were awfully good. I really thought they could take the whole thing. I'm getting more and more nervous. I want us to win. We've worked so hard this year. Last year, our team ended in fourth place and came home empty-handed, but with the determination to make sure they placed this year.

The judge begins to announce second place, saying what an accomplishment it is, adding, "With that said, it's time to announce the team who earned runner-up." She opens the envelope as I hold my breath, "East River Rapids, Cougars! Congratulations!" The judge is beaming. I can't believe it! We got 2nd place! Our whole team stands up, screaming with excitement and runs over to accept the trophy. They take a quick official photo and make us sit back down immediately. It's hard to contain ourselves. We are all so excited.

"I can't believe it!" Trina says. "We haven't placed in years, this is awesome!" Then she suddenly looks mildly disappointed and adds, "I wish we won, though." Our team gets hushed by the judges. We need to be quiet so they can announce the winner. We calm down and wait quietly to hear who the winner will be.

As the judge describes how close the call was this year, it makes me feel like next year is really in our sights. Opening the envelope, everyone is on edge when she announces, "The winner for the third year in a row, Oakdale High School, Bulldogs! Congratulations, once again, you were the team to beat and will be heading to Orlando for Nationals!" Cheers, applause, and congratulations surround their team. They were terrific, I can't deny that. A ping of jealousy bubbles up. Now more than ever, I know exactly what I want next year: first place. Everyone is congratulating each other on their performances this year, and it's a nice feeling to know we performed our best. Coach is walking towards me, and I wonder what this is going to be about.

"Becky, can we talk?" Coach pulls me aside, out of the way of all the people swirling around us.

"Yeah, what is it, Coach?"

"I just want you to know that you really helped the team today. You really know what it takes to come back from defeat. After that one bad performance, you were so down I wasn't sure you would ever get your confidence back. Today, when the team needed you, you stepped up and managed to give us your best performance. That's what we need in a leader. I want you to know I won't forget that. We will need leaders next year, and I'm hopeful you'll be one of them." She says and gives me a hug.

"I'm honored. And shocked. Thank you!" I say as she hugs me.

"You're welcome. Now go find your family and celebrate!" Smiling at her, I nod my head in agreement before running off to find my parents. Everyone is so excited and wants to see the trophy up close. It's still a huge trophy for second place, and we are so proud of it. Everyone is taking a million pictures with different groups of people in front of the trophy. We managed to get a photo of everyone, including Ally and Kelly, who didn't dance this year. My mom makes sure to get a picture with just Ally, Trina, and myself. It's the photo I'll cherish most. Once everyone gets their chance to see the trophy, it's time to head home. Once in the car, exhaustion hits me as I fall asleep on my way home.

Chapter Seventeen
Moving On

I slowly wake up, wiping my eyes and looking at my phone. It's Christmas morning, I can't believe I slept in! I fix my ponytail and run downstairs ready to start our family tradition of sipping on a warm drink while opening gifts. Mom hands me a hot cocoa and shows me my pile of presents in the corner by the fireplace. Jen is home for her Christmas break, and it's awesome having her home for longer than just a weekend. She's sipping on her cocoa while Mom opens her last gift. Dad is sitting on the couch, drinking his coffee, and smiling as Mom holds up the new purse we got her. He always opens his gifts last. He enjoys watching all of our excitement first. As Jen starts opening her gifts, Mom is ready with her camera. She always takes pictures of everyone, even though we look terrible in our pajamas, make-up-free, and sporting our bed heads. Someday, we will appreciate these photos, though. Stevie gets a present, too, and sticks his head right in his gift bag. He gets distracted and starts to play with the tissue paper, so we have to help him open the rest of his gift. Squeak, squeak, obviously he found his toy Santa. He runs off with his toy and continues squeaking it in the corner. Christmas morning is the best. Even as I get older, I still love it.

After the opening of gifts, everyone gets showered and ready before Grandma and Grandpa come over for brunch and more gifts! We start the process all over again, holding up each item, giving hugs, and getting our photo taken. At least in these photos, we look presentable. Stevie gets treats this time, so he has no problem finding his gift bag, which I'm sure smells delicious to him. During brunch, we reminisced about the year we had, followed by rehashing funny family stories and laughing at them for the 100th time. Grandma and Grandpa are packing away their gifts. It's already time for them to leave.

Stevie starts barking and I know Nate must be here. We are going to a movie tonight and I totally lost track of time! Running into the bathroom, I quickly fix my hair and make-up before heading downstairs.

"Hi," I say, as I see him in the entryway, giving my mom a poinsettia. He looks over at me as my mom is thanking him, and shoots me one of his gorgeous smiles.

"Merry Christmas, Becky," He says.

"I'm going to put this over by the tree. It's beautiful and so thoughtful, Nate." My mom says and gives him a hug.

We decided not to exchange gifts this year. It was my idea because I couldn't think of anything to get him. Things were so weird between us leading up to Christmas break that it would have been a last-minute shopping trip anyway. We decided to just go to dinner and a movie instead.

"We are going to re-do our first date." Nate says as we drive to the movie theater, "Well, minus Chris having to drive us and Ally interrupting our almost first kiss." He says with a laugh.

"That's true. Tacos and a movie." I agree. It's not like we really had a choice since it's Christmas and not many places are open, but I love the sentiment.

"And I think it's nice enough out for one more stop." He adds, and I'm not sure what that means, but I have an idea. There was only one other place we went on our first date.

Nate parks the car, and as we walk through the parking lot, he takes my hand, leading me in the direction of our bench. As we walk over to it, he says, "This was the best part of our first date."

"Our bench," I say, knowing where he is leading me.

"It might be cold, but it wouldn't be a true recreation of that night without us stopping here for a minute." He says. I love this romantic side of him. He's so sentimental, probably because he grew up hearing the love stories of his grandparents and parents.

"It was my favorite part of that night, too." I say in agreement. Once we sit, we're in the exact spots we sat on that first night so many months ago. Strange, there's no snow on the ground for Christmas, but lucky for us.

"Whenever I think of that night, I always remember how many times I almost kissed you. It's time we finally make that happen." Nate leans in to kiss me softly. Ever since we made up, he kisses me differently. It just feels like we are closer now.

"It's about time I did that here," he says with a laugh.

"I agree. It's about time." I say, and I mean it. I'm starting to shiver, though, and Nate notices.

He wraps his arms around me, rubbing my arms to warm me, and says, "I love you, Becky."

"I love you too."

"Ready to head inside, or was there anything else about our first night we need to revisit?" I ask half teasing and half in case he has something else planned.

"That's it; let's go inside. I'm freezing!" Nate exclaims, and we literally run to the taco place. As we eat, we laugh about how many tacos Mark ate that first night. We talk about the homecoming dance, and now that we've told each other we love each other, my drunken slip is hilarious to both of us.

"I can still see your face." Nate says, then mimics me, adding, "I loveee…" He starts laughing, clearly picturing my face, reliving that moment from homecoming. Every single time Jen sees him, she manages to bring it up. They are always laughing about it. I'm never going to live that one down.

"You and Jen will never let me forget it! My face must have been terrible." I say with a laugh.

"It wasn't that you looked bad; it was just that…I can't explain it. It was so funny, though." He says, still laughing. "I knew I loved you way before that moment. But, that really sealed the deal."

"Well, I'm glad you found it so amusing," I say and throw a piece of wrapper at him.

He swats the paper away, "I'll never forget it."

We talk about all the fun moments, followed by all the annoying moments we shared, most of which involve Stacy. I wish he would just explain to me why he feels the need to humor her, but he always says the same thing: 'She's been through a rough time.' If I ask what that means, I simply get a sad look, 'I wish I could tell you, but it's really her story to tell.' Never knowing what he means, I still truly believe nothing is going on with them. We then get to the point where I lose my necklace, and I start feeling uncomfortable.

"I'm so glad you're back to yourself. I just didn't know how to help. I never want to lose you again." Nate says.

"I know. I'm sorry. I hated the way I felt so insecure when I lost that necklace. The best thing that came out of it is that I believe in myself now. I also know I can open up to other people; that brought me even closer to you and our friends."

"Well, I've decided in honor of what you discovered, I'm giving up my lucky underwear from now on." He teasingly whispers the words 'lucky underwear' as if it's some major secret that nobody in the restaurant should hear. "If you don't need a good luck charm, neither do I."

"That is the sweetest thing I've ever heard!" I lean over and give him a little kiss. I swear he is too good to be true.

After Christmas break, we arrived back at school, and everything is going so well. The dance team is having a pep rally to celebrate our second-place achievement. It'll be my first performance in front of the school since my disaster performance. People are going to be watching me closely today. It's time to redeem myself. The whole school knows about my terrible performance, whether they were there or not. It was the talk of the school for a solid week. Today feels like a test; I have something to prove, and I have to do it without my necklace. Getting nervous before a performance is normal for me. Now, when I reach up near my heart, it reminds me that I am all the luck I need. Taking a deep, calming breath, I think, 'Thank you.' Grandpa is right. It calms me the same way the necklace did. They announce us, and we run into the center of the gym. The music starts, and we all drop. This time, I perform without missing one step. I've redeemed myself in front of the entire school.

The crowd cheers for us as we take our final pose. This routine is a show-stopper. I'm energized by all the applause. As the coach announces us to come forward one by one, the crowd cheers enthusiastically. Ally's name is announced, and as she hobbles out to the center stage wearing her brace, the crowd goes wild. Coach continues to announce the rest of the juniors, followed by Trina. Then, "Becky Lewis," unexpectedly, the crowd cheered the loudest I've heard all day. They wanted me to redeem myself today, too. At least that's how it felt, and I'm overwhelmed by their support. Taking our seats, the pep rally continues. Next up is the fall sports team's turn to announce their MVPs for the year. Each coach will give a short speech on the season, followed by the MVP winner.

The soccer team MVPs are being announced. They start with the freshman soccer team. Everyone is mostly interested in the varsity soccer team. Nate doesn't expect to be nominated at all. Sophomores never win. He voted for Mark since he took him under his wing early on, and Mark is one of the best players but also a great teammate. The varsity soccer coach is announced, walks up on stage and starts talking about the team's season. They had so much success, and many of those players will still be here next year. He explains how they chose their MVP this year. The varsity teams chose their MVP by having the players vote anonymously.

He starts introducing the MVP, "The person the team voted for this year doesn't surprise me at all. He was tested to his limit at the beginning of the season. He worked hard to earn the trust and respect of the team. He led by example, showing up every day ready to play, and gave the team 110% at every practice and game. He never once complained, but instead, he sought out solutions when something wasn't working. Not only did he earn the trust of every player on the team, but he also earned my trust and the title of Varsity Soccer MVP. Nate McNeil, you are this year's MVP." Everyone in the stands cheers in appreciation. This is totally unexpected. The soccer team exploded, and Mark was so excited he was cheering as if his team just won the World Cup. It brought tears to my eyes, knowing what Nate had been through with that team. This would mean the world to him, and he is obviously emotional while standing on stage, taking in all the applause. MVPs are almost always seniors, and this is a huge deal.

As the pep rally ends, Nate is leaving the stage. His team is surrounding him while congratulating him, giving him hugs and high-fives. I'm dying to run over to him, but I know he deserves to have this moment with his team. Hanging back, I see him looking for me. He spots me and runs over, grabs me, picks me up and spins me around in celebration.

"I'm so proud of you! MVP!!" I'm yelling as he spins me.

He sets me down and gives me a kiss. This is pure joy and celebration. "I can't believe it." He says.

"You deserve it. I'm so happy for you."

"It's just where I started this year, and then to get MVP. I'm speechless."

"Well, from the reaction of your team, they love and respect you very much. Mark was going nuts!"

Nate laughs, "Yeah, even I noticed Mark's reaction."

As we hugged each other, I noticed Stacy staring at us from a distance. I'm sure she is waiting to congratulate him. I ignore it, I'm done letting her bother me.

That night I went to Nate's for dinner, and afterward, we decided to watch a movie. It was one of those super chill weekend nights that I love. During the show we pause it so Nate can to the bathroom, and his mom comes over to talk to me. I could tell she was waiting to have a moment alone with me.

"Hey, Becky, can I ask you something? Is that girl in the red dress from Nate's birthday party still after Nate?" Interesting, I wonder why his mom is asking me about this.

"Honestly? Yeah, I think she is, but I trust Nate. Why?"

"I've run into her a few times, and she always talks to me, almost like she's pretending to be Nate's girlfriend. It's bizarre and concerning. I always wondered if she had anything to do with what happened between you two around Christmas." I knew she was referring to when I was pushing Nate away.

"No, I wouldn't say that was her fault. It had more to do with me. I was being self-conscious. I don't feel insecure anymore, and I kinda feel sorry for Stacy. She seems so insecure lately, and I know how terrible that feels. It's like she always needs the attention and approval of a guy." I say, surprising myself that I told his mom all of that.

"Yes, she lacks self-confidence, I would agree with that. Well, I reminded her that he already has a girlfriend, so she can stop with the pretense. I just wanted you to know I think she is up to no good. She was falling over drunk on his birthday and hitting on him in front of you. I don't want her anywhere near my son."

"Who? What did you do?" Nate asks.

"Oh, nothing to worry about." She says, giving me eyes like, 'don't say anything.'

"We were just chatting about some of the more troubled kids in our grade," I say. Well, one troubled kid, anyway.

As soon as his mom is out of earshot, he asked: "What was that really about?"

"Stacy, your mom is not a fan."

"Oh, yeah, I know that. She has had enough of the girl in the red dress that is for sure." Nate says with a laugh. "She loves you, though." He adds and gives me a kiss on the cheek.

"I'm glad. She seems like she can be pretty stern if you get on her bad side."

"Nah!" Nate says, then thinks about it and adds, "Well, maybe." He says with a wave of the hand, like who knows? We cuddle up and watch the rest of the movie with no more discussion of Stacy.

Chapter Eighteen
Sweetheart

Sweetheart Court nominations are the talk of school this week. It is the only thing to look forward to during the cold winter nights in Michigan. The top three guys and top three girls in each grade make the cut for the final vote. Winners of this vote will be on this year's Sweetheart Court. Excitingly, Nate and I are both in the top three! Last year, I remember being so envious of Stacy. Jealous that she was lucky enough to be on court with Nate. Suddenly, I start picturing us together on the sweetheart court, walking hand in hand, but just as I am about to get wrapped up in my thoughts, a knock on the door interrupts me. One of the girls from the dance committee walks into Mr. Whitman's class.

"Sorry to interrupt, but we have permission to take the votes this period." She says to Mr. Whitman, then looks at our class and adds, "Vote for one guy and one girl. I will pass this around and put your vote in the box, be quick. I still have to make it to a bunch of classes." She holds up a box with a slit in the top where we will place our paper votes.

Each person gets a paper with the names of the nominees. Stacy is also nominated, I don't know why anyone would vote for her this year. She is very pretty on the outside but isn't particularly pretty on the inside. My name is directly across from Nate's on the list, so I circle them both in one big circle, smiling to myself.

"You better have voted for me," Nate whispers as he leans over to me.

"Oh yeah? Well, maybe I did, and maybe I didn't." I say with a wink and teasing smile, which makes him laugh.

At the end of the day they will announce who will be on the court. Hopefully, if Nate wins then I will be with him. I would hate if it was Nate and Stacy. I know I'm supposed to be full of my newfound confidence, but she just gets under my skin. Lately, whenever I look in her direction, I find her staring at Nate. It just can't be Nate and Stacy on court together, I don't know if I can handle it.

At lunch, everyone is talking about who they voted for, and people keep coming up to me, saying they voted for me. The same is happening to Nate. We might have a chance! Nate leans over and says, "I hope it's you and me, together."

"Me too," I say.

Stacy walks over to our lunch table. "Hey, guys, good luck with the whole court thing. I know it's your first time being nominated, Becks. Nate and I are pros at this, right, Nate? A repeat of last year?" She asks, looking at Nate and trying to flirt. She clearly expects them to win again.

"We'll see what happens," Nate says with a fake smile.

"See you after they announce the winners." She says to me, pretending to be sweet but not pulling it off.

As she walks away, I ask, "Why does she do that?"

"She's just trying to get under your skin. Don't let it bother you. That's what she wants."

"I'm surprised she is still trying after what your mom said to her."

"What's that?"

"I forget exactly, something about you already having a girlfriend so she should stop pretending." I try to repeat what his mom said.

"Wow," he laughs. "No wonder you said you don't want to get on my mom's bad side. I think Stacy is really weird around my mom. I've never heard her talk about anyone the way she talks about 'the girl in the red dress.'" He says the words 'girl in the red dress' like it's something from a horror movie.

"Your mom is never going to wear red again," I say jokingly, trying to lighten the mood. It works; we both start to laugh.

As we leave the cafeteria, Stacy runs into us once more. "I can't wait to be by your side on court again this year, Nate! And, good luck, Becky."

"Come on, Stacy..." Nate sounds super annoyed, and I'm shocked. He usually tries to blow her off nicely, but he's clearly sick of all her talk.

Stacy's jaw drops, and she just makes a hmph sound, turns, and walks away.

"Wow, Nate, didn't you just tell me not to let her get under my skin?" I say, teasing him.

"Nothing else seems to be working. She's so disrespectful. I can't keep being a friend to her if she keeps acting this way." He shrugs, but I think he has every right to be angry with her.

"Well, she doesn't seem to get your more subtle hints," I say with a shrug, trying to stay out of it.

It's now the last hour of school. The announcement is being made on who will represent each class on Sweetheart Court this year. They finished announcing the freshman, and continue to read the list, saying, "The sophomore class has voted for Nate McNeil and Stacy...oh, sorry. Nate McNeil and Becky Lewis. Congrats to Nate and Becky!" Everyone in class turns to me and says congratulations. Stacy Wyse was voted on court for the junior class. That must be why they accidentally said Stacy instead of Becky at first. That's my hope at least. I'm scared to celebrate too much, though, just in case it was a mistake.

"Thanks, everyone," I say as the bell rings.

Nate and Stacy are talking down at the end of the hall, and I head towards them.

"But, they said my name…" I hear Stacy say as I approach them.

"Hey, how's my sweetheart?" Nate asks when he sees me and puts his arm around me. Stacy looks truly annoyed at this.

"I'm just saying, maybe we should go to the principal's office to make sure it's you and Becky." Stacy says, exasperated, "No offense." She adds as she looks at me dismissively.

"None taken. We can double-check if you'd like." I say. Nate looks at me, shocked. Honestly, though, I would feel better knowing for sure. It was a weird way to hear the announcement.

"Okay, let's go," Nate says.

Nate and I follow Stacy down the hall. She is definitely a girl on a mission. She seems a little over-confident that she won. We get to the office and ask the secretary.

"Oh, yes, I have the final results right here. It is Nate McNeil and Becky Lewis." The secretary says and shows us the tally. I beat Stacy by 10 votes. She tries to grab it from the secretary, whose reflexes are too fast. "I can't let you take this, sorry. Congratulations, Nate and Becky." The secretary says, looking at us.

"Thanks," Nate and I say at the same time. If I still had the necklace, I would have believed everyone voted for me because of the charm. This is much more meaningful, and I realize I'm glad I no longer have it. My thoughts are interrupted by Stacy, who is completely over reacting.

"It doesn't make any sense!" Stacy yells, arms folded in protest.

"I don't know about that." Nate says, "It seems like our class got it right to me." Nate says, and I chuckle at that. He is feisty with her today.

"You're a jerk!" Stacy says and slams open the door as she stomps away. She seems genuinely hurt, but I know Nate is just frustrated with her.

"I was just teasing, sorry, Stacy!" Nate calls after her. I look at him, and he looks a little upset. "I shouldn't make her feel bad. She's just really bothering me today. I've tried to be nice to her, but she has no respect for our relationship. Honestly, she makes it almost impossible to help her."

"She'll get over it," I tell him, knowing she will. I'm curious about what he is helping her with, but I don't bother to ask. Already knowing what he will say, which is, it's not his place to tell me what is going on with her. He makes it sound like it has to do with Blake, but they've been broken up for months now! I just need to let it go and celebrate being on Sweetheart Court instead.

As we walked out of the office, I noticed how quickly the students cleared out of all hallway. Down the hall, Stacy is talking to someone who is on the dance committee. Pretty sure she doesn't realize her voice is carrying in the empty halls as I hear her yell, "You promised me!"

"I tried! I changed as many as I could, but Becky still won, okay? Deal with it." The girls says and starts to walk away in a huff before she turns around and adds, "You know Stacy, nobody likes you anymore. It's no surprise you're not on court. Ever since Blake, you've changed; we all see it."

"This is horrible. It was my last chance with Nate. It was supposed to be me!" Stacy yells at the girl, but the girl continues to walk away without another word. Nate and I look at each other, both knowing Stacy tried to rig the vote. I'm not surprised. Of course she tried to cheat her way onto sweetheart court, she would do anything to be close to Nate.

Nate is cringing. "That was crazy. I feel bad about her and Blake, but I don't know what to do anymore. Thank God I'm not on court with her again." Nate says, shaking his head. "I just don't understand why she has to keep pushing things. If she just let it go, we could be friends.”

“No wonder she was so confident all day and kept making those comments about being on court with you,” I add. I can tell something is weighing on him about Stacy, but I just don't understand it.

Nate just shrugs his shoulders. “She said it was her last chance. Maybe she will leave me alone now.”

Ally and Trina are down the hall, and they run over. “Congratulations, Becks! You too, Nate. We were thinking we could help you pick out your dress. Let’s go shopping tonight!”

“Definitely!” I say, “My mom will want to come too, I’m sure.”

Nate seems full of joy as I exclaim, “I can’t wait to go shopping for my dress!”

“Good luck! And, just one thing though, maybe not a red dress?” He says with a smirk. “You know, because of my mom.”

Laughing at that, I agree, “No problem!”

Tonight is the night of Sweetheart Court. We will be announced during halftime of the varsity basketball game. Nate keeps telling me how gorgeous I look while holding my hand as we wait to be announced. He looks so handsome in his suit, like an old-school movie star. Very dapper. No matter how long we’ve been together, there are still moments when I can’t believe he’s my boyfriend. As we wait in the cafeteria, grandma and grandpa stop by to see us.

“How are the lovebirds?” Grandpa asks. It’s his nickname for us now.

“You look beautiful.” Grandma says, “And handsome,” she adds, looking at Nate.

Grandma gives us both a hug, "We'll be cheering you on." she says

"Thanks, grandma. I feel like the luckiest girl in the world." I say as I squeeze Nate's hand.

"Well, I can certainly see why!" Grandma says, then whispers to me, "He is awfully handsome."

"Did I just hear you say you're the luckiest girl in the world? I told you, it was never the necklace. After all, if you're lucky enough to be Irish, you're lucky enough!" Grandpa says, laughing. He gives me a big smile. "Can't wait to see you two out there!"

Grandpa gives Nate a teasing nudge and adds, "You're the lucky one, you know?"

"Oh, believe me, I know," Nate says with a laugh as he pats Grandpa on the back in agreement.

Our parents walk into the room and give us hugs. My mom and Nate's mom are taking a million pictures of us. They keep making us change positions for different photos. Our dads are talking in the corner, and I imagine my dad is telling one of his jokes.

"Everyone!! We will be announcing you in 10 minutes." Our principal yells.

"We better get to our seats! You guys look great! We'll be cheering for you!" Our parents say as they give us hugs and head to the stands. My sister's here with Leslie and Chris, who are saving seats for everyone in the gym.

The principal comes to get us. We wait outside the gym door as he walks into the entrance of the gym to start announcing Sweetheart Court. He announces the freshman, and they walk out to the center stage as the crowd cheers. We are up next, "The sophomore class representatives are Nate McNeil and Becky Lewis." My heart flutters at the sound of our names.

We walk out to center court holding hands, and the crowd is deafening as they cheer for us. My family is sitting alongside Nate's family. They're all waving, whistling, and cheering for us. The sight of them together warms my heart. I've had a lot of moments on center court this year. The good and bad memories flash through my mind. Looking over at Nate, it's the first time the applause is for the both of us, together. He looks over at me and shoots me a smile. That smile used to only live in my daydreams; this is real and so much better.

After the game, we all gather together again in the cafeteria. My sister comes over, hugs me, and says, "It was so fun to see you and Nate out there together. You were beautiful. I'm so glad I was here to see it." It's always special when she comes home to celebrate with me.

"Thanks, Jen," I say in her ear while she hugs me tight.

"We were thinking we should all come back to our house and hang out for a while." She says, which I think is perfect.

Nate's family, along with Leslie and my grandparents, all come over to my house to celebrate and relive the evening events. Our two families blend together with such ease; it makes the time go by quickly. It is really fun, everyone is laughing with my grandpa, who is telling his hilarious stories of his younger years. He was pretty wild back in the day, and never holds back when telling a good story. He's always the last to leave a party, unless grandma doesn't give him a choice. Hanging out, we were truly enjoying each other's company until it's time for Nate's family to leave.

"You guys looked so lovely out there today. I'm so glad I got to spend more time with your family. Your Grandpa is a riot!" Nate's mom says as she hugs me goodbye.

"I know it. He is always the life of the party," I say while hugging her back.

"I had a great time tonight, Becks. I really enjoyed your family." Nate's dad says as he gives me a hug.

"Love you, can't wait for tomorrow," Nate says quietly as he kisses me on the cheek and winks.

"Love you too," I whisper back, smiling so big my face hurts.

Our families are all hugging each other goodbye while Stevie is demanding to be picked up so he can be in on the action. Everyone gives him a pat on the head before leaving. My family goes out on the porch to wave goodbye to Nate's family as they pull out of the driveway before we turn back inside.

"Well, that was a fun night. I really enjoy his family," Grandpa says.

"You enjoy them because they like your stories," Grandma says, giving Grandpa a teasing nudge. He laughs at that, and he knows it's true.

"Oh, you're right about that!" He says, then adds. "We should go too. It's late. We're going to be tired tomorrow!" We hug them goodbye and tell them to drive safely. Grandpa had a few more beers than usual, so Grandma is driving, which she rarely does.

"We'll be fine," Grandma says reassuringly. We watch as they back up and head home before heading to bed ourselves. Resting my head on my pillow, I'm quickly asleep with a full heart, knowing I'll have sweet dreams tonight.

Oversleeping after last night, I barely have time to hang out with my sister before it's time to get ready for the dance. Jen has to head back to college today. She has some party back at school she's excited about. It's a bummer she won't be here all weekend, but still means the world to me she came home to see me on court with Nate.

Ally and Trina arrive at my house to start getting ready. We decided to get ready together. Talking excitedly about the night ahead and singing along to music as we finish up our make-up, we're so excited. Ally helps me with my make-up this time since I still don't know how to do it myself. She finishes up my make-up and tells me to look in the mirror.

Turning around to look in the mirror, I catch my reflection and can't believe my eyes. My face looks vibrant, with a glow that brings my pale skin to life. The color of the eye shadow makes my green eyes pop. They look bigger and brighter than usual. Wow, I look gorgeous!

"Oh my gosh, Ally, how did you make me look so good?!" I ask in astonishment.

"YouTube, I love practicing with videos. It's so fun! When I was first learning to do make-up, that's all I did. I'm addicted to them now." She says.

Trina comes over, "Let me see!" Turning towards her, she smiles, "You look amazing."

Trina and Ally always wear make-up, so when they get ready for a dance, it isn't as shocking. Unlike me, who doesn't wear much make-up at all, my face totally transforms. Tonight is no exception. I feel amazing. We all get dressed and wear similar-colored dresses. Mine is a pink champagne color, Ally is wearing pale pink, and Trina is wearing a blush-colored dress. Our pictures together will look phenomenal since our dress colors blend so nicely. We're huddled around my full-length mirror, putting on our final touches.

Stevie starts barking, letting us know the guys are here and we look down the hall towards the stairs. "Hey, little man," Nate says to Stevie in the entryway.

"Hi, Nate, Mark," Mom says. "The girls are still upstairs getting ready. Do you want anything?" Knowing they are comfortable with my parents, I don't worry about running downstairs to meet them yet. Instead, I go back to check on the girls, who are almost ready.

Stevie barks again, and I can hear everyone welcome Austin. All the boys are here, and we are ready. Time for our grand entrance. "The guys are here!" my mom yells.

"We're coming down," I yell back, and look at the girls.

"The guys are going to die when they see us." I say excitedly. They smile in agreement and follow me down the stairs.

My favorite thing is seeing the expressions on everyone's face when first seeing us all dressed up. Nate already saw me in my dress, but his expression was still one of admiration as he looked up at me. "You are so beautiful." He says.

Mark and Austin say similar to Ally and Trina. My mom immediately starts arranging for us to be placed in different positions for photos. After she is satisfied with the pictures, we head to the dance.

Arriving at the dance, we get our photo taken before heading straight to the dance floor. We all love to dance and always have so much fun together. None of us care about what anyone else thinks. We dance the night away. Nate and I have Sweetheart court responsibilities. Leaving the group to complete all our court tasks, we first get our photo taken with the other court couples, followed by a slow dance with the Sweetheart Court couples after they announce us on the dance floor. Unlike last year, this time, it isn't Stacy who gets to slow dance with Nate for being on court; it's me. Now I can see why she wanted to be on court with him so bad, she would have had him all to herself this whole time. Once all our duties are over, we find our group of friends and dance the night away with them.

Dancing alongside Trina to our favorite song, we are singing along, and having a blast. A few people away I notice Stacy. She's dancing with a group of girls I don't recognize. A slow song comes, changing the vibe, and she sits down at a table. Nate finds me and takes me in his arms to dance. It's strange to see her sitting alone. It isn't like her to be dateless, and I'm not sure if she has danced with any guy tonight. I know how it feels to lose faith in yourself. It's horrible, and I wouldn't wish that on my worst enemy. I might understand Stacy a little better than I'd like to admit. Suddenly I felt bad for her and hope she will find a way to believe in herself again.

She wasn't like this last year. She was confident and nice. Really, I wonder what happened.

Nate interrupts my thoughts, "I can't believe how much has happened this year. I'm so glad I'm here with you." He kisses me sweetly, and before I know it, the song has ended. We only have half an hour left of the dance, and it consists mostly of upbeat songs. In the blink of an eye, the night is coming to a close. The six of us dance together in a circle for the last song of the night.

After the dance, we head to Ally's so we could hang out longer. It's nice since she lives so close to Trina and me. At Ally's, we turned on the music, but nobody felt like dancing anymore. Instead, the guys started telling funny stories about each other that I had never heard. Austin is hilarious, recounting the time Mark got stuck in a porta-potty at a music festival last year. He's reenacting how he had to help pull the door open, followed by Mark stumbling out of the porta-potty and into the crowd. It had us in tears, laughing. Mark had to give it right back and started telling funny stories about Austin and Nate. Ally and Trina are crying from laughing so hard. Now, all of us are bent over in laughter. Hard to say if I was laughing more at the stories or because of the girls contagious laughs. It was such a blast, even though we weren't at some big college after party this time. We were having the best time until Trina's alarm went off, alerting us it was time to head home to make curfew.

Nate drives me home, which is just a few blocks down the street from Ally's. "Tonight was so much fun; those stories were hilarious. Austin's reenactment was the funniest thing I've ever seen." Nate says.

"Did you know that story?"

"Nope. I'm sure Mark doesn't want too many people to hear that one. Austin would only tell people he knows that Mark trusts. He's good that way." Nate says, and it makes me happy knowing the trust we have within our group of friends.

Chapter Nineteen

Truth

Stevie's barking wakes me up from my sleep, so I run over to the window to see who is here. My grandparents are pulling into the driveway. It's a perfect distraction for me today. As I walk downstairs, still in pajamas, Grandma looks up and asks, "How was the dance? Looks like you had a late night." She says, noticing my outfit. We walk over to the dining room table to sit and she leans in, wanting to hear every detail.

"It was so much fun! We all got ready together here, so we had lots of girl time before the dance and afterwards went to Ally's to hang out until curfew." I tell her all about the dance and show her pictures.

"I bet Nate thought you were beautiful," Grandma says with her warm smile as my parents and grandpa sit down with us for brunch.

"Yes, he did. He kept complimenting me all night. It was so much fun, we danced the whole night!" Remembering how much fun we had, I add "I'm so lucky to have the best friends and boyfriend ever!"

"You see! I told you! It was never the necklace." Grandpa says approvingly, joining our conversation with his joyful smile. "I knew Nate shouldn't give it back to you!" Grandpa adds, proud of himself.

"Joe!" Grandma exclaims and hits his arm with a swat, which means he needs to stop talking. She has to do this often with him since he tends to accidentally spill the beans without realizing it.

"What?" Grandpa says, rubbing his arm and protesting the swat he got from Grandma. "It's true, isn't it, honey? You don't need that necklace." He shoots me a look as if asking for some backup in his defense. "It was never about the necklace," Grandpa says again, exasperated. Once more, he turns to me to defend him. Clearly, he has no idea what the big deal is. Grandma, on the other hand, is looking at me cautiously as if she is awaiting my reaction.

"Yes, I believe that now," I say, confused. "What did you mean you told Nate not to give it to me? He has it!?" Unbelievable, this can't be right. How could Nate have the necklace? No way. It's not possible.

Grandma is giving Grandpa a death stare. She knows exactly what is going on. Clearly, Grandpa has told a truth that he should have kept to himself.

"Honey, it's not as bad as it sounds," Grandma says reassuringly.

"Okay, so what's going on?" I ask her, unsure if I want to hear the answer.

"Nate has the necklace. I told him not to give it to you, though, because you're doing better." Grandpa says he's finally caught on to his mistake.

"Nate has the necklace?! How? Since when?" I ask, completely dumbfounded and starting to feel a sense of betrayal.

"Only since the competition," Grandma says encouragingly. For some reason, she seems to think that will make me feel better. It doesn't.

"Since the competition?! That was months ago! You all knew that Nate had my necklace this whole time? I can't believe it. You were all lying to me! Why would you do that?" As this new information hits me, a million emotions flood me at once, and all of a sudden, I just have to get out of here. "I gotta go." Upset, I get up from the dining room table and run upstairs to my room. Needing time to process this, I run away to be alone.

"Becks…Becks!" Mom and Grandpa are both yelling as I leave the room.

This doesn't make any sense. I lost the necklace between the cafeteria and the gym the day of my performance. Nate helped me look for it, did he find it then? Grandma said he had it since the competition, she must mean regionals. He would have given it to me, I know it. Grandpa said he told Nate not to give it to me, but why would Nate ask my grandpa? This makes no sense at all. Looking at my texts, there are two new ones, Nate sent me a couple.

N: Can we go to the diner today?

N: I have something I need to tell you.

My heart jumps into my throat. Nate has something to tell me today, too. This day is not going as expected. I just need to lie down for a minute and think. Tears start to fall; the people I love most have been lying to me for months. I am hurt, angry, and very confused at the same time. I need to know what really happened.

"Becks?" Mom asks quietly as she knocks on my door. Wiping my tears away quickly, I respond to her.

"Yeah," I say, "You can come in."

"Honestly, Becks, I knew nothing about any of this. Your grandpa feels terrible. You know he is only ever doing what he thinks is best for you." She says, and I nod, knowing that it's true. She continues, "Don't be mad at Nate; he was only taking the advice of your grandpa. They both love you." Mom says, looking at me with concerned eyes.

"I know they do, but I just don't understand. How could they lie to me? They saw how unhappy I was. I just don't understand why they would do this to me." Tears start to fall down my face again. I'm so hurt, and it's bringing back memories of how miserable I was without the necklace.

"If you want to understand, you'll have to talk to Grandpa. Will you? He is very upset. And, Grandma is still yelling at him." Mom says. Picturing grandma yelling, softens my anger, she's probably saying something like 'Joe, you have such a big mouth' and 'how dare you hurt your granddaughter.' I knew grandpa, and I knew he would never hurt me. I need the whole story, it's time for the truth.

"Okay, fine." Getting up, I wipe away my tears before heading downstairs.

"Becks," Grandpa says, eager to apologize as he reaches out to give me a hug. "I'm so sorry. I guess I thought you knew by now."

"I just don't understand." That's all I could say before Grandpa started to explain.

"It was at the competition. Remember when I found you and we talked before your performance? I told you how it wasn't the necklace, but instead that you started to believe in yourself. It's that belief in yourself that matters. I've always known that Becks." Grandpa says.

"Yes, I get that, Gramps, but why didn't you or Nate tell me he had the necklace? I don't get why you would do that!" I'm so confused and frustrated.

"Well, when I talked to you, I didn't know Nate had the necklace. On my way back to my seat, I ran into Nate. He just arrived and was frantically looking for you. He told me he just found your necklace and had to give it to you before you performed. I stopped him." Grandpa says, looking down. "I'm sorry, Becks, but you were finally believing in yourself. You would be perfect without your lucky charm. I told Nate that you were ready, and if he gave it to you, it would do more harm than good. I explained to Nate that we talked and that your spirits were high. It took a lot, but I convinced him not to give it to you. I assumed he would have told you about it by now."

Processing this new information, my thoughts are racing, wanting to make sense of it. Nate found it on the day of the competition. It's hard to believe. "Does Nate still have the necklace?" I wonder aloud.

"I don't know," Grandpa says. "I just know he had it, and I'm the reason he never gave it to you."

"So Nate has been lying to me this whole time?" I say in disbelief. "Why wouldn't he just tell me? It's been months now!" My voice cracks, sounding more hurt than angry.

"Don't be mad at Nate, sweetie. Nate loves you. He was just doing what he thought was best."

"He also didn't give me a say in the matter either; he just decided for me. I can understand why you told him not to give it to me. But, don't understand why, after all this time, Nate never told me about it."

"You'll have to ask Nate. But…Becks, promise me you'll listen to him with an open mind. He loves you, and maybe he made a mistake, but people make mistakes. Nobody is perfect, remember? Remember when you were first dating Nate? How relieved you were to find out that he wasn't perfect after all? Don't hold it against him now. Promise me." Grandpa says with such sincerity I realize just how much he likes Nate.

"Okay, Grandpa," I say, knowing that at this point, I just need to hear the truth, all of it.

Grandma peeks around the corner at us. "How is it going in there?" she asks.

"It's okay, Grandma. I think I understand now, at least Grandpa's part."

She walks in and sits by me, "I told Joe how stupid it was to bring that necklace up. He should have told you a long time ago, I kept telling him that. It never ends well when he opens his big mouth and spills the beans! Someone was going to get their feelings hurt, I just knew it." She gives Grandpa one of her looks, and shakes her head at him.

"It's okay, Grandma," I say, knowing Grandpa will be in trouble with Grandma the rest of the day. She's protective of me and hates to see me hurt. "Don't be too hard on Grandpa," I add, she laughs at that as she gives me a hug.

"Now, don't screw up what you have with Nate over that stupid necklace. That lucky charm is turning into a curse if you ask me!" She says with a laugh.

Laughing with her, I think she might be right about that. "I already promised Grandpa I would listen to Nate with an open mind."

"And an open heart," Grandma adds with a nod. "You should talk to him sooner rather than later. Get the whole story before you start getting upset with only half the truth."

She taps me on the back like, 'You got this,' stands up and says, "I think it's time we head home, Joe."

"I love you, Becks," Grandpa says as he stands up to leave. Walking them to the door I give them hugs before they go, showing them they are forgiven. They both remind me to give Nate a chance to explain once more before they walk out the door, and I promised them I would.

"Well? What happened? Are you going to talk to Nate?" Mom asks.

"Yeah, Grandpa explained everything. They both want me to give Nate a chance to explain his side of the story. But, mom, he has been lying to me for months!" I complain.

"I agree with them; keep an open mind. You and Nate have something really special, and we can all see that. I don't want you throwing it away because he made a mistake. Grandpa was the one who stopped him originally, and you forgave him."

"But Grandpa hasn't had the necklace this whole time!" I argue, trying to prove my point.

"Becks, you need to hear Nate out. Keep an open mind." Mom repeats, and in my mind, I hear grandma's words 'and an open heart.'

"I'm going to text him and see if he can come over."

"Sounds like a good idea," Mom says with an encouraging smile.

I head to my room to text Nate.

B: Hey, can you come over?

Bubbles show up on my phone, alerting me he is writing a reply.

N: Yeah, I have to finish up some errands. I'm helping Dad. I'll text when I'm done here. ☺

Trying to piece everything together is hopeless; parts of this story are missing, and I need more information. Information that only Nate knows. When did he find it? Where did he find it? Why didn't he give it back after my performance? Was he ever planning on telling me the truth? I'm nervous, I want us to get past this, but I don't know if we can. What if this is the end of us? My heart aches at the thought. Without a doubt, I will listen to him with an open heart and mind. Honestly, I don't want to lose him again.

Jen will know what to do. I reach for my phone and call her. It rings twice before she picks up the phone, "Hey, how was the dance?!"

"It was awesome, but this morning sure hasn't been," I say, my disheartened tone gets her attention.

"Oh no, what's wrong?" Jen asks, and everything I just learned comes flooding out of me. Patiently, she listens to me.

"You guys will be alright. I know it." She says, matter of factly.

"How? Am I supposed to just let it go and pretend it doesn't bother me that he's been lying all this time?"

"Of course not! You talk to him, tell him everything you just told me. Honestly, Becks, I can understand where Grandpa and Nate were coming from. It wasn't the right way to handle it, but it's not something to break up over either." Jen says.

"It feels like a betrayal."

"Becks, this wasn't an act of betrayal; it was an act of love."

"Love, huh?" I say with a scoff.

"Yes, just because it seems like the wrong thing to do doesn't mean that it wasn't done with the best of intentions. They did this out of love for you and nothing else. I know that, deep down, you know it too. Talk to Nate, and forgive him. You guys will be fine." Jen says, and I hope she is right.

"Thanks, Jen. You always make me feel better."

"You're welcome!" She says, sounding proud of herself.

As I hang up with Jen, Stevie starts barking. My heart races, knowing Nate must be here. He had texted while I was on the phone with Jen. I'm still upset with him, but I feel myself forgiving him already. She's right. I just need to talk to him and get the full picture. I know I was wrong in the way I acted when I lost the necklace and pushed him away. He forgave me for that, and these mistakes are just us being human and figuring things out.

"Hey!" Nate says, looking up at me with his smile. He is on the floor playing tug of war with Stevie, and that warms my heart. I already want to forgive him. Please let there is an explanation for this, I think to myself.

"Hey," I say while walking down the stairs. He stands up and gives me a kiss on the cheek. "I need to tell you something, Becky." Nate always calls me Becky. Everyone else calls me Becks for short. It feels special in a way, and I love that he does that.

"Yeah, we need to talk," I say, and I notice my mom eavesdropping from the living room.

"Let's go downstairs." We need some privacy to talk. Sitting on the couch, we turn on the TV for background noise.

"Nate, I know about the necklace. Grandpa accidentally spilled the beans today." Blurting this out, I could feel tears start to well up in my eyes. Please let him explain. I'm so hurt, but I want so badly to forgive him.

He leans in and hugs me, but I don't hug him back. As he pulls away, he looks me directly in the eyes and says, "Becky, I love you, and I'm so sorry. I should have told you earlier, but I wanted to be sure."

"What in the world does that mean? Sure of what exactly?" I'm upset and can't hide it.

"Well, I wanted to be sure you didn't need it anymore. I wanted to give it to you right away. But also thought you should have time to prove to yourself that good things happen without the necklace. So, I kept it safe. If something happened and you needed it again, I would have given it back." He looks down, "Maybe that was a bad decision. After last night, I knew it was time to give it back to you. No matter what, I knew you believed more in yourself than in the necklace. You were so happy and confident."

Taking this in, I'm trying to listen to him without judgement. In some ways, I realize I'm the one who got into this mess. I put so much energy into believing in the necklace when, the whole time, I could have just believed in myself. Nate interrupts my thoughts.

"Becky, I don't want to lose you. I can't lose you again." He says, and his face is full of emotion. He looks scared and vulnerable. Instinctively, I reach out to hug and comfort him. I hate seeing him defeated like this. Pulling away to look at him, his face is full of uncertainty.

"When did you find it? Where did you find it?" Still needing answers, I began to ask the questions weighing on me.

"I found it the day of the dance competition. Mark and I were meeting up with a group of guys to play some basketball at the gym in the morning. I was sitting on the bench during a water break, and a bright light caught my eye in the corner of the gym. I walked over to see what it was, and there it was. Your necklace. It was just lying there. I couldn't believe it! I left the game immediately, went home, and got ready as fast as I could. I hit the road in a hurry to get it to you in time. I was planning to ride with Mark to the competition but

I didn't even wait for him. When I parked, I got your text that you were dancing after all. As I was running in the door, I was in a panic, knowing you needed the necklace as soon as possible. I was wandering around, trying to find you, and that's when I ran into your grandpa. I told him what was going on and that I needed to get the necklace to you immediately. He told me not to give you the necklace, that it would ruin all your progress. You were finally believing in yourself, and you didn't need it anymore. Neither one of us wanted to see you go through what you had just experienced. We knew it wasn't the necklace that was bringing you luck. After a while, he convinced me it was the best thing for you. Watching you perform, I knew he was right. You were back."

"So why didn't you just tell me that after the performance?" I ask, exasperated. I just couldn't understand what he was thinking.

"I was going to, and then you told me that you loved me. Honestly, Becks, I was so happy, and I was dying to tell you that I love you too. I just didn't want to ruin it by bringing the necklace back in the picture. For the first time, you explained that you thought our relationship started because of the necklace. I didn't want you to second guess my love for you. I was worried you would think it was because the necklace was there after all. I love you, Becky. That has nothing to do with the necklace."

"I know that Nate. I love you too," I say, feeling bad that he doubted me. This situation has affected everyone, and that makes me feel terrible.

"You have to remember where you were at the time. I just didn't want to mess anything up."

"Okay, maybe I wasn't ready that day. But it's been months now. You could have told me a million times." It's nagging at me. He's been lying this whole time.

"Originally, I was just going to give you a little more time without the necklace, like a few days. I figured if your grandpa was right, it might be good to wait a little bit for you to gain more confidence without it. Looking back, I realize that might have been a dumb idea. After I waited, I started to worry. If I gave it back too soon, what if you just started to believe in it again? It was messing with me, and all I knew was that I never wanted to see you hurt ever again. Really, Becky, I was just scared it would hurt you again." His eyes are sincere, and I know he means well. I can feel myself starting to soften to what he is telling me and what my family has been telling me. He did this out of love for me. Interrupting my thoughts, he continues to explain, but I know I'm already forgiving him.

"The thing is, the longer I waited, the more I worried that you would end up mad at me for keeping it from you. I was becoming afraid that when I told you, I'd end up losing you again. Honestly, I'm still scared of that. I can't lose you again, but after last night, I knew it was time. It was such an amazing night. I couldn't hide it anymore, no matter the consequences. Please forgive me, Becky, please. I'm so sorry." He says with pleading eyes, his concern is palpable.

"You could have told me, and we could have talked about it. Instead, you just hid it from me. It reminds me of when you lied, telling me you never brought Stacy to the tree when we all know you did." As I say it, I realize it has been nagging at me in the back of my mind. It's another small lie, and I need to hear the truth. I need this explanation.

"First of all, I need to clarify that situation with Stacy. I was at the tree by myself. I had a bad day and went there to be alone. It was this summer during soccer, and I needed to get away. I went there to think, and at the time, Stacy and I were together. She just happened to see me there, so she joined me. I didn't bring her there. I didn't tell her the story of my family or the importance of that spot. I just let her sit with me for a while because what else was I going to do? I didn't like her being there; it felt all wrong, and that's when I knew for sure it was time to end things with her. That's all that happened. And, second of all, YOU are the only girl I've ever brought there. I wanted to share that spot with you, as my girlfriend." Frustration and agitation are in his voice. As he talks, I know he is telling the truth. I know he is sick of this Stacy situation. Well, now I'm positive Stacy overheard Leslie talking about the tree with me. Every chance she got, she tried to rub it in my face. Now I know he was right. She was making it sound worse, hoping we would fight.

"I understand. I just wish you had told me that a long time ago. You're right. She was making it sound way more significant than it was. You know she has been rubbing that in my face every chance she gets, right?" I sigh in frustration. "This whole thing could have been avoided if you would have just explained it to me. We can't keep having these misunderstandings. Can we promise to just tell each other everything from now on?" I ask, looking up at him for reassurance.

"I know, you're right. I promise, no more secrets from now on. I really didn't realize that Stacy being at the tree bothered you so much, not until we fought after you lost your necklace. But I never got the chance to explain it to you after that day. I just hope you can understand where I was coming from."

"I do now. Since we are getting everything out in the open, can you please tell me what is going on with Stacy? Why does she always need to talk to you alone?" A huge lump hits me in my throat. Terrified of this answer. I realize suddenly that this is why I never pushed him on this more, the fear of hearing he still has feelings for her. I need to know. We need to get everything out in the open.

Nate's body tenses, and he lets out a sigh. "Becky..." he says quietly as if he is weighing his options.

"You have to tell me something that makes sense, Nate. I know you say that it's her story to tell, but you have to give me something." I'm almost begging for an explanation while praying it isn't that he still has feelings for her.

He sounds nervous and says, "Blake is..." and his voice trails off.

"Blake?" I ask, surprised, not expecting him to bring up Blake. Nate stopped explaining and he looks as if he's searching for the right words.

"You have to promise not to say anything, and you have to understand that I was just kind of pulled into this because I saw him... he was...aggressive with her. She was talking to me about class, nothing flirty at all, and Blake freaked...he grabbed her arm and yelled some nasty things to me. He pulled her aside and, she looked scared. I intervened before it got any worse, and after that, she started confiding in me. Now that they broke up though, he's left her alone. I think she's just after me to make her feel...safe? I don't know, I want to help her, but she makes it almost impossible the way she acts. I can't stand it." His body relaxes, and he lets out a sigh. I'm shocked. I had no idea that he was dealing with all this.

"You should tell someone, like, an adult." I say.

"I did, actually. I ended up telling my coach because he could tell something was bothering me and I thought it was okay since he didn't know either one of them. I promised her I wouldn't say anything, but I didn't know what to do. After my birthday party, I ended up telling Chris about everything. I was worried it would get worse for Stacy after they broke up. Chris needed to know so he could help me talk to Blake, and we set him straight the morning after my birthday. It seemed to work."

"I wish you had told me. Everything makes so much more sense now."

"I wanted to, but Stacy made me promise. She kept saying she was handling it and it wasn't that bad. He never actually hurt her, as far as I know, but I know he scared her. She was afraid to break up with him, and he seemed to have some control over her. Every time she pulled me aside, she was confiding in me. I just didn't know what to do and felt like it wasn't my place to tell people. I was worried that if people were gossiping about it that would make it worse for her. I didn't want her to end up getting hurt. Like, physically hurt." He stops talking, and we sit in silence. He's deep in thought but then suddenly continues, "I just don't know. I still don't know if I'm doing the right thing. I had to tell someone, and got advice from my coach. After that day she tried to cheat her way on sweetheart court, I just couldn't deal with all the crap she was pulling. In frustration, I reached out to coach again, and he got their names out of me. After talking to me, he told her parents and the principal. They made a formal complaint to the school about Blake." He sounds exhausted as if he has been carrying a huge weight. "You can't tell anyone, not even Trina or Ally, okay? I mean it."

"I promise. I'm so sorry you were carrying all that on your shoulders. I'm stunned, really. I had no idea. I thought she just wanted to get you back."

"Well, she does!" He says, laughing, "I feel like the Blake situation has been mostly over, the school can help protect her now. She's still using it to get me alone, which I wouldn't mind if I thought we were friends. She just keeps pushing too much. Sometimes she does need something important, but other times it isn't. It's impossible to constantly be at her beck and call. I tried making it clear I only wanted to be friends, but she's making it too hard. That's when I started getting snippy with her because I felt like no matter what I said, she was relentless. I feel horrible. I've been keeping an eye on Blake, and now that the principal knows, I can go to him if I need to." Nate has been carrying this huge secret for months, and I feel terrible for ever doubting him.

"Should I talk to her?" I ask, suddenly understanding everything and wanting to help. I feel horrible that I was so dismissive of her. I don't know what to do.

"No, she doesn't want people knowing. She thinks rumors will start, and it'll just make things worse. Her parents are making her see a therapist now that they are aware of what has been going on. I really hope that will help her. Blake is in real trouble too. I know he has to do certain things in order to stay at school. I don't know what the details are with all that. I've told you too much. Can we please stop talking about this now? It really is something that is private to Stacy." He looks drained, and it's obvious how much this has been weighing on him. I nod, we can be done with this.

We hold each other for a while before he lets me go, reaches into his pocket, and pulls out the necklace. Shining in the light, it's the four-leaf clover that started it all. My first thought was how small it seemed compared to what was happening with Stacy. My second thought was, could it actually be magical? Is it enchanted after all? It did help me believe in myself, and that's why my dreams came true. Now that I've learned that lesson, I have a sense that it has lost its magic.

"Here," Nate says as he hands it to me gently as if it's delicate and precious.

"I don't even want it anymore." Once it's in my hand, it feels all wrong. "It feels like it doesn't belong to me now."

Nate looks confused. "You don't even want it?"

"It feels like it doesn't belong to me anymore. It's strange." Looking at it as it lies in my hand, it feels like it belongs somewhere else.

"That's kind of how I felt about having it." He says sheepishly, then asks, "Becky, can you forgive me? I never meant for any of this to happen. I know I've made a mess of things by not giving you the necklace or explaining the Stacy situation. I don't want to hide anything from you ever again, even if I think I'm protecting you from being hurt."

"Of course, Nate, I don't want to go through anything like this ever again. No more hiding things, no more lies. From now on, we tell each other everything, no matter what." Looking at him, knowing that we can get through this, I lean closer to him, wanting to be wrapped in the security of his arms.

"I promise," Nate says and takes me in his arms. We hold each other for a while, saying nothing. "Forgive me?" he whispers, breaking the silence.

"Forgiven. I love you so much, Nate. I know you were trying to do the right thing, even if I wish you would have told me everything.

I understand it all now." As I say it, I feel a sense of relief wash over me. I never wanted to lose Nate, I love him, imperfections and all. Finally, I understand where he is coming from.

"I love you so much, Becky." He says with overwhelming emotion. He starts kissing me with a sense of longing. I could feel his emotions on my lips, the fear of losing me, and the relief of forgiveness all at once. As he pulls away, we look at each other; both of us have so much emotion in our eyes. No need to say anything; we've already said it all. We cuddle up in each other's arms and stay for a long while, wanting to be close to each other. Finally, I break the silence.

"Nate, I really don't want to keep the necklace. It doesn't feel right anymore." It's been in my hand the whole time, ever since he gave it back to me. It feels out of place. I keep thinking that maybe it is a lucky charm that finds the person who needs it. Once that person learns whatever lesson they need to learn, it's time for them to let it go. It's my turn to give it up, because someone else needs it now.

"You've been through a lot with that necklace, so whatever you feel is probably right. So...what are you thinking?" He asks.

"Would you keep it for me? At least for a couple more months, in case I change my mind? If I feel the same way in a couple of months, then maybe we leave it somewhere and let fate take over? If someone is meant to find it, they will."

"That sounds perfect," Nate says and kisses my forehead.

He decides to stay for dinner, and my mom is thrilled that we aren't fighting. I can hear her talking to Grandma on the phone, and she's telling her things are okay with us. It's cute to see how much my family likes us together and how much they were pulling for us to get through this.

Chapter Twenty
Let Go

Nate and I waited for three months and decided we were going to leave the necklace behind this weekend. First thing first, though, and today is Ally's birthday party! She is having a party at her house, but nothing as crazy as Nate's big blowout. At her house is our group of friends, as well as the girls from both dance teams and their boyfriends. There were more girls than guys at her party, for sure. Her parents are barbecuing in the backyard, and games are set up for people to play.

The guys are in a major competition. They created their own Cornhole tournament. Since there isn't an even number of guys, Kelly is playing, too. Nate and Mark are playing against Blake and Kelly. It's so weird to watch, knowing everything about Blake. Now, it's so easy to see the tension between him and Nate. Blake is flirting with Kelly, she brought him to the party, and that is scary knowing what I know. Even though she's not my favorite, I still worry about Kelly, and wouldn't want her to get involved with Blake. After learning the truth about Stacy, I never told anyone else what Nate shared with me that day. One thing I've learned is that you never know what is going on in someone's life. I wish I could warn her to stay away from Blake, but I don't think she'd believe me since were not on the best terms. Kelly has that mean streak to her. I'll never forget her smile after Ally got hurt at regionals. Ally forgave her, and I can too.

Ally's parents interrupt my thoughts by bringing out the cake. Everyone starts singing 'Happy Birthday' as they stop what they are doing to join in. Ally looks so happy as she blows out her candles. The cake will be served shortly, but first, her parents announce that they want to give Ally her gift. She literally runs to the front yard, and squeals of excitement fill the sky. She got her new car, the one she was talking about on that first double date so many months ago. Jumping up and down with excitement, Ally hugs her parents over and over again. Everyone is checking out the new ride, which is a brand new Volkswagen Jetta with leather seats inside. It is perfect.

Overhearing Mark, he quietly says to Nate, "Well, my gift isn't going to impress her now." Poor guy, he couldn't possibly compete with a new car. He got her a heart-shaped necklace with her birthstone. It must have been pretty expensive, judging by the way he was talking about it earlier.

Once the car excitement wore down, we were served cake. All of us were sitting together as Ally opened Mark's gift. We all watch as she gives him a kiss and jumps into his arms with pure joy. Relief washes over Mark's face, along with a huge smile, and I know he thinks the money was well spent. Ally is going around, showing off her necklace to everyone. Mark is so proud, and it is adorable.

"I guess I could compete with a car, after all." He says to Nate with newfound confidence. Between bites of cake, Nate nods approvingly.

It's awesome to see how happy Ally is, and I tell Mark, "You did well. This is the happiest I've ever seen her!"

He smiles proudly and nods toward her. "Seeing her like that makes it all worth it."

As Ally's party winds down, our group helps clean up. Austin and Trina are in the backyard picking up the games while Nate and I are carrying the leftover food inside.

"You guys want to go for a ride in my new car?" Ally yells over to Trina and Austin. It's crazy it took her this long to ask. Popping her head inside the door, she asks me and Nate the same thing.

"We'd love to Ally, but we are supposed to go to Nate's tonight for a bonfire with the family. Do you guys want to come?" I ask.

"Oh, yeah! I'll drive everyone else over to Nate's and meet you guys over there." She says excitedly.

"Enjoy the ride! We'll see you over at Nate's." I yell back as Nate, and I head out to pick up a few extra drinks and S'more ingredients since we have additional people joining us. I love bonfires at Nate's.

Sitting alongside Nate at the fire reminds me of that first bonfire at this house. I was so nervous about meeting his parents and couldn't believe that I was actually inside his house. For once, I wasn't just looking at it from the outside. It felt like a small miracle when I was invited over that first time. Now, it feels like a second home. I'm so close with his family and really enjoy spending time with them.

Leslie breaks up my thoughts and asks me where I got Nate's keychain. She wants to give one to Chris for his birthday. Nate asked me about it earlier as well; they ordered it for their parent's anniversary, which is coming up. A new tradition in the McNeil family that started with me. Nothing could make me happier.

"You know they got their parents the keychain, too? They are giving it to them for their anniversary." I whisper to Leslie, followed by, "I'll send you the link."

She smiles, "Those two are such romantics." she says, talking about Nate and Chris.

"Yeah, we are lucky," I say and then point to their parents, who are dancing to the song on the radio in their kitchen. "I wonder where they get it."

"Yeah, they definitely get it from them," Leslie says, smiling. We watch their parents dance for a little longer until they stop. They're heading to the door, Ally and the gang must have arrived but now there is no movement in the house.

"I think Ally is showing them her new car," I say, and that makes Leslie laugh.

"I'm sure she is." She says, teasing since we know how excited Ally is about her car.

"Hey guys! We brought the leftover birthday cake!" Mark says as he walks out the slider door, followed by, "Ooo, S'mores!" He is always easy to please as long as food is around.

The gang joined us at the bonfire, telling us all the things they liked about the new Jetta. Ally is so proud of her birthday gift. As I look out at my friends sitting alongside Nate and his family, I'm full of appreciation. It wasn't that long ago that I was sitting on the bus feeling invisible, wishing I was more like Stacy after freshman year. I'm happy just being Becky and no longer wish to be like someone else. I'm no longer hiding myself from the world. I'm confident and open, finally feeling good in my own skin.

Mark starts teasing Ally about the time he tried to teach her to golf. "I was trying to teach her how to hold the club, and she kept working on her grip to perfect her swing. It didn't work out so well, though, did it?" He asks Ally, with a smirk, "I'd say her new grip was a failure." Mark starts laughing, and you can tell he is envisioning her as he explains, "She totally missed the ball, swinging as hard as she could and threw the golf club. I remember thinking, wow, she threw the club pretty far. The ball would have gone flying if she actually hit it." He is poking at her, and they are both laughing.

"Yeah, it was pretty embarrassing. The ball was still sitting at my feet, but the club went flying. It wouldn't have been too bad, except other golfers saw it. After that, I just drove the golf cart until Mark got on the putting green. I would just put my ball next to Mark's and practice putting." Ally finishes the story, and Mark is laughing and teasing her. We can all totally picture Ally throwing her club.

This is followed by a story Trina had of Ally and a wardrobe malfunction at one of their summer dance competitions. The stories kept coming, and it was turning into a bit of a birthday roast for Ally, as we were all trying to embarrass her. It was hilarious until, in the middle of the laughter, Trina's alarm went off. We all know that means it's curfew time. Everyone automatically starts to pack up.

"Hey guys, I have some news before we leave," Trina says; she seems kind of hesitant, and I wonder if she found out she isn't going to be competing with her new dance studio. They tell the girls early at this studio so they have more time to prepare. I knew it was coming up from Ally, but Trina had decided she didn't want to talk about it until she found out. I look over at Ally, who shrugs, like, 'I don't know.'

Everyone stops packing up and looks at Trina eagerly. Austin goes over to her and puts his arm around her. His face is giving it away. He looks so proud.

"I found out today I am competing this year with my new studio. I'm going to the international ballet competition! I didn't want to take away from Ally's night, but I wanted to tell you while we were all together." Trina says as we all start hugging her and congratulating her.

"Finally! You have always deserved this! I am soooo happy for you!" We are holding hands and jumping up and down. "I can't believe you have been waiting all day to tell us, and now we have to leave!?! We need to celebrate!"

Ally agrees. "You didn't have to wait because it was my birthday! It would have been perfect to celebrate together!" Ally's injury has healed now, but it has put her at a disadvantage, and she didn't even try to compete this year because of it. "I will help you prepare, anything you need! This is the BEST news! We do need to celebrate."

We decided to figure out a celebration next week since we all really need to pack up and leave to make curfew. I take a second to look around at my friends and all the happiness that I'm surrounded with, and I can only think, 'Thank you.'

It's obvious to me that it's time to move on and away from the necklace. Realizing the choice to believe in myself is always within me has changed everything. My friends are so amazing, and I love seeing everything work out for them. There is something very comforting in that, thriving along with the people you care about. It turns out I do have some of my Grandpa's lucky genes. After all, as he would say, 'If you're lucky enough to be Irish, you're lucky enough.' I just needed to believe in myself to see it. I'm convinced that the necklace ended up on the beach that day, fatefully waiting for my grandpa to find it and bring it to me. It found me when I needed it. The more I think about it, the more I believe the necklace will find its way to someone else who needs it now. Believing this makes me excited to leave it behind.

"Where should we leave the necklace?" I ask Nate once in his Jeep while he's driving me home. I really hope it will continue to be passed along from person to person, helping people along the way.

"You're grandpa found it on the beach, right?"

"Yeah, but that was really lucky. It could get lost in the sand so easily."

"Well, maybe outdoors somewhere then. It's warm now. People will be walking the trails." He suggests.

"That sounds like a good idea. Somewhere near your family's tree? It would have to be a spot closer to the path so it's more noticeable." Imagining leaving the necklace behind, I try to picture the perfect spot, but nothing comes to mind. I have faith I'll know it when I see it.

"That should work. We can have a picnic out there and then walk the path until we feel like we found the right spot," Nate says with a satisfied smile. "Let's do it tomorrow. It's supposed to be a nice day to be outside."

"Okay," I say and feel relieved; we have a plan. He brings me home after our night at the bonfire and simply says, "See you tomorrow."

At home, I keep reminiscing about this year. The school year is coming to an end. At the end of the year, I will not be sitting alone on the bus looking out at everyone else. Instead, I'll be out on the steps making plans with my friends. Turning off my bedside light, I know tomorrow will bring me peace, and luck to someone in need.

Today is the day we are going to leave my good luck charm behind. I hope more than anything that someone else finds it and it changes their life the way it changed mine. Stevie's barking downstairs. Nate must be here. Looking out my window, his jeep pulls into the driveway and I head downstairs. Before bed last night, I told my mom what we were planning to do with the necklace today.

"I hope you find the perfect spot." She says as she gives me a wave on my way out the door.

"Thanks, Mom, I know we will," I say as I wave back. Mixed emotions fill my mind, but I am positive this is what needs to be done. I run outside and jump into Nate's Jeep.

"Hey," I say, giving him my best smile, trying to hide my nervousness.

"Hey, are you ready for today?" He asks and seems unsure of what I'll say.

"I am. I feel good about it. Why? What are you thinking?" I ask, curious if anything has changed for him.

"I think it's the right thing to do. I'm glad you didn't change your mind; now, let's hope we find a good spot for it." Nate says with a reassuring smile.

"We will! Don't worry, I'm ready. I won't be changing my mind." I say confidently. The necklace is in fate's hands now.

We drive over to the park. Nate's mom has packed lunch for us to take on our picnic. Our cooler is packed with sandwiches, fruit, and homemade cookies. As we walk the path that leads us to the tree, my eyes are looking for a spot to call out to me, but nothing does. Reaching the tree, Nate puts down the plaid picnic blanket. Trees are surrounding us with vibrant green leaves now, unlike the colorful ones of the fall. The river is higher from all the spring rain, making the water rush over the boulders with intense energy. It's more powerful than it was the first time we came here. Looking out at the river, it flows forcefully downstream, but I still find it peaceful. The sound of the flowing river is soothing in the background while we sit at our spot. We eat our lunch sitting so close that the sides of our bodies are touching. Being close to Nate brings me so much comfort, making the view even more perfect.

"You know, this was really nice of your mom to pack us lunch, but I kinda miss the burgers." I say to him, remembering our first picnic here.

"I knew that was a good call the first time we came here." He says, laughing, "Burgers from the diner really aren't picnic food, though. This seems more appropriate." He adds with a shrug and a laugh. We talk about our plans for this summer. I won't get my license until later in the summer, but Nate is planning on visiting the cottage as often as he can. Ally, Trina, Austin, and Mark are going to come out to the lake this year too. It'll be the first year where I can actually stay in touch with people and have visitors who can just drive out to the lake. For the first time since elementary, I won't be a nervous wreck on the first day of school. The amount of change that happened to me this year is remarkable. Looking over at the necklace, I quietly say, 'Thank you.' Gratefulness washes over me, and even though I don't need it anymore, I'll never forget the lesson I learned.

Leaning my head on Nate's chest, he says, "I wish we could carve our initials right there." He points towards the tree at a spot just under his parents' initials. He then adds, "Someday," and kisses my forehead. Butterflies, he gives me so many butterflies. This is his way of telling me he wants me in his future. It's exciting but scary, we are so young. This year alone, thinking of the amount of change and growth I had in just one year, who knows what the future will hold for us.

Turning towards him, "Someday," I say, in agreement with him. We are both looking at the tree now. I can't help but imagine our initials on the tree, and it feels so right.

"I have an idea. After we find the perfect place to leave the necklace, I have a surprise for you," Nate says, suddenly seeming excited. I know whatever the surprise is, he just thought of it.

"Okay," I say, curious what surprise he just thought up for me. Nate starts packing up; our time under the tree is done for today. As we pack up, I start to wonder if I'm doing the right thing with the necklace. Suddenly, the wind starts blowing. It feels like it's blowing in two directions at once, surrounding me. It hasn't been windy at all today. Instinctively, I close my eyes. The wind feels like a sign meant for me, encouraging me to let go. It makes me feel at peace. Opening my eyes, I see Nate standing with the blanket and backpack, ready to go. His arm outstretched, handing me the necklace, and I know what I have to do.

I have the necklace in one hand and Nate's hand in the other as we walk along the trail. We continue to walk further down the path away from the tree, keeping our eyes open for a perfect spot to leave the necklace. "I want the right person to find it," I say, mostly to myself. I know I can't question this. I have to believe in fate.

"We don't have control over who finds it, but we can put it somewhere that it will more likely be found." Nate says, then adds, "What about over there?" He points out a bush, and I try to lay the necklace on it in a way that's noticeable, but it keeps falling through the leaves, so we give up on it and continue on our walk. Just up ahead, there's a wooden bridge that goes over the river with benches for people to rest and enjoy the view.

"Somewhere over there?" I ask, pointing out the benches to Nate. As he spots the bench up ahead, he nods his head in agreement.

"Yeah! I think we can make that spot work." He says as he looks along the path towards the bridge.

Walking along the path, my eyes inspect each tree and bush along the path, intently looking for the perfect spot. In my heart, though, it feels as if there will be a perfect place near the bench. As we approach the bridge, it's easy to see why there is a bench placed here. It's a beautiful view of the river. The closer we get, the louder my heart starts thumping. This is it. This is where my necklace will be left behind. A mix of emotions consumed me: sadness, anxiety, and hope all hit me at the same time before a strong sense of peace washes them all away. It's the feeling I get when I know I'm doing the right thing.

"Are you ready?" Nate asks, followed by, "You seem quiet."

"Yeah, I'm ready." My tone was upbeat and was meant to reassure Nate. I am optimistic, even if I am being a little reflective.

Sitting on the bench to appreciate the view, we both notice the same tree. It's across from us, and it is closer to the path, making it stand out. Smaller, bare branches hang down at exactly the right height, directly in our sight when sitting on the bench.

"What if I hang it on those thin branches?" I ask Nate.

"I was thinking the exact same thing. It's right where you would look if you were sitting here. It would be noticeable, and it would stay on those branches for as long as it takes." He says.

I walk over to the tree and can easily reach the branches from the path. Holding the necklace in my hand and whisper 'Find someone who needs you' to the necklace. It makes it easier to leave it behind with the hope that it will help someone else the way it helped me. One of the thicker branches holds the chain, with the pendent hanging lower. There is another two-pronged branch that hangs lower, and it is the perfect place for the pendent to sit.

"Well, can you see it?" I ask.

"Sometimes. It's noticeable when the light hits it a certain way." He says.

"That sounds right; that's exactly what my grandpa said when he found it. The light caught his eye."

"That's how I found it in the gym, too," Nate says, nodding in agreement.

"It's pretty miraculous that my grandpa and boyfriend both found this necklace." As I say it, I know I believe it was meant for me, at least for a time. Now, that time is done.

"I guess we were the ones meant to find it," Nate says, standing next to me, looking at the pendant hanging from the tree branches.

"Now, it's someone else's turn. It will find the person who needs it the most." I say, feeling satisfied.

"I think you're right," Nate says as he walks over and wraps his arms around me. All I feel is happiness, and I know it's time to move on.

"So, where are we going now?" I ask, remembering his surprise.

"You'll see," Nate says with his smile, which makes me melt. He takes my hand as we follow the path back to his jeep.

As we drive down the road, I keep wondering where we could be going and what the surprise could be. It wasn't a planned surprise, I know, because I saw his face the moment he thought of it. As we continued to drive, I started to realize where we were going — the plaza, the location of our first date, and many other dates that followed.

"Are we going to the plaza? Are you hungry for tacos or something?" Teasing him, trying to get him talking so he'll slip up and tell me. I can't stand not knowing where we are going. It's my best guess.

"Well, that's not the plan, but I'm always willing to eat some tacos." He teases back. He pulls into a parking spot closer to the playground area, and I know for sure we are going to our bench. I'm not sure what the surprise would be, though. Nate grabs something out of his console but I can't tell what it is. I have no idea what he is planning. Jumping out of the jeep, he walks over to me, taking my hand in his as he leads me to our bench.

It's a nice day out, and kids are playing on the playground. The bench is too far from the playground for any parents to sit there while the kids play. It's always empty as if it's placed there just for us. It's placed so that it has a beautiful view of a wooded area. I notice an entry point into the woods and realize there is a path through the woods. That must be it. I always wondered why this bench was placed at this spot, and I realized it probably had something to do with the path.

"Have you ever walked that path?" I asked Nate, wondering if the path was going to be part of my surprise.

"Honestly, I never knew it was there." He says, then adds, "We can explore it sometime."

"I love our spot," I say, smiling at Nate as I sit down. "This is a nice surprise."

"Just being here isn't the surprise." He says, smiling, and reaches into his pocket to pull out his Swiss army knife. "This is."

"A knife? What does that mean?" I can't help but laugh — I have no clue what he's thinking. A knife is my surprise?

"It hit me when we were saying 'someday' we could carve our initials on the tree. But, Becky, we can carve our initials on our bench today. It's our own spot, without all the tradition attached to it. It's ours and ours alone." Nate says, smiling proudly.

"You want to carve our initials onto our bench?" I ask, astonished. It feels so special, like the most romantic thing in the world.

"Yes, it's our spot. It's perfect." He says, giving me a sweet kiss before adding, "I love you, Becky."

Tears are welling up in my eyes, and a teardrop falls down my face. All I feel is an overwhelming love for Nate. "It's perfect," I say and kiss him, tears and all.

He wipes away the tears falling down my cheeks. Slowly he pulls away and looks at me, "You okay?"

Nodding, I lean in to hug him again, saying, "I'm just so happy. I love you so much." I'm holding onto him so tight and never want to let go.

"You are squishing me." He teases with a laugh, and I finally let go.

Nate gets out his knife and starts carving our initials R.L + N.M for Rebecca Lewis and Nathan McNeil. Watching him, as he is carving with such pride, fills me up. We sit back and look at our creation. As I look at our initials, I'm transported to our first date, our multiple 'almost-kisses' on that first night in this exact spot. Remembering the conversation we had and how Nate opened up to me about his struggles with the soccer team. Thinking of him taking me here on Christmas day to finally kiss me at this special spot, I lean over and say, "I love you, Nate McNeil."

"I love you, too, Rebecca Lewis." He says, smiling as he leans in and kisses me.

As we walk away from the bench, I have a sense of comfort, knowing our initials are etched in time. It feels permanent, and I know that no matter what happens to Nate and me in the future, we will always have our bench.

Epilogue

Stacy

Stacy is sitting in the living room, trying to distract herself from her life, but as always, her mind is racing. It's constantly replaying everything that happened this year. The sun is peeking through the window, beckoning her to come outside and escape the stale air of indoors. She can hear her parents talking in the kitchen, and it sounds like they are discussing her again. "She's going to therapy, and we've done everything we can. I'm sure some of this is just teenage hormones, too." Her dad is trying to convince her mother that there is nothing to worry about. She has to get out of this house.

"I'm going for a walk," Stacy yells to her parents while already halfway out the door. She does catch the worried look on her mother's face before closing the door behind her.

"Just be home for dinner," her mother calls out.

It was a beautiful day out, and she needed time to think. She knows why her parents are worried. Honestly, she is worried, too. This year, everything changed. She changed, and now she doesn't know how to get herself back. She needs to fix things, fix everything that happened this year. That requires her to admit to herself all the things that got her to this point — too many mistakes to count.

At the end of last year, she thought her sophomore year would start with Nate at her side, and they would be a couple. She loved all the attention they got at the end of Freshman year. Nate always made her feel special, and she was on top of the world when she was with him. She never understood why Nate broke things off with her over the summer.

Once she was single, it wasn't long before Blake came into the picture. He was an upperclassman and the starting quarterback. It seemed unbelievable he was paying attention to her, even though he didn't like her friends. She remembers him clearly, "I can't be hanging out with little freshman girls all summer. You're cool, but those other girls, they are so immature. You can't keep inviting them to my friend's parties." He always emphasized 'freshmen' even though they were going to be sophomores. It made her feel like he saw her as older and cooler than her friends.

At first, she was flattered and felt special, like only she was cool enough for him. It didn't take long before she pushed her friends away and only hung out with Blake and his friends. If she started to miss her friends and tried to hang out with them again, Blake would quickly remind her that they weren't cool enough. After hearing that enough times, she started to believe it herself and eventually didn't miss her friends anymore. That's where it all started to go wrong. She excluded herself from the people who really cared about her, and now she's completely alone.

Around homecoming Blake got angry because he saw her talking to Nate after one of their classes. Maybe she was flirting with Nate a little, but she didn't mean anything by it. She was really into Blake. Blake came over and pulled her away from Nate. It was aggressive; she had a mark on her arm afterward, and it was the first time he really scared her.

Blake yelled something cruel at Nate, but she was too shocked to remember what he had said. The tone was seared in her memory, the rage in his voice. Once he got Stacy alone, he whispered in a seething tone while still gripping her arm. "You're my girl. Mine. If you ever slut it up around school again, I swear I'll..." He didn't finish the sentence, but he did squeeze her arm even harder to get his point across. She got the point.

"Okay, I promise." Her voice sounded meek and frightened. She wasn't doing anything wrong with Nate and wanted to yell back at him, but was too afraid to protest while he was so angry. It was then that Nate intervened, obviously concerned with what he witnessed. From that moment she knew she could confide in Nate. That night, she called Nate, and he was worried about her. He saw how angry

Blake was, and he wanted to tell someone, but she made him promise not to, convincing him to keep her secret.

The real problem was that once she finally saw Blake's true colors, she was alone. She had pushed away all her friends. How could she go running back to them now that things weren't working out with Blake? They were giving her the cold shoulder, and she deserved it. She didn't realize how much being with him was changing her. She was becoming someone she didn't even recognize. The only friends that she had left were Blake's friends. She couldn't confide in them; the only person she could talk to was Nate. He saw what happened, and he understood. She was trying to put up a brave face, but it didn't work. Instead, she just became desperate and mean. She felt so alone and became obsessed with the idea of getting back together with Nate.

Feeling the way she did when she was with Nate last summer is all she wanted, and she thought he could bring that happiness back to her. She kept holding on to that thought, especially since Nate was being so supportive. They were always a fun couple, loved by everyone. He was so carefree around her. How he ended up with Becky is beyond her, of all the girls, she never would have picked her. They are polar opposites, and honestly, Nate is way too popular to be dating a girl like Becky. She hated seeing them together.

The warm sun was welcome on her face and stopped her rambling thoughts. Looking around, she realized she'd walked all the way over to the park while lost in thought. The tree-lined river was in sight, and she decided to keep going and walk the path along the river. It shouldn't be too busy today. Noticing the tallest tree nearby, this spot hit her as familiar; it was near the spot where she had run into Nate that day last summer. That special spot she heard Becky and Leslie talking about after homecoming. When she approached the spot where she saw Nate last summer, she glanced towards the tree. Stacy's heart ached. She ached to be the girl she was last time she was here with Nate. She ached to return to that fun-loving girl she was last summer. She wanted to be happy again. Not able to look at that spot any longer, she turned down the path to get it out of sight.

She started to walk deeper into the woods, and her thoughts were racing; fighting back her tears was hopeless; she couldn't stop them from falling down her cheeks. She used to be so happy, but this year she is completely alone. How does she find her way back to the person she once was? She never had to 'try' to be popular; she just was. The more time she spent with Blake and his friends, the more she began to look down on others. It made her feel powerful, but it also changed her into someone she doesn't like very much.

Now she just misses her friends, her real friends, the ones she's known since elementary. Overwhelming sadness engulfs her. It's the first time she has been really honest with herself, and her tears won't stop now as she continues to walk further down the path.

Thankfully, the path is empty today; she doesn't want anyone to see her like this. She can only imagine what her tear-stained face must look like. She's been walking along the trail for hours, absentmindedly, and is now deep into the woods. Looking around, she realizes she is much further into the woods than she had planned, and she better turn back.

On her way back, she tries to think of ways to patch things up with her friends. She needs to tell them everything. Someday, she will have to apologize to Becky, too; she shouldn't have tried so hard to steal Nate. That will have to wait, though; she's not ready to face Becky yet. As she was thinking about how to right her wrongs, she noticed a bench near the river and decides to sit down. She needed to rest for a minute, feeling exhausted both physically and emotionally. Once sitting, she realized she should have worn better shoes. She wasn't planning on walking so far, and her feet are starting to hurt.

Sitting on the bench, she watched the river cascade over the boulders. It was serene here, just what she needed. It felt so good to just sit alone and finally not have the urge to cry. She knew she was going to try to make amends with everyone, and that felt good.

Closing her eyes for a moment to take in the nature sounds, the wind blows. The breeze felt reassuring, and not just because it was hot outside. It brought a feeling of peace to her. It was as if the wind was coming from two directions at the same time, surrounding her. It wasn't a windy day, and she wondered if it was a sign of change coming her way. As she opened her eyes, something caught her attention as the trees moved with the wind; it sparkled in the light across the way from where she was sitting.

She was drawn to it and felt compelled to find out what was catching the light like that. As she approached, she saw what looked like a pendant caught on a tree branch swirling in the wind, catching the light as it moved. She reached out to grab it and wondered how it could have ended up there. It was definitely a pendent; taking it in her hand, she saw that it was a dainty four-leaf clover. A sign of good luck. She couldn't believe it. It's just what she needed; it really felt like it was there to give her the courage she required. She knew it was time to apologize to her friends and work towards forgiveness.

She put the necklace on and suddenly knew everything was going to be okay. She couldn't help but reach up and touch the necklace lying around her neck. As she felt the four-leaf clover between her fingertips, she felt that maybe, for the first time this year, her luck was about to change.

www.ingramcontent.com/pod-product-compliance
Lightning Source LLC
Chambersburg PA
CBHW041048310726
48978CB00011BA/472